Camp HOPE

Sara L. Foust

Published by Silver Lining Literary Services, LLC
106 Offutt Rd
Clinton, TN 37716
www.saralfoust.com

Second edition. Printed in the United States of America.

First edition printed 2017.

ISBN: 978-1-732-9047-6-7

Cover by Diane Turpin at dianeturpindesigns.com

All Scripture quoted is from the King James Version of the Bible.

For my family.
You guys are the most supportive, loving, encouraging bunch of people a girl could ask for. I am so blessed to have each one of you!

And now abideth faith, hope, and charity,
these three; but the greatest of these is charity.

I Corinthians 13:13 (KJV)

Chapter 1

The long-awaited call came in the pre-dawn hours. When the farmhouse sagged and dared not breathe. Amy Dawson dug herself out of a deep sleep to answer. “Hello?”

“This is Diane with Child Protective Services. Would you like to take a placement?”

She bolted upright. This was it. After all the terrifying training classes, the long weeknights worrying about her decision, the moment was finally here. What was she supposed to ask? Amy took a breath to calm her shaking hands. “Can you tell me about the child, please?”

“Mattie is a nonverbal four-year-old. She’ll be coming from another foster placement. They’ve decided they can no longer keep her.”

“In the middle of the night?”

Diane clicked her tongue. “It’s complicated. Would you like to take her?”

Amy took another deep breath. “Why doesn’t she talk?”

“Doctors believe she can speak but chooses not to. Oh, and one more thing. She’s a type I diabetic, so she needs a strict diet and insulin. Are you familiar with the disease?”

Was she ever. Memories like dark photographs flashed in her mind. Injections twice a day, every day, whether her mother was conscious or not. “I’m familiar with it. Anything else I should know?” Could she handle caring for a child with diabetes? The memories that would barrage her?

“There isn’t much information to go on.”

Amy expected that. They’d taught her as much in classes. Especially with a middle-of-the-night placement. What if she couldn’t keep Mattie safe once the summer campers arrived? What if she couldn’t adhere to a strict schedule with the medicine?

“Ms. Dawson?”

None of it mattered really. Not if she listened to what her flying heart was telling her. “How soon can you get here?”

“Great. Give me an hour.” A long pause and Diane shuffled papers. “Maybe longer considering where you live.”

Amy chuckled. “That’s what everyone says. I’ll be ready.”

How her life was about to change. The solitude she’d been fighting to build all these years was about to be penetrated by a sweet child in need of help. Though she was the same age as most of the other people in the Parents as Tender Healers classes, they had been mostly young couples with experience raising children of their own. She knew how to be a good camp counselor. She'd been doing that half her life. What if she failed miserably as an actual parent?

Amy slipped on her fuzzy, blue socks and padded downstairs. The silence so oppressive it nearly scalded her ears. She wanted to shout down the hill and tell Sam the news. But it was too early. A smile slipped onto her face. Wouldn't her best friend be surprised when she checked in before morning chores?

Amy brewed a pot of coffee and took her mug and journal to the front porch. With the sounds of the quiet, summer night filling the air, she curled up on the swing and poised her pencil to write.

May 22, 2016

You're finally coming! I never thought I'd get through all the scary classes to become a foster mom, but then I did and had to wait seven whole weeks. But it doesn't matter, because you're headed this way, and I'm so excited. I only hope I can be a good foster mother for you and help you heal. Maybe you'll get to stay a while.

Amy put down the pencil and sipped her coffee. Moths flitted around the porch light, and fireflies blinked on the lawn. Stars glimmered in the vast, black sky, a million of them visible from her farm without any city light interference. Somewhere in the distance a coyote yipped.

Why was Mattie nonverbal? Training taught Amy ninety percent of all children in foster care had received some form of abuse. And she'd certainly seen kids at the camp over the years she suspected had past traumas. Could that be what held the poor little girl mute?

Amy shivered. It would make sense. All her own years of trauma taught her a few things. Screaming, begging, and whining didn't help. She squeezed her eyes shut. No. Those memories weren't going to cloud this happy moment. She was about to be a stand-in mom for a little one who desperately needed to feel safe and loved. Who knew how long Mattie would stay, but Amy would make the best of it. Maybe she could even get the girl to start talking.

An hour and a half later, headlights dotted the road into Camp Hope. A silver Camry pulled up beside Amy's SUV. A tall, thin brunette exited the driver's seat, waved once, and opened the rear door.

Amy waited on the top step, her breath paused in her chest.

Diane helped a skinny girl in a My Little Pony nightgown climb from the back seat. The graceful woman scooped Mattie up, brushed her dark hair from her face, and carried her to the steps.

"Amy, this is Mattie. Mattie, this nice lady is Amy."

Mattie raised her head from Diane's shoulder and peeked at Amy.

"Oh! I have something for you. Hang on just a second." Amy raced into the house, grabbed the stuffed animal from the dining room table, and returned to the porch. She held out the purple dragon and smiled. "Here ya go."

Mattie reached out and gently grabbed the dragon's glittery wing. She tucked the animal under her right arm and stretched her left toward Amy.

A lump formed in Amy's throat. Such beautiful, big, scared eyes. Amy took Mattie in her arms and ran her fingers through the child's long hair. She weighed almost nothing. Certainly not what a four-year-old should anyway.

"Here's her medicine." Diane handed over a black cooler with a shoulder strap. "And I'll get the papers for you to sign."

Amy settled onto the porch swing once more and wrapped a blanket around Mattie's back. It would take some getting used to having such a quiet child around. The kids at Camp Hope were rarely silent. Excited shouts, loud laughter, and mile-a-minute jabbering usually filled Amy's summertime days.

But not her farmhouse. Maybe the quietness wouldn't change as much as she'd expected.

Diane retrieved a manila file and a bag from her car. She set the bag at Amy's feet. "Mattie's belongings."

"That's it?"

"More than what most kids come with. Probably all stuff the previous foster family bought for her."

"How long was she with them?"

Mattie nuzzled deeper into the crook of Amy's neck.

"About five weeks."

"Why can't they keep her?"

"Decided they are getting divorced."

"Just now?"

"Yep. Can't give many more details, but there was apparently a pretty big fight. Clothes on the lawn and everything." Diane sighed. "Just like on TV. The husband left. Wife called us. And here we are." Diane pursed her lips but held in whatever words may have come next. "Sign here." Diane laid the thin, blue folder on the swing next to Amy.

"Can you sit on the swing next to me?" Amy tried to lift Mattie from her lap, but the little girl's arms tightened around Amy's neck. She took the pen and held the papers in front of her around Mattie's torso. Her signature was messy, but it was legible.

"We'll check on you in a few days. If you need anything, feel free to call your resource parent support worker. There's a list of Mattie's doctor's appointments in the folder here."

Amy nodded. A few days? That seemed like an awfully long time to entrust a child to a brand-new foster parent without checking in. She had her support worker's number on the fridge but barely knew the woman. She'd only met her twice and briefly then.

"Mattie's biological mother has already signed her custody over to the state, and she wishes to remain anonymous for now. We are working to track down Mattie's father, but he has been MIA for months."

How could a mother sign over her rights, just like that? Amy didn't have biological children, but she couldn't imagine letting them go to anyone without a fight. But who was she kidding? Jewel probably would've let Amy go in a heartbeat, if the price had been right. She didn't exactly remember her mother fighting much when Great-Aunt Zena had taken over custody.

Diane pulled out of the parking space and disappeared down the long driveway into the morning that was just starting to lighten.

Mattie trembled, so Amy pulled the blanket tighter. The child's slight frame relaxed and her breathing slowed. She must've been exhausted.

Amy swung slowly until long after dawn broke. Excitement and nervousness filled her. What would the coming months bring?

Chapter 2

June 13, 2016

I like to think I am like the green spring grass. Short, yes. But also never cut. Never cropped. Full of goodness and nutrients. Growing. Changing.

I am not.

I'm much more akin to the crunchy, brown, end-of-summer grass. Bowing. Exhausted. Beaten by the scorching sun. Dehydrated by the relentless blue sky.

The sultry wind blows in waves over the fields. Grass much taller than usual this time of year. It's well past time for Sam to do the first cutting. But repairs, endless repairs, have left little energy for baling hay.

The next wave of campers will arrive soon. Coming in like the wind—fresh and strong. It's my favorite time of year. Mattie still hasn't said a word, but we are making progress with nodding and shaking her head, and occasionally a smile. It's a start, at least.

Hesitant footsteps sounded from within the house.

Amy pushed her glasses up her nose and shut the pencil in her journal. "I'm out here, Mattie."

The screen door slammed, and Mattie padded around the corner in her new princess nightgown. Sam had bought it for her on the last trip into town for supplies.

Amy stretched out her arms, and Mattie climbed into her lap. "How are you this morning?"

Mattie curled into a smaller ball.

"I'm still tired too. Campers are coming today. Remember me telling you about how busy it's going to be soon?"

Mattie nodded.

"Today's the day." Amy rocked Mattie and gazed out over the farm. What happened to this sweet, beautiful child? "You know, bad things happened to me when I was little too. If you want to talk, I'm here to listen." She said the same thing every morning. Maybe Mattie would never speak. "Let's get some breakfast so you can take your medicine, okay?"

She put Mattie on her feet and kissed the top of her dark brown head. "I love you, Mattie."

Mattie dashed into the house.

Amy finished her scrambled eggs and stared at Mattie nibbling on a piece of toast. Mousey, timid little girl. Amy was much like her as a child. Trying to be as small as possible so the grown-ups in her life wouldn't notice she was there. If only that had worked, Amy might not have the mental scars.

The back door creaked open, and Sam peeked in. "Mornin', Amy. Miss Mattie."

Amy nodded toward the elder woman.

"Any words yet?"

"Nope. But that's okay."

Sam removed her cowboy hat, and a long, blonde braid fell to her shoulders. Her tan skin spoke of years of hard, outdoor work. What would Amy do without her? She was the closest thing Amy ever had to a sister. She rarely thought about the age gap, but Amy imagined a real sister would be closer. Someone she could share all her secrets with. Someone who would never dream of hurting her. Or leaving. Not that Sam would ever hurt her, but she was almost the same age now as Aunt Zena was when she died. How much longer would Sam be around?

"I'm fixin' to start the tractor up and get mowing."

"Oh, good. We'll take care of the morning chores at the barn for you. Won't we, Mattie?"

Mattie's thin lips curled at the corners.

"Have you eaten breakfast?"

"Three hours ago." Sam chuckled and replaced her hat. "I'd take a thermos of coffee, though, if you've got it."

Amy filled the old, green-speckled thermos and handed it to Sam with a smile. "Thank you for all you do."

"I promised your Aunt Zena I'd take care of you, didn't I?"

"Indeed you did."

Sam slipped out the door, and Amy turned to the fridge. "Come on. Let's do your shot real quick so we can go to the barn."

Mattie tiptoed to the fridge next to Amy and lifted her shirt to reveal her pale stomach. Amy hated having to hurt her, but not receiving her insulin would be even worse. Mattie didn't make a sound when the needle entered her skin. Crazy how a four-year-old could take her meds without as much as a whimper. Amy's mother had been so dramatic all those years ago. Each injection Amy had to give Jewel brought at least one tear and snippy complaint along with it.

"Ready to go feed the horses?"

Mattie nodded and sprinted out the door.

Amy slid her boots on and grabbed some marshmallows for treats.

Mattie skipped down the dirt trail a couple yards ahead, her brown hair bouncing on her shoulders.

The hazy mountains in the distance framed the old, red barn. Humidity hung heavy in the air and made it hard to breathe. Amy wiped the sweat from her brow on her shirtsleeve. Today was going to be a scorcher. Could they break tradition and start out the first day of camp with a swim in the pond? No, better to stick with the schedule. She tapped the folded-up paper in her pocket. It crinkled beneath her palm. She knew the list by heart, but it was better to have it on hand just in case.

Campers arrive at four, settle into cabins, and meet at the fire circle at five. Orientation with volunteer leaders at five-thirty while the campers eat in the dining hall. Campfire and marshmallows from six to seven. In cabins by eight. Lights out by nine. Schedules meant predictability. Predictability meant safety.

Amy flung open the tall barn door and inhaled the sweet, musty scent of molasses, alfalfa, and horses.

Honeydew nickered from the stall closest to the door.

"Don't worry. I've got breakfast. And marshmallows."

Mattie skittered down the hallway and stopped in front of Moonpie's stall. The chestnut mare seemed to be her favorite.

Moonpie's head appeared over the wall. She sniffed the top of Mattie's head, and the little girl flashed a rare, toothy smile.

Amy made her way down the hall, stopping at each door to dump in a scoop of feed. When she reached the end nearest the loft ladder, she opened the door and stepped in with her favorite horse. "Good morning, Cobalt. Have a good night?"

Cobalt rubbed his head against her arm and resumed eating. His ears remained pinned toward the rear, and his tail whipped back and forth. Every few bites, he jerked his head out of the trough and gazed through the window.

"What's the matter?" She paced the four corners of the stall. No snakes. Nothing out of place. Maybe a deer ran by, and Cobalt caught enough of a glimpse to spook him some.

She slid his door shut and put her hand on the vertical ladder. "Be right back down, Mattie. Stay here, okay?" She climbed two rungs and stopped. Oh, wait. There were only a few bales of hay left. Better save them for dinner. She tossed the horses each two flakes from the bale already in the feed room. They'd probably not be happy about half-rations, but a little was better than none.

Jack Evans leaned back against the hay, stretched his legs, and crossed his feet at the ankles. Streaks from the dawn sky pierced through the cracks in the barn. With a long yawn, he pulled his ball cap over his face and closed his eyes. There would be time for a quick nap. The all night walk up the mountain had exhausted him. He hadn't remembered it feeling like such a climb as a teenager. But he was here now, and after a short rest, he would find Amy and surprise her.

Would she be happy to see him? He hadn't exactly been the friend he promised through the years. He winced as he remembered the last letter he sent. Too many years ago to count. He had promised to stay in touch and failed miserably. Amy had been better off without him anyway.

What brought him here now? He asked that question a few dozen times as he hiked in the dark. Still, no answer came. He was driven to see her. But why, he didn't understand. *Lord, I hope you know what you're doing.*

A voice filtering up the ladder made him sit upright. She was here and going to climb the ladder and discover him lurking in the barn. This was such a dumb plan. He should never have come. His heart thundered in his ears as sweat broke out on his brow.

A boot thumped on the bottom rung.

There wasn't anywhere for him to hide in the nearly empty loft. He backed into a deep shadow in the corner and held his breath as though if he did that, she wouldn't be able to hear the pounding of his heart. Amy's head didn't appear through the opening. Her voice faded from the barn, and he expelled the breath he had been holding.

He caressed the scar on his cheek. So much had happened since Amy last saw him. The ugly scar was all anyone ever noticed when they looked at him. Would Amy focus on it too? It would be natural if she did. But it would be painful to see the judgment in her eyes. The questions he would be forced to answer or risk looking distant and shady.

No. She wouldn't be happy to see him. He had to leave. If he could hide out until dark, he could sneak away, and she would never know he'd been there. He paced to the far wall and peered through the rectangular, glassless window.

Amy's trim form disappeared into the trees.

The sight of her caused a knot in his chest. That beautiful, wavy, brown hair. It had been so soft between his fingers all those summers ago. But he had no right to ever let it run through his hands again.

Hurry up, night. He needed to escape before he started something he couldn't see through. Before he failed again.

"Everyone buckled?" Sam called over her shoulder.

A chorus of excited "yeses" rang out from the campers.

She flashed a smile into the rearview mirror and put the bus in drive. The children's foster parents faded into the background. Their chatter turned toward the adventure ahead at camp.

No matter how many summers—and she'd seen a lot of them—Sam spent with Camp Hope, it never failed to thrill her when a new season began. Her lifelong best friend, Zena, had envisioned this place when they were but teenagers. Being alongside her for its creation and success had been a blessing. It never mattered that Sam took backstage to Zena, and now Amy, for she could see the promise instilled in these young minds, and that in itself was worth it all.

Had she really just turned fifty-two? How had the time flown by so quickly? It seemed a lifetime ago when she and Zena first dreamed of a home they could belong to for life. As foster children in a slow system, they had time to dream. The group home they shared provided food and a roof but never the sense of family they both craved.

Camp Hope had become home long ago. A place to take pride in, and now that Zena was gone, Sam had more responsibilities than ever. Whether Amy knew it or not, Sam had her back and would until she left God's green earth. Sam glanced in the mirror at the anxious, smiling faces of the girls in the van. The first group of campers for summer, 2016. She sighed and smiled. More lives touched, and she played a role. *Thank you, Lord, for allowing me to still be a part of this magic.*

Pieces of the conversations in the rows behind her drifted to her ears. None of the girls that visited here seemed to have normal conversations. They were already too experienced, too worldly for their words. Sam understood it well. The way a pre-teen's life changed when she was ripped from her parents. Since she had been a child in the system, things had changed drastically. She'd seen a lot by twelve, but these girls saw even more. Drugs, rape, violence, death. Too much of the sadness of life and not nearly enough of the joy.

Sam grimaced as her thoughts wandered to the boys they neglected. There were just as many young boys in need of a place of serenity as young girls, but Sam couldn't begrudge Amy the decision. After Zena died, it was the one thing Amy adamantly changed. Sam knew how hard it was for Amy to make peace with her childhood. To try to look at the young boys not as a threat but as in need of their services. Amy banned boys from camp to protect the girls, but still, it hurt Sam's conscience. Maybe someday things would change, but for now she'd stand by Amy's decision and pray Amy healed from her unseen wounds.

The excitement in the rear seats picked up steam as she turned onto the gravel road leading to Camp Hope. The wooden sign at the foot of the mountain pointed them in the correct direction, but, of course, Sam didn't need the arrow. The women volunteers chatted quietly over the seats. They seemed as nervous as the children. They'd do fine, no doubt, just like they all did. And they'd leave changed too, after time with these strong, resilient girls.

Chapter 3

Amy and Mattie walked hand-in-hand down the grassy path. Ancient hemlocks lined the twisting trail. A mockingbird chirped in the branches overhead.

A few steps later, they emerged into a large meadow with five rustic cabins situated in parallel lines. Their small front porches each held a swing. A place for the girls to visit and relax. The kids that came to Camp Hope needed that. None of them had an easy, happy-go-lucky life.

Amy entered the first cabin and grabbed a broom. "You hold the dust pan for me, okay?"

Mattie took it and squatted at the door to wait.

She swept the spiders from the corners and the stink bugs from under the two bunk beds. Straightened the bedding and tucked in the sheets on the full-sized chaperone's bed. Refilled the soap in the bathroom and added a new roll of toilet paper. Mopped the floors and threw open the windows. Those tasks done, she set out to repeat her efforts in each cabin, with Mattie trailing at her heels.

The first round of camp always stirred up old memories. Some good. A lot bad. Amy's stomach churned. Excitement combined with anxiety made her heart fire rapidly in her chest. Only an hour until Sam would arrive with the bus load of kids and volunteer supervisors. Twenty girls, five women. Then she wouldn't have time for memories of her own. Just building new ones for the foster children attending camp.

Amy dumped the mop water from cabin number five over the porch rail. "Time to go to the house," she hollered.

Mattie didn't emerge from the cabin.

"Mattie?" She stepped back into the dim room. Wasn't she just here playing on the bed? Amy lifted the dust ruffle. Nothing. She flipped on the light in the bathroom. Empty. She returned to the porch and shouted. No response. Of course there was no response. Mattie not speaking sure made it difficult to locate her.

Amy licked her lips with a dry tongue and wiped her sweaty palms on her pants legs. Maybe Mattie already went back to the house? Amy ran up the hill, making a full circle, and swung open the front door.

She stopped at the kitchen and leaned against the frame, taking a deep breath to calm her frayed nerves.

Perched on the edge of a chair at the counter, Mattie used a butter knife to spread peanut butter on

Ritz crackers.

Thank goodness. “You scared me, sweet girl.”

Mattie shrugged her shoulders but didn’t turn.

“Feeling yucky? I’m glad you came to get yourself a snack.” Amy patted Mattie’s back. “But next time can you at least tug on my shirt and let me know you’re leaving?”

Mattie nodded once and resumed making her crackers.

Amy’s smile faded as she watched Mattie. Though she was glad Mattie recognized her low blood sugar, it was heartbreaking she’d had to learn to fend for herself at such a young age. How many four-year-olds would be so adept at feeding themselves? What had Mattie’s life been like before? It was a question Amy had asked over and over since the beautiful little girl’s arrival.

The camp van’s horn sounded out front.

Amy’s eyebrows shot up. “They’re here.”

With peanut butter on her fingers and cracker crumbs on her shirt, Mattie leapt off the chair and raced Amy to the front door.

Sam waved from the driver’s seat with a huge smile on her face. Amy suspected this was her favorite time of year too.

“Welcome to Camp Hope, girls. We’re excited to have you here.”

Twenty faces, some smiling, some grimacing,

stared back at Amy from their seats on the huge logs circling the fire pit. The adult volunteers scattered among them waited for instructions. All five of them newbies. Not too surprising. It was harder and harder to find grown-ups with few personal ties to these children who were willing to sacrifice a week of their time.

Mattie hugged Amy's leg, making a hot spot where her buried face exhaled onto her jeans.

"I want each of you to know this is a safe place. Our volunteers, Sam, and I are here if you need anything. We will have a ton of fun this week, but we will also have one-on-one sessions with each of you, if you wish. If you want to talk, we are available. That's what we are here for." Amy paused and drew a breath. As she made eye contact with the children individually, fear radiated from each. All of them suffered some sort of trauma. By the end of the week she could impress upon them the bond they all shared. The fact that no one was "normal," so everyone was.

"Amy," Sam whispered and nudged her in the side.

Right. Not the time to get lost in melancholy thoughts. "Our first order of business is your inaugural dinner with us. Our kitchen staff has prepared homemade pizza with ice cream sundaes for dessert."

Several of the girls cheered.

Amy smiled. "I, too, was in your shoes once upon a time. My fifteenth summer, my mom was taken to jail, and I ended up here with my great aunt, Zena. She is the one who envisioned this place, started it when I was a small child, and I continue in her footsteps. You are part of a very special group of people, you know. If you have any questions, please feel free to ask me or Sam. She will lead you to the dining hall. Adult volunteers, please remain for further instructions."

Amy waited until the campers' heads bobbed out of sight over the hill. Their voices faded into the late afternoon. She grinned at the women. "Thank you for volunteering. It means a lot to us and helps keep our costs low so foster families can afford to send their children here. As many of you know, these children aren't like others. They are wounded. We must treat them with respect and patience at a higher level than ordinary children. The kids here have experienced more in their childhood than most of you have in your adult lives. I've got a few precautions to remind you of.

"Safety is the most important thing. It is your job to make sure the campers assigned to you are where they say they are going to be. We've had runners in the past. Let's try not to repeat that again this year.

"Number two. No one is to swim without adult supervision.

"Number three. No bullying will be tolerated. It is grounds to send a camper home. This is a safe haven where these kids can make positive memories. Anything else will be shut down immediately.

"Number four. In the case of an emergency, help is not close. We have a fully stocked first aid kit in each cabin, with more supplies in the main house, and

Sam has years of hands-on experience with various injuries. She is a fantastic asset in a crisis.

"That should be it. It means a lot to us, and to these kids, that you are here. Go enjoy dinner."

The women headed in the direction of the dining hall, conversing in low tones.

Once they were out of earshot, Sam stepped from the shadows. "What do you think?"

"There's a few."

"If anyone knows how to get them to open up, it's you."

Amy pursed her lips. "I don't know. Never can tell with these kids."

"You manage to mentor at least two every summer. I'm sure this year will be no different."

"I'm going to give the horses their evening meal. Can you take Mattie with you to dinner?"

Amy strolled toward the barn, humming softly and scanning the names of the campers on her list. Would she be able to help any of these unfortunate girls? Would any of them open up and try to trust her? It was too soon to tell. Pre-teens could be so stubborn. So guarded.

Cobalt's ears didn't perk up when Amy fed him. "What in the world is going on with you today?" She patted his neck. "You'd better not be sick, mister."

He nuzzled her shoulder and nibbled at his food.

"I'll get you some hay, but if you don't perk up, I'll be forced to call the vet. Oh, yes. First thing in the morning."

Cobalt swished his long, brown tail, snapping her

back with the tips.

Amy laughed. “What? You don’t want me to call the vet?”

She climbed the ladder. With her feet firmly planted on the loft floor, Amy grabbed a bale of hay, tossed it down the ladder hole, and stood with her hands on her hips. Only ten bales left. Hopefully, Sam would have new bales ready to restock in a few days. If it didn’t rain.

She turned to leave, but movement caught her eye. Probably another rat sneaking into the short stack of hay. She grabbed the rake and rounded the corner of the bales.

Her jaw dropped open, and her heart leapt into her throat.

Not a rat. A man. In cowboy boots, faded jeans, torn T-shirt, and ball cap. Sleeping on her loft floor. She flung the rake and scooted away from him. Her feet plunged her down the ladder, her sweaty hands barely managing to keep a grip on the wooden rungs.

She raced for the house. Barring the old door behind her, she grabbed the walkie-talkie. “Sam, keep the campers in the mess hall. Bring Mattie to the house right now, please. But don’t go by the barn.”

“What? Why?”

“No time to explain. Don’t panic. Tell them not to panic if they hear sirens. Get the karaoke machine out and let them sing or something.”

Why was there a man in her barn? And how did he get there? She lived thirteen miles and a steep mountain from the nearest house for a reason.

Hank Wainwright's radio crackled.

The dispatcher's voice filled the small space of his patrol car. "Closest unit please report to 151 Farmstead Road, Briceville."

His heart sped up. He knew that address. Not the closest unit by far, but he snatched up the radio and depressed the button. "Sheriff Wainwright responding at 17:46. Emergency traffic." He flipped on the siren and blue lights and pressed the pedal harder.

Hang on, Amy. I'm coming.

His usual tactics had never worked on Amy. And he'd tried. He'd approached it from every angle he could imagine. Amy was unmovable. Each time she refused him over the years, it only made him more determined to break through her walls. Was he really interested in her anymore? Or was it the challenge that lured him? She tugged on his heartstrings. He couldn't help thinking how she reminded him of a gangly, newborn giraffe. Adorable, but vulnerable. Trying so hard to blend in with her surroundings and walk without falling that she stuck out all the more prominently.

He rarely made it up to her farm. He'd gotten that message, at least. The fiery darts Amy hurled at him the last time he surprised her and showed up on her doorstep were enough to keep him away unless he had an invitation. Like now. She needed his help. He desperately wanted to be her hero.

The more Amy hid on the top of this mountain, the more mysterious and alluring she became. Like a luxurious prize on top of a tall, mountainous pedestal. He dreamed of her. Longed to rescue her from the prison she'd built around herself. To serve and protect.

His uniform usually did the bulk of the work for him with the women. Not with Amy. Everything about her screamed, "Help me, but don't touch me." And each fiber within him responded like a taut wire, aching to find release under her strong, slender fingers. If he kept trying, he would wear past that outer wall eventually. Penetrate the armor to find the emerald inside.

He took the corners with respect. His patrol car hated this road with all its ruts and switchbacks. But Amy needed him, so he pressed the accelerator in the straights. Gravel pinged off the undercarriage, and a cloud of gray dust swirled in the rearview.

The sight of Amy waiting on the porch stirred his stomach into currents like whitewater rapids.

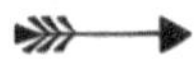

The police siren echoed up the mountain long before Amy could see the cruiser. In the forty-five minutes since she had called 911, Mattie had taken her evening insulin and gone to sleep without a fuss. Amy watched the barn like a hawk while Sam watched over the campers. The man had not emerged.

A trail of dust followed the blue and white car, rising to coat the summer leaves with a thin film of silver-white powder. The siren stopped wailing, and Amy breathed a sigh of relief. Mattie wouldn't be awakened by its blaring, and most importantly, maybe the squatter wouldn't have time to run.

Sheriff Wainwright himself stepped out of the car and waved. "Miss Amy, what's the trouble?"

Surely the dispatcher already told him her emergency. She cleared her throat and leaned against the porch rail at the top of the stairs. "There's someone in my barn. Asleep in the loft. He's trespassing."

"Righto. I'll check it out for you." Wainwright tipped his hat and spun on his heels. He strutted down the path, whistling.

Amy took a deep breath and shook her head. He looked like a dumb peacock. Would he ever understand she had absolutely no interest in dating him? He didn't have to show off for her. It would never change her mind.

She had tried letting her guard down and letting someone in. Once. Jack had been ripped from her life. Even as a teenager, the wound stung. She had no need for a man in her life. She clung to the sweet memories of that summer, and that was enough for a lifetime.

Her grip on the rail tightened as Wainwright disappeared into the shadowy barn. He hollered a few times, and then the silence lasted for too long. Had something happened? Maybe the man had managed to sneak out?

Sheriff Wainwright's bowed head and tense shoulders appeared first at the door. The man from the loft trailed him on the right and a step behind, hands cuffed in front, shoulders sagging. Oh, good. Amy sank onto the top step and slid her shaking hands under her thighs.

They shuffled back to the car and paused at the passenger door. Wainwright removed his hat and held it in front of his chest. "Do you want to press charges, Miss Amy?"

"I'm . . . I'm not sure."

The handcuffed man's chin rose, and he met her gaze. Hazel eyes, dark eyebrows. Her heart fluttered. Was it her imagination, or was there something familiar about those eyes? A jagged scar stretched across the man's nose, over his left cheekbone, and ended in an abrupt round bulge.

"No, but I want him removed from my property."

"Ten-four." Wainwright opened the door and placed a hand on the man's head.

The man grabbed his hat bill with two fingers and tipped it in her direction. "Much obliged, Amy."

That movement. That subtle tip of the hat. And the drawl. She knew that accent. "Wait."

Sheriff Wainwright stopped, and the man stood up, head hung and vein pulsing in his neck.

She approached on heavy, slow feet. "Jack?"

His head bobbed once.

She brought her hand to her chest. "What are you doing here?"

He shrugged.

Wainwright's tone bristled. "You two know each other?"

Jack ignored Wainwright and raised his eyes to

meet her gaze. "It's been a long time."

Amy's pulse bounded, like hail falling on a tin roof in a summer storm. She didn't have to count. Fifteen years and ten months since she'd last laid eyes on him. Thirteen years and two months since his last letter.

Wainwright shoved his hat back on his head. "You still want me to haul him off?"

Amy searched Jack's face. The same boy she knew, but harder. More handsome, despite the scar. Jack would never mean her harm. "No. Release him."

"Wastin' my time," Wainwright mumbled as he undid Jack's cuffs.

Jack rubbed his wrists. "Thanks." He stepped away from the cruiser and shoved his hands in his pockets.

Amy didn't know what to say, so they stood, silent, side by side as Wainwright got into the car, slammed the door, and sped down the driveway.

Jack kicked at the dirt with his right foot. "Listen, I'm sorry about this. Not exactly how I pictured it all going." He touched her elbow with his fingertips.

She jerked away. Her elbow stung from his touch. Just like it used to. "I didn't know what happened to you."

"I know. I'm sorry."

"You're okay?"

"I'm getting there. How about you?" Jack peered into her eyes.

She looked away. "I doubt I'll ever be okay,

really. But I survive."

He pressed his lips into a thin line and nodded.

He understood. He was the only one who ever did. "You hungry?"

Amy refilled Jack's coffee mug and slid another piece of pizza onto his plate.

"Thanks."

Seated across from him, she waited as he wolfed it down. Must've been a while since he had an actual meal. He was awfully thin-looking. But then again, he was a petite teenager too.

Mattie's brown eyes and wrinkled brow flashed around the door-frame and then ducked out of sight.

"It's okay, Mattie. You can come in."

She padded into the kitchen in socked feet, yawned, and climbed into Amy's lap.

Jack's eyebrows rose. "Your daughter?"

"Foster daughter." Biological daughter would've meant Amy had to be intimate with a man. That wasn't going to happen. No way.

"Ever been told she looks an awful lot like you?"

Amy giggled. "People see what they want to see."

"Suppose that's true."

Amy introduced Mattie and Jack.

Mattie glanced up at him and re-tucked her face into Amy's shoulder.

"She doesn't talk."

Amy rose and opened a drawer while balancing Mattie on her hip. She dug through screws, bolts, twisty ties, and other random junk until she found what she sought. She placed a silver key on the table in front of him. “Here’s the key to the apartment above the garage. Yours if you want it.”

“You don’t even know me anymore.”

She stared into his eyes for a moment. “I know enough.”

Chapter 4

The ache in Sam's lower back woke her again. Too many years of horses and hard work and her discs were deteriorating. Amy didn't know, and Sam wouldn't let on until she had to. She could hide the grimaces and pain a while longer. At least until summer was over.

Stray stems of dry grass decorated the kitchen floor, dimly lit by dawn. She had to finish cutting today, before the weather had a chance to change. She needed to get to the feed store too. They were low on grain for the horses. They needed groceries and to restock supplies for the first aid kit. A new prescription of insulin awaited Mattie. So much to do! Hopefully in the lull of mid-afternoon, she'd be able to sneak away.

Would Tom Wainwright be in town today? She hadn't seen him the last two trips, thank goodness. Third time's a charm, right? She guffawed and slipped on her boots. Luck was likely to not be on her side much longer.

She made her way to the dark and nearly-empty dining hall. The click of the door echoed through the uncarpeted space. “Good morning, Lou.”

The brunette woman near Sam’s age emerged through the swinging door that led to the cooking area. Lou jumped and nearly dropped the basket of silver forks she carried. “Sam, you nearly gave me a heart attack.”

Sam chuckled. “Sorry. Got any extra coffee? Lights ain’t on up at the house yet and I’m out.”

“You and your coffee. C’mon in.” Lou held the door open for Sam to pass. Lou filled Sam’s Thermos and screwed on the cap. “Something else on your mind?”

Sam told her eyebrows to unwrinkle. They didn’t listen. “I’ve just got a feeling this morning. Don’t know what it is.”

Lou scooped up a basketful of spoons and nodded.

“Will you do me a favor? Keep an eye on a couple of the campers for me when they’re in here.” Sam described two of the older girls she had noticed on the drive in. “Something about their attitude made me single them out. We haven’t had trouble here in a long while. Seems like it might be about time for something to go wrong.”

“Don’t go gettin’ all doom and gloom on me now.”

Sam absentmindedly massaged her lower back.

"Don't say anything to Amy. Okay?"

"I'll be your spy, friend, but try not to worry so much. It'll make an old woman of you." Lou chuckled.

"Always something to worry about, Lou. Always."

Amy placed the hot cast iron pot in the middle of the wooden picnic table and removed the lid. "Breakfast is served."

Sam leaned forward and inhaled the savory steam. "Smells delicious."

"One of Aunt Zena's favorite recipes. Bacon Impossible Pie."

Mattie held out her paper plate.

"You think it smells good too?" Amy smiled as she dished casserole onto the girl's plate.

With large helpings on each of their three plates, Amy sat across from Sam and Mattie. Her gaze drifted toward the mess hall down the hill as she chewed. No need to worry. The volunteers and kitchen staff had everything under control. The first morning of letting chaperones supervise always made her a bit nervous. But they had to learn to fly solo if this week was going to be successful. Amy and Sam couldn't possibly oversee every single moment.

"I still can't believe you let him stay," Sam whispered between bites.

"I know." Amy dropped her gaze to the plate before her. She didn't understand what had made her offer the apartment either.

"Are you sure it's a good idea?"

"No."

Sam's gravelly voice rose. "What made you do it, anyway?"

That summer. "History." Amy cleared her throat. "You don't remember him, do you?"

Sam shook her head with a mouthful of casserole.

"I've never been able to forget him." Amy snapped her mouth shut as Jack appeared in the side garage door. A shiver ran up her back, stirring her heart to beat faster. His mouth remained the same. Full, beautiful lips, heart-shaped dip gracing the upper curve. She remembered those lips.

Sam waved and spooned another serving of breakfast onto her plate. She picked up her coffee cup and, with plate in the other hand, strolled silently toward the mess hall.

Oh great. Alone with him again. Well, except for Mattie. But, she might as well be alone. "Are you hungry?"

"Starved."

Same question. Same answer. "Have a seat. There's plenty."

"Thanks." Jack slid onto the bench near Mattie and took the plate Amy offered.

Amy fiddled with her fork but couldn't bring herself to meet his eyes. "Sleep well?"

"Mmm-hmm."

"That's good." What exactly was she supposed

to talk about with a man she hadn't seen in almost sixteen years? A man, no less. The first one on the premises for more than a few minutes in a very, very long time.

Mattie finished her last bite, and Amy exhaled. Perfect excuse for them to leave the table. "I need to give Mattie her medicine, but you stay here and eat as much as you like." She took Mattie by the hand and resisted the urge to run into the house.

Why did she have the feeling Jack watched them as they walked away? She shivered again. What was she thinking letting him stay?

The sun danced through the treetops in patches, already warming the fire pit circle. The yawning campers stared at Amy from their seats on the massive logs with doubt in their eyes and full bellies.

"Good morning, girls." Amy grinned at the apprehensive-looking group. "Don't worry. Nothing too scary planned this morning. We're going to do some trust exercises."

Several of the girls exchanged glances and rolled their eyes.

"I know, I know. You've seen it all before. But, I promise, this will be fun. Sam has the list of how we've broken you into smaller groups. To get to know each other better, we've intentionally mixed you up from your cabin groups."

Sam read the list of names aloud, but Amy

couldn't listen. Her eyes were on Jack as he walked down the hill toward their group. The tall grass brushed his snug blue-jeans, and the cloudless blue sky framed his shoulders and handsome face. Oh, boy. When had she last had thoughts of anyone being handsome? It'd been a while. A long while. She shook her head and strengthened her fading smile.

"All right, split up into groups. I will take two, Sam will take two, and we'll get started."

Jack stepped beside her. "The place looks exactly how I remember it. Seems a little smaller though."

"Not much has changed. Except Aunt Zena."

"How long's she been gone?'

"A little over two years." Amy's voice hitched.

Jack placed his hand on her shoulder. "I'm sorry."

She took two steps back. "Thanks."

His hand fell to his side, and his brow wrinkled.

"Okie-dokie, ladies. To the barn." Amy led the way with ten girls and two chaperones following. Jack brought up the rear.

"He's cute," one of the campers behind her said. A second girl giggled.

He was cute. But that wasn't where these girls' thoughts should be. Or Amy's. She picked up her pace.

Honeydew waited at the hitching rail outside the barn. She munched on some loose hay, tail swishing at the flies, weight balanced on one rear foot with the other resting under her belly.

Amy whistled as they approached. "Never a

good idea to sneak up on a horse, girls."

Honeydew's head shot up, and her ears perked forward. She whinnied her reply.

Turning around and walking backward to address the group, Amy began, "Now she knows we're coming and we won't startle her. Horses rarely try to hurt us, but they are big and some scare easy. When they are scared, their reaction is to protect themselves by running away. A tied horse can't run, so it ends up in a big mess most of the time. I don't want you or Honeydew hurt."

Most of the girls nodded. Two of them, Sally and Emily, wouldn't make eye contact with Amy at all. They stared at the ground. Those were the two that needed a friend most, she'd bet. Someone to voice their fears to, to confide in. She would make sure they worked together this morning.

Jack hung at the back of the group. Clearly, Amy was uncomfortable with his presence. It wasn't too late to leave. She'd probably be relieved.

Why had she offered the apartment to him? Probably kindness. Not because she really wanted him to stay. Maybe she just felt bad for him, like all the others. But being near her again was intoxicating. It muddled his thoughts. He couldn't stay, but he couldn't walk away either.

Amy smiled at the girls, sending his pulse into overdrive. Over a decade had passed, but Amy's beauty hadn't changed one bit. His reaction to it had changed, though. Last time he'd been around her, it was as an immature teenager. Now, though, now was something entirely different. He suppressed a groan. He was in big trouble, wasn't he?

Amy continued with instructions. "All right, let's get started. Elise and Gretta, you will be first. You will learn to saddle the horse."

Elise crossed her arms. "What's the trust part of this?"

"Ah, that's the fun part. You and Gretta saddle and someone else gets to ride. In order for them to get on Honeydew, they have to trust you did a good job. And I have to trust you don't want them hurt. Right?"

Elise smirked. "Right."

The sarcasm the young girl exuded made Jack's eyebrows quirk. He wouldn't trust her to saddle the horse for him.

"Jack, maybe you can help this morning?"

Jack snapped to attention. Really? She needed his help? He straightened his shoulders. "Sure thing."

"Why don't you go ahead and get Moonpie out of her stall? That way we can have two groups of three going at once and the others," she shot a glance at the fidgeting pre-teens, "won't be milling around as long."

His spirits rose. He could be useful. He touched the bill of his cap with two fingers and nodded in Amy's direction. He entered the barn and scanned the brass nameplates on the stalls. They'd all changed since he was here as a boy. His favorite used to be a beautiful dun named Wrangler. He remembered one afternoon when he had saddled Wrangler and taken off into the forest. Never to return. If he could have gotten into those mountains with his favorite horse, he could have lived off the land forever. No more foster home. No terrible uncle. Just freedom and independence.

He chuckled as he haltered Moonpie. He'd barely made it ten feet into the woods back then when footsteps had approached.

"Where ya headed?" Amy had asked.

"Nowhere. Everywhere."

"Mind if I come too?"

He'd stopped Wrangler in his tracks and turned to face her. "I thought you weren't going to stop me and now you want to come? With me?"

"Why not? Nowhere sounds safe and everywhere sounds exciting."

In the late afternoon sunlight, her long hair glistened. Her heart-shaped lips full and pouting. He shook his head. "Changed my mind."

"Oh, good. Come on then. Before Aunt Zena catches us."

Amy had a power over him that summer. A power no one else had before or since. She believed in him. No one in his life thought he was worth anything. Just a lazy rebel. Amy saw past the façade to the drive underneath.

A lot had changed since then, though. He ran his fingers over the scar. He'd been so many places. Seen so many things. And not accomplished anything.

Amy seemed much more distant. Harder. She'd changed a lot about Camp Hope, it seemed. If he gathered correctly, campers only stayed a week now. And no boys. No men on sight. He couldn't say he blamed her after her childhood. Maybe he should have, but he hadn't expected that.

Amy willed her eyes to focus on the task at hand, not to watch Jack as he brought Moonpie from the barn. There was nothing dramatic about his narrow gait. Nothing to scream at her about his presence. Yet it was torture not to watch him draw nearer.

Ever since he'd been forced to leave Camp Hope, she'd longed for his return. And now here he was, and she couldn't tease out how she really felt about it. Other than scared. His presence definitely elicited a tingling sense of fear. Jack brought the past with him.

"Okay, girls. Now for the fun part. You've saddled the horse for Kelsie. It's time for you two to help her mount."

Kelsie took a step back. "Uh-uh. I can get on by myself."

"There's something special about these saddles." Amy pointed to the dangling side straps. "No stirrups."

"Are you afraid?" Elise sneered.

The color faded from Kelsie's oval face.

"We will not tease each other. Remember, this is a safe place." Amy took Kelsie's hand in her own and led her closer to Honeydew. "Stroke her neck, like this."

Kelsie touched Honeydew's neck with trembling fingers.

"She is as gentle as a kitten. I promise she won't hurt you. And I'll be right here." She squeezed Kelsie's hand. "Jack, can you help the next group saddle Moonpie while I teach Elise and Gretta how to get Kelsie onto this horse?"

Amy met his eyes for a split second.

He nodded and looked away.

"Kelsie, stand on your right leg and bend the other leg at a ninety-degree angle." Amy bent her knee and demonstrated. "Grab the saddle horn with your left hand. Elise and Gretta, you will grab Kelsie's calf, gently please. On the count of three, Kelsie, you will bounce onto your toes, and they will pick you up. Swing your right leg over the horse and get settled into the saddle."

Kelsie stepped back. "I can't do this, Ms. Amy."

"Sure you can. You just have to trust yourself, the horse, and your friends."

"Don't trust anybody," Kelsie muttered.

"I know. I'm asking a lot. But can you at least try?"

Kelsie shook her head. "Why don't you show me how?"

"You guys aren't big enough to lift me."

"He could help you." Kelsie pointed at Jack.

Have Jack help her? Stand close to her. Touch her. Amy's stomach plummeted. "No," she whispered and cleared her throat. "He's busy."

Kelsie crossed her arms over her chest. "Then I

ain't getting on that horse."

"Looks like Ms. Amy doesn't trust anyone either," Elise said.

Gretta snickered. "Especially not a man."

Tears sprang to Amy's eyes. "That is enough. Lesson over. Find your chaperones at the mess hall."

How dare they! Amy's cheeks burned as she watched the girls' somber retreat. As soon as they were out of sight, her shoulders slumped. Who was she kidding? They were right.

"You want me to put Moonpie back?"

Jack's simple question made her jump. She would not let him see her weak. She spun and raised her chin. Over Honeydew's back, she met his boring gaze and nodded once. "Please."

"Sorry for causing you trouble. It's the last thing I intended."

"What did you intend, Jack?" Heat rose up her throat. "I haven't seen you in fifteen years. I didn't know where you were or if you were okay. Maybe you had died, for all I knew."

He hung his head. "I'm sorry."

She shouldn't have yelled. Amy took a deep breath. She swung onto Honeydew's back and squeezed her sides. "Yah!"

Honeydew bolted from her drowsy position and raced down the trail into the forest.

Branches tore at her hair and stung her face. It didn't matter. She had to get away from Jack. It was too much. He was too much. How was she supposed to teach these girls anything when her every thought revolved around him? Where had he been all these years? Why had he tossed her aside? Never written. Never called. Until now.

Sam's drive into town always seemed so much longer in the dark. Good thing the Wal-Mart pharmacy stayed open late.

The familiar blast of cool air lifted the strands of sweaty hair around her face as she entered the front doors. Her list was a mile long. She turned the buggy into the coffee aisle and stopped short. Tom. Could she try a different row before he saw her?

"Sam, hey!"

Nope. "Hi, Tom. How's Evangeline?"

Tom's top lip momentarily disappeared behind his bottom one. "She's . . . fine."

What was that about? Sam wrinkled her brow. "Saw the sheriff yesterday."

He thrust his shoulders erect and smiled.

"We had a stranger in the barn. Can you believe it? I knew it was about time for some trouble up at Camp Hope. Been quiet too long." Why was she telling him this?

"I'm sorry to hear that." He paused, and his eyes softened. "Happy birthday."

A blush crept up Sam's neck. She dipped her head. "Well, I'd better get to it." She needed to get away from him before the jumpy crickets in her stomach made her do or say something foolish.

Imagine, at her age, still getting flustered near a married man whom she'd known for more than thirty years. One whose wife she respected. It was pure nonsense.

Sam rushed away from Tom, away from the feelings she hoped to leave on the tiled floor where only the coffee cans and bread could see them. It had never worked before when she ran into Tom. Maybe this time would do the trick?

Chapter 5

June 14, 2016

Jack's here. At Camp Hope. I never, in a million years, thought I'd see him again. And how is it that after all this time, he still has the ability to make me weak in the knees? We had a rough day with the campers. I didn't finish their horse trust exercises. It's been a long time since one of them got in my head like that.

Amy's head snapped up as light footsteps approached. What was Mattie doing out of bed? She uncurled her legs and placed them on the porch boards. She took a deep breath as the swing stopped creaking. A slight wind rustled the crepe myrtles on the other side of the dark banister. "Mattie?"

"No, it's me." Jack rounded the corner of the house and stopped.

"What's wrong?"

He looked at his boots and shoved his hands in his back pockets. "Can we talk?"

Amy crossed her arms over her chest and nodded.

He stepped closer.

Her shoulders tensed. What did he want?

"I'm leaving. I never should've come. I'm sorry."

"Leaving? When?" Heaviness flooded her. He couldn't leave. He just got here.

"Now." He turned to go.

She hadn't noticed the mandolin case strapped to his back until he spun. "Jack, wait." She rose from the swing. "At least wait until morning. Then Sam can give you a ride to the bus stop or something. No sense in you hiking out of here in the middle of the night."

"I hiked in here in the middle of the night." He winked.

A smile tugged at her lips. "Indeed you did." What was it she couldn't say? Please stay? She didn't want him to leave? "Just, please wait."

The cicadas buzzing filled the summer night air.

"Do you still play?"

He grinned and took the case from his back. "What was your favorite song again?" Taking the mandolin from the case, he drew the pick across the strings. "Oh, yeah. Red River Valley."

How had he remembered? Amy collapsed into the swing. Sweet music surrounded her. Drew out even more memories of their time together as kids. Even as a fifteen-year-old girl, she had recognized how much she loved him. Was it possible those feelings still existed in some deep, hidden part of her? Maybe she hadn't done as good a job banishing them as she thought.

Jack finished the last note and dropped the mandolin and pick to his side. He smiled sheepishly from under his cap bill.

"That was beautiful," she whispered. She couldn't stay out here on the porch with this handsome man in the light of the summer starlight, with her heart in her throat, a minute longer without being lulled into a sense of contentment. "I'd better get to bed. I'll see you in the morning, and we'll arrange for Sam to drive you out. If that's still your plan by dawn."

She spun on her heels and retreated into the side door. Lifting the gingham curtain, she peeked out the darkened window.

Jack stood stock still, rooted in place with his old mandolin in one hand and a strange look on his face.

A deep breath calmed her aching heart. That was too close. Never again would she let herself feel for any man what she felt for Jack a decade and a half ago. Men couldn't be trusted. Love couldn't be hoped for. Healing couldn't come. Not with all she'd been through.

Grocery shopping wore Sam out a whole lot more than it used to. She slipped into her favorite rocking chair on the front porch and gazed at the half-cut field with a cup of fresh coffee in hand. She'd let the hot shower massage her tight muscles, and it felt heavenly. Her cell phone beeped, and she picked it up to find a message from Lou.

"Forgot to tell you. Overheard a couple girls talking about that man Amy let stay in a way young girls should not be talking. I got onto them. You were right to watch them. They mentioned something about the horses, but I couldn't hear the rest."

Of course they were talking about Jack. The whole camp was buzzing with the news of an attractive man living in the apartment. Sam shook her head. Young girls who didn't get to be young and innocent. What a shame it all was.

The horses, eh? It had happened before that campers decided to ride without permission. She pried herself from the rocking chair and slipped her boots back on. They hugged her feet a little too tightly at this hour of the night after such a busy day.

"Aw, c'mon, Sam. You act like you're elderly or something." Her voice fell into the empty night. She felt old. And growing older every day.

Her gaze wandered over the family graveyard as she passed. A smattering of headstones circled by a white, metal fence under a single shade tree. The grass waved tall in front of the names, barely visible under the pale starlight. When would she find time to mow there too? Sam sighed. She really could use another helping hand.

Movement on the path ahead gave her pause. Two shadowed forms emerged from the direction of the cabins. "Who's there?"

"It's Kat and Beth. We've got missing campers."

Sam smacked her open palm with her fist. "I knew it. C'mon up to the house."

Amy bolted upright and pushed her sleep-tousled hair from her face. Something was wrong. A hesitant knock sounded at the door.

"Amy?"

"Sam? What's wrong?" She slipped a sweatshirt over her pajamas and opened the door.

"Got some campers missing."

"Again?" When would the girls who came here learn? "Okay. Let me get dressed."

Five minutes later, Amy met Sam on the front porch. The chaperones from cabins four and five shifted from foot to foot and whispered to each other under the poplar tree in the yard.

Amy approached them with a flashlight in her hand. "Ladies, what happened?"

"I woke up," number four's chaperone began, "and had two empty beds. I went to cabin five and woke Kat up. She has two missing campers too."

Kat nodded. "I'm sorry. I can't believe I slept through them sneaking out."

"This isn't the first time this has happened. But they usually turn up quickly. We are so far away from anything, they give up and come back. No one likes to hike in or out of here." Except Jack. Amy shined her light on the garage apartment's black window. No sign of him. "Who's missing?"

"Elise, Kelsie, Gretta, and Gypsy," Kat said.

Of course Elise and Gretta were involved. "Okay. Go back to your cabins and keep an eye on your other girls. Sam and I will start looking. The swimming pond is usually a favorite. We'll keep you posted."

Sam nodded and clicked her flashlight back on. "I'll check there first."

Amy touched Sam's elbow. "Thanks. I'll check the barn." With one last glance at Jack's window, Amy headed down the hill.

The door stood open. Strange. She or Sam always closed it before bedtime. She stepped through the door and switched on the overhead light. Four stall doors gaped open. Oh, great. She peered into the tack room. Saddles and bridles didn't dot the walls like they should have. The girls had clearly decided to go on a midnight ride. Those stinkers were in so much trouble when they returned.

Sam stepped into the barn. "No sign of 'em at the . . ."

"Yeah. Moonpie, Honeydew, Vasper, and Nate are missing."

"Well, at least they took the slow, gentle ones."

Amy chuckled. "True."

"What now?"

"We wait. They always come back."

Sam's lips pressed together into a thin line. "Except that once."

Amy dipped her chin. “So you do remember Jack.”

“That was Jack? This Jack?”

“Yep.”

Sam shook her head. “Hope we don’t have to call Sheriff Wainwright.”

“It’s not a matter of hope. It’s a matter of common sense. It’s dark. Even if they make it to Briceville, what’re they going to do when they get there? Nothing’s open, and it’s a long ways to the next town.”

“I’ll take a little drive and see if I can spot them. But what’s to say they ain’t out on the trails?”

“Those girls don’t really know anything about trail riding. Earlier they were too scared to mount up. I bet you’ll find them on the road. This isn’t an escape plan, it’s a stunt to get under my skin again after their lesson earlier.”

“What happened?”

She’d panicked when Gretta touched on the truth. “Nothing.”

Sam raised one eyebrow.

“Really, it’s nothing. I’ll go tell Kat and Beth not to worry.”

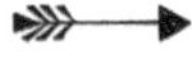

Amy paced the path from barn to house. What was taking them so long? The stars glittered overhead, taunting her. They could see where the campers were. And all she could see was the ticking of time on her watch. 2:03 AM. Where was Sam?

The distant crunch of gravel finally reached her ears. Oh, thank goodness. The clip clopping of the horses' shod feet accompanied the approaching camp van. The headlights illuminated three horses with all four girls. Three horses?

Amy jogged to meet them at the front porch steps.

Sam cut the van and exited. "Off the horses. Now."

The girls complied and left the reins dangling. If the tone in Sam's voice was any indication, they didn't have a choice. The horses munched grass and caught their breath while the girls' gazes remained fixed on the ground.

Amy put her balled fists on her hips. "What were you thinking?"

Their eyes remained downcast. Not an utterance spoken.

"You four are in big trouble. First thing in the morning."

"Please don't call our foster parents." Gretta's voice held a slight tremble.

A knife twisted in Amy's breast. Gretta was afraid of her foster parents. Did she have good reason? Amy shook her head. "I think we can deal with this in camp. But you will go straight to your cabins and stay there until morning. Do you understand?"

Four heads nodded their reply.

"Where is Vasper?"

"We didn't take him," Elise said. "He was in his

stall when we left."

Sam accompanied them in the direction of the cabins while Amy took the reins and led Moonpie, Honeydew, and Nate back to the barn. It didn't make any sense. If the girls had only taken three horses, where was the fourth? Had he managed to get out somehow?

With the horses back in their stalls, Amy inspected the latch bolt on Vasper's door. Intact. No signs of a way Vasper could've escaped. Amy's brow wrinkled. What in the world happened to him?

Jack.

The answer came to her on the whisper of the wind.

Had he decided to leave tonight after all? But steal Vasper? It wasn't like him.

Amy huffed. What did she know about the man he'd become? Not a thing. Maybe it was like him. How dare he take advantage of her hospitality!

Amy stomped back to the house and up the apartment steps. She banged on the door. As she suspected, there was no response. She used her spare key to unlock the door and swung it wide. The room appeared tidy, the bed made. His mandolin was gone.

Amy sank onto the bed. He had left. Even after their talk, he had left. Again. She should've known. Why had she let her guard down so easily? She was different now. Not some dumb kid. She was blind to have let him stay.

Amy plodded to the house and crawled into bed, not bothering to undress again. It was only a few hours till daylight. Why bother? Exhaustion stole her into restless sleep and nightmares about Jack and the missing campers.

Amy gently pushed Mattie's door open. "Are you awake? Breakfast time." She took two steps toward the bed and gasped. No little lump in the middle. Had she snuck out of the house early? "Mattie?"

No reply.

Great. Another search party. All she'd done for the last eight hours was look for people. Couldn't anyone just stay put?

She searched the closets and nooks upstairs. Mattie wasn't in the bathroom either. Downstairs Amy opened each cupboard, swung open the laundry room doors, and pushed the furniture from the walls. Mattie had never hidden in any of these places before, but what did she really know about her after only a few weeks? Had something scared her and she'd chosen to hide? Or maybe she'd simply wandered out of boredom?

Amy ran to the pond and stepped onto the walkway stretching into the middle. What if Mattie had drowned? She ground her teeth together and peered into the thick water, but she wouldn't have been able to see the bottom no matter how her eyes strained. There was no sign Mattie had been there. No flip-flops on the boardwalk or anything. The only way to be certain would be to dive in and try to reach bottom, but she had a feeling this wasn't where Mattie had come. Mattie was hesitant around water, fearful because of her inability to swim.

Next, she sprinted to the barn and climbed into the loft. She checked behind the sparse bales of hay and in the darkened corners. She descended the ladder and checked each stall one by one. No sign of Mattie anywhere. Each minute that passed without finding Mattie, her heart sped faster. A tense knot forming in her throat made it painful to swallow. Where was she?

By the time she made it to the cabins, an aching sense of urgency pushed against her chest. Mattie had strayed before but never where Amy couldn't find her. Usually Mattie only went back to the house for snacks or to the barn to pet Moonpie.

"Sam," Amy called into the walkie-talkie.

"Baling hay. What's the problem?"

"I can't find Mattie." The tremble in her voice gave away her panic.

"Be right there."

Amy gazed over the meadow at the waving grass and the mountain peaks, level with their farm situated atop a plateau. If Mattie wasn't in any of the buildings, how would they ever find her? There was so much empty forest. So much dangerous, endless mountain land. If Mattie had wandered into the woods alone, how would they know where to start?

Sam's tractor stopped in the middle of a row of cut grass. She sprinted for Amy and reached her side, panting, with concern dimpling her forehead.

"Where've you looked?"

"Everywhere."

"She's here somewhere."

"Jack's gone too." Amy wrung her hands together. "What if he took her?"

"Now, don't think like that. She'll turn up."

"And if she doesn't?" Amy hugged her stomach.

Sam's fingers pressed into Amy's forearm. "She will. Go check the house again. I'll cover the barn and pond one more time."

Tears filled Amy's eyes. "She doesn't know how to swim." That was one of Amy's goals for this summer. Everyone should know how to swim. What if she never got the chance?

"Go on."

Amy turned from Sam with heavy footsteps and tears clouding her vision.

The house, though filled with sunlight, felt empty. She once again searched each room to no avail. With a sigh, she fell onto Mattie's cold bed. "Where are you, sweet girl?"

Downstairs the front door creaked open, as if on cue.

"Mattie?" Amy placed her feet on Mattie's fuzzy, purple rug. Something crinkled. She stooped to pick it up. "Grape bubble gum?" Odd. Mattie didn't chew sugary gum. She stuffed it in her pocket and flew down the stairs. It wasn't Mattie that waited at the door. It was Sam with a grave look on her face.

"What? What is it?"

"There's no sign of her anywhere. Vasper's still

gone." Sam paused and took a deep breath. "I think it's time to call Wainwright."

Chapter 6

Amy whipped out her cell phone and punched in the number.

"Wainwright speaking."

"It's Amy. I've—"

"You again, eh? Looks like you want me up there more than you let on." He chuckled.

She could picture the wry grin on his face. If she could reach through the phone and smack him, she would. "No, you don't understand. Mattie's missing."

"I'll be there as soon as I can."

"Sam, please go watch over the campers. No use in panicking everyone. Yet."

"Well," Wainwright said, "what's going on, Amy?" He placed his right foot on the bottom step, leaned in, and draped his arm across his knee.

There was far too much sparkle dancing in his eyes. "I told you on the phone. Mattie's missing."

"That so?"

Amy rose from her seat on the top step and crossed her balled fists over her chest. "That's so."

"Have you looked everywhere?"

"Of course I have."

Wainwright made a note on his pad. "What about that louse you let stay here? What was his name?" He smiled. "Oh, right. Jack."

Amy's gaze darted to the barn. "He's gone."

"Well, well, well. Things are getting interesting 'round here."

Her blood scalded her veins. "Are you going to do your job, Sheriff? Or what?"

Wainwright held up both palms and wrinkled his brow. "Calm down, little lady. I'll look around and see what I can find. Bet you wish you'd let me arrest him now, don't ya?"

One more condescending remark and Amy would punch him in the throat.

Sam stepped between them. "Wainwright, I've known you since you were a snotty kid. There's no need to talk to Amy like that. Just do your job, or I'll call your mother."

Wainwright's grin faded. He spun on his heels, retrieved his hat from the patrol car, and stomped to the barn.

"Thank you," Amy said.

"Please. That man ain't got a lick of manners.

Shame too. His momma is such a sweet woman."

"I can't just sit here while he checks all the same places we've already looked. Does he think I'm lying?"

"Wainwright's the kind of man that needs to believe the plan is always his idea. But once he gets a notion, he runs with it." Sam placed her hand on Amy's forearm. "It's going to be okay. Let him do his job."

Amy nodded and bit back her frustration. Where hadn't they looked? She gazed out over the forest and tried to remember her favorite hiding places from childhood.

The old tree fort.

She hadn't been there in a decade. Was it even still hanging in that giant oak tree? She'd sought refuge there more times than she could count as a teenager. And spent countless hours there telling Jack all her secrets and shames of the past. Maybe Mattie had discovered her hideout. "I'll be right back."

Sam opened her mouth but closed it again and nodded.

Amy crossed the driveway, squeezed through the barbed wire pasture fence, and jogged to the forest's edge. Sweat trickled down her back. The cooler air under the canopy of trees would've been sweet relief from the sun's rays had she not been so worried. A few hundred yards later, she stared at the rickety board floor of the tree fort somehow still suspended on crooked oak branches. The board and rope ladder creaked under her weight but held firm.

The warped floor felt surprisingly stable. And clean. Without glass in the windows, shouldn't there be a decade's worth of leaf litter and spider webs? She paced to the window looking toward the farmhouse. A boot print stood out in the thin layer of dust underneath. Someone had been here. Watching the house from the vantage in the trees. Amy shivered. Jack? He clearly wasn't the same person she knew as a kid. But kidnap Mattie? In the past few hours she'd gone from trusting him enough to invite him to stay to wondering if Jack had stolen Vasper and then kidnapped her sweet girl. The boy she fell in love with could never turn into a person that could kidnap a child. Could he?

At the opposite corner, Amy stooped to shake out a blanket. Still colorful and intact. Not dusty. It had to be new. A piece of paper fluttered to the ground. She stooped to pick it up. Another grape bubble gum wrapper. She held it to her nose and inhaled. A memory like an electric shock cascaded through her mind.

Pinned against the barn wall, splinters poked through Amy's t-shirt. She struggled to speak with him pressed tightly against her. "What do you want?"

Red's strong hands squeezed tighter on her biceps. Dried spit clung to the corners of his mouth. "Taking what I want. Ain't that what you've learned too? No one wants you. No one loves you. So when we want something—"

"I'll scream." Amy opened her mouth and took a breath deep enough to let out a scream that would wake the neighbors.

His thin lips pressed against her mouth. Hot, wet, unpleasant.

She turned her head and flared her nostrils.

"Go ahead. I'll say it was you that begged poor little ole me." He faked a sad expression.

"Aunt Zena wouldn't believe you."

"Oh yeah? I know what you are. Heard you talking to Jackie-boy."

Amy's eyes grew wide. "You . . . you—"

"That's right. Now it's my turn to have a taste."

"Please. Just let me go."

His grip tightened again.

Her fingers tingled with numbness. Bile rose into her throat as his lips found hers again. Her braces cut the insides of her lips, and the taste of his grape bubblegum invaded her mouth. No. She was supposed to be safe here. Aunt Zena had promised.

A voice rang out from the doorway. "Let her go."

Amy slammed backward into the tree house wall. The entire structure shook as her body quaked. She had worked so hard to block that memory. The taste of his awful grape gum. The smell of his sweaty body. The feel of his putrid lips on hers.

She shook her head. Jack didn't take Mattie. Someone far more evil did. She had to find her before it was too late. Amy knew all too well what Red was capable of. She may never heal from her scarred childhood, but she could save Mattie from going through it too.

Amy sprinted for the house and met Wainwright at his patrol car.

"No sign of—"

"I know who took her."

Wainwright looped his thumbs through his utility belt. "You do, eh?"

"Yes. I don't know his real name." She pulled the gum wrappers from her pocket and held them out for Wainwright. "We called him Red when he worked here."

Wainwright smirked. "You're an investigator now?"

"You're not listening—"

"This Jack fellow." Wainwright leaned into his car and pulled out a stack of papers. "He has a rap sheet, you know. Petty theft. Evading arrest." He flipped to the last page and held it out for her to see. "This one is especially interesting. Aggravated assault."

"What?" Amy crumpled the gum wrappers into her fist and slowly took the papers he offered with her empty hand.

"It's not a huge leap from aggravated assault to kidnapping."

"No. He wouldn't."

"I think you're letting your childhood crush get in the way of your judgment."

How did he know that? "I . . . He wouldn't do something like this. These charges are from when he was nineteen." She shoved the papers into Wainwright's hand. "The gum wrappers. Red always chewed this gum."

"Lots of people chew gum, Amy. They could even be Mattie's."

"Mattie doesn't have sugary sweets. She knows better."

Wainwright waved a dismissive hand at the wrappers. "I'm calling in backup. Is there anything else missing?"

Amy bit her cheek.

"What is it?"

"A horse."

Wainwright frowned. "Lots of backup."

Chapter 7

"He's not listening to me, Sam."

"I know. You said that before." Sam refilled Amy's mug and placed it on the table in front of her.

With her legs curled under her, Amy lifted the cup and took a sip. "It wasn't Jack."

Sam sighed. "How can you be sure?"

"I just know." Had Aunt Zena told Sam about Red's behavior all those years ago? Amy couldn't meet her friend's gaze.

"Okay. You know. Even if it wasn't Jack, they will find the trail. They're bringing the dog."

Amy nodded. The dog, yes. It would find Mattie's scent no matter who she was with. The evening sun pierced long rays through the windows, casting shadows in the kitchen. "They need to hurry. If she hasn't had her insulin at all today, she'll be in real trouble."

"They are doing their best, I'm sure." Sam opened the fridge. "Here, I forgot your creamer."

"Thanks." Amy held out her cup and allowed Sam to add a dollop of Italian Cream. "Wait," Amy said as the door swung shut. She rose from her seat and pulled open the door. "The insulin. It's gone." But that didn't make any sense.

The syringes too. They were gone from the counter. How had she not noticed before? Relief flooded her. Whoever took Mattie, took her medicine too. At least she wouldn't have to worry Mattie would be suffering from her diabetes.

Sam sighed. "Well, we can thank God for that at least. But how did they know to take the insulin?"

"I don't know."

"Did Jack see you give Mattie any shots?"

The tree house. With binoculars, the kidnapper could've watched through the window. "Well, yes. He knew she needed insulin, but there's more."

"Oh?"

"I checked out the old tree fort. I think someone's been watching the house."

"Did you tell Wainwright?"

"I tried. He wouldn't listen."

"As soon as we see him again, we will tell him."

Amy closed her eyes. It would be dark soon. They couldn't wait. "I'll go find him now."

"Last I saw him, he was scouting down by the pond waiting on the dog team to come."

She leapt from her chair. She had to try again.

"One more thing."

Amy spun to face Sam.

"We need to make a decision about the campers. We can't pretend nothing's happening any longer."

Aunt Zena would scold her for an unsuccessful week. But Amy couldn't watch them and search for Mattie at the same time. "Send them home."

Sam pressed her lips into a thin line and nodded.

Amy made a beeline for the pond. No sign of Wainwright. The greenish water troubled her. How could she be sure Mattie wasn't lying at the bottom? She shook her head. That wouldn't explain why the insulin was gone. Mattie was alive. Kidnapped, but alive. For now.

She walked the tree line, scouring the ground for clues. If Red or Jack took Mattie on Vasper, there would be prints. Follow the prints, find Mattie.

Unless Jack took Vasper and left. And Red took Mattie on foot.

Amy's lungs contracted until she couldn't breathe. She bent over and put her hands on her knees. Squeezed her eyes shut and pictured Mattie's beautiful, rare smile.

Thank God the kidnapper took the insulin? How could Sam say that? Amy could thank God if Mattie hadn't been kidnapped in the first place. No sense thanking Him, though. He did whatever He pleased. Even when it meant an innocent child got hurt.

Amy opened her eyes and stared at the flies buzzing a pile of horse manure. Fresh manure. They hadn't used this trail in weeks. The girls that ran the night before were on the other side of the farm, down the road. Not in the woods. A thrill ran through her. This could be the clue they needed. It hadn't even been a whole day. If the dog hurried, they could find Mattie tonight.

"Wainwright!"

His muffled voice answered from the direction of the cabins.

She jogged to the cabins but stopped short when she spotted Wainwright in front of the group of anxious-looking girls. "What are you doing?"

"Just questioning them. They might have seen something."

"Without even asking me?"

"I thought you'd want me to do whatever it took to find Mattie."

His words bit her. Of course she did.

"They told me an interesting story. Seems you didn't give me all the details about last night."

"Them deciding to go on a midnight ride doesn't have anything to do with Mattie."

"And I'm sure you called their parents."

Amy gritted her teeth.

"You didn't? I'd bet they'd be interested to know what happened."

"There was no need."

"There is now. I have to recommend you send all the campers home."

"We already —"

"And I'll need a list of their contact information if I have further questions."

She remembered Sam's words. It ached to

concede, like a vise twisting her intestines. But, like it or not, she needed his help. "Of course. Good idea."

Wainwright's face lit up, and his chest swelled. "Okay, girls. You can go to the mess hall after you gather your things. We will arrange transport home soon."

The wink he gave them made Amy's stomach turn. Maybe he would listen if she used her sticky sweet voice. She forced a smile and took him by the crook of the elbow. "I have something I'd like to show you."

He cleared his throat. "Okay."

She led him to the trail head and pointed out the manure.

He squatted to inspect it. "It's fresh."

"Yes."

"You're sure none of the girls rode this way?"

"Positive."

"We will start the dog here then. I need something of Mattie's for them to smell. They should be here in a few minutes."

"Thank you." Amy backed away three steps. "Whoever took Mattie, took her insulin too."

"Interesting. That's a good thing though, right?"

"Considering the situation, there aren't any good things. But that buys us a little time to find her."

He nodded and stood erect.

Finally, he'd listened to her.

He closed the gap between them with one quick stride. "What do you say we spend some time catching up? Until the other day, I hadn't seen you in months."

Really? At a time like this? Her daughter, foster daughter, was missing, and he wanted to "catch up?"

"How about dinner after this mess is over?"

The itch to strike his haughty chin tickled her fist again. It took every ounce of control she possessed to reply politely. And even then, her words burned her throat. "Wainwright, I appreciate your help with Mattie. But I can't go to dinner with you. Not now. Not ever."

His cheeks tinged red. "Shame. We'd make a great pair."

Ugh. No we wouldn't. "Thanks for the offer. I'd better get back to help see the campers off." And away from him before she exploded.

Sam leaned against her kitchen counter and drew a deep breath. She'd feigned needing to come to her cabin to take Tylenol for her aching head. It was aching, but the truth was she needed a moment to breathe. And pray. Mattie was missing. Poor, sweet, little Mattie.

If she'd been more diligent keeping an eye on things around camp, maybe the kidnapper wouldn't have had a window to steal Mattie from her bed. Sam was supposed to protect Amy and now Mattie. She'd promised Zena she would. Great job she was doing. She hadn't tried hard enough to make Amy send Jack home.

Sam remembered him as a teenager now. The

scar had thrown her off. He had been somewhat deer-like. Fear-filled eyes and a manner that said he'd bolt at the first sign of trouble. Jack wasn't a brave child or a troublemaker. But that was a long time ago. The scar on his face was evidence of time's change. He'd probably gotten it in some brawl.

Lord, please, I beg you, protect Mattie. Bring her home to us.

That short prayer was all she could muster. Her head throbbed, her back ached, and her heart wrenched as if it were tearing in pieces. Tom's face danced through her mind. His comforting presence would have been welcome. Sam shook her head. Not in this lifetime. He was married to another woman, and Sam was destined to be alone. She didn't need a man, anyway. Not as long as she had God and her own strength of will.

She summoned courage she didn't feel. It was time to gather the campers and get them home.

The cafeteria filled with children had never been so quiet. The four chaperones hugged the back wall with frowns etched into their stony faces. "Girls, I'm sorry it's turned out this way. As you know, Amy's little one is missing. We know it has nothing to do with any of you." Sam paused and passed her forced smile around the room. "But we need to focus all our efforts on getting Mattie home safely. I will talk to Amy when this ordeal is over. Maybe we can have a redo week. Sound good?"

The girls mumbled and nodded their replies without mirroring her half-hearted grin.

"Okay, chop, chop. Let's get you home. Your foster parents will be waiting in town where I picked you up."

The drive into town remained as silent as the cafeteria. Soft music playing on the radio was all that filled the disappointment.

"Sam," Kat began, "I'm so sorry this has happened. My husband works for TWRA. Maybe they would have a way to help with the search." Kat laid a hand on Sam's forearm. "I'll ask him as soon as I get home."

"That would be great. Thank you." Was all of this really real?

Sam pulled into the parking lot at the store in town. The group of foster parents huddled near their crookedly parked cars, whispering and shaking their heads. "Ladies, your rides await." She hoped her attempt at sounding light and pleasant was succeeding.

The girls exited the van and gathered their bags. With stooped shoulders, they found their foster parents' vehicles and disappeared one by one inside. With each one, Sam's heart sank a little deeper into her chest. They had never canceled a single week of camp. Never had to send a whole group home before. There was nothing left to be said, so the foster parents quietly drove away.

"Sam."

She jumped and spun toward Tom's voice.

"I heard what happened. I know he ain't really supposed to, but Hank needed to talk when he came by the house last night." Tom scratched his bearded chin.

"I've never seen him so upset, so downhearted before. I'm awful sorry." Tom took a step closer.

Sam's breath caught in her throat. "Thank you," she managed to squeak out.

"I've seen the way my son acts when he's around Amy. Like a blame fool, if you ask me. I don't understand it myself altogether, but I think the boy's afraid of getting hurt so he acts like an idiot so there won't be any chance. I'm sorry for that too."

"Wainwright can apologize for his own behavior."

Tom smiled. "You'll let me know if I can do anything to help?"

She nodded. Why was it that when she was alone with Tom, somehow she forgot about Evangeline? *Lord, forgive me.*

Hank stepped through the colorful doors into the cooler nighttime air. It had been hard to tear himself away from Amy's place, but he couldn't miss his great-uncle's funeral either. Though they hadn't been close, his mother expected his presence. Why was it every time the preacher spoke, he felt as if he was in the hot seat? Even at a funeral.

His mother slipped her arm through the crook of his elbow. "Come on, Hank. Drive me home."

"Ain't you riding with Dad?"

"We need to talk." She beamed a smile up at him.

Great. This couldn't be good.

He escorted her to his truck and tucked her into the passenger seat. Another deep breath and he was behind the wheel.

"Mary Beth asked about you again this morning. I bumped into her at the grocery store. When are you going to ask that nice girl out?"

Ah, that was it. "Not interested, Mom." What he needed to do was get back up to Amy's. The Amber alert was sent out an hour ago, but if Amy was right, no one would spot Mattie on the roads.

Her tone lost its lighter inflection. "It's time to move on. Amy isn't interested in you. She's made that plain. How long are you going to badger that poor woman?"

His mom had always been direct, but ouch. Dad must've mentioned to her how much time he'd spent on top of her mountain today. She must not have heard the details this time. "I'm not badgering." He was looking for Amy's little girl. Word would spread soon enough of the kidnapping, but until then he wasn't going to get into an argument over semantics with this stubborn mother of his. "Besides, you told me Dad had to ask you a bunch of times before you accepted a first date."

"There was a difference there, son. I liked your father. I wanted to go out with him, was just playing hard to get." She chuckled.

"How do you know that's not what Amy's up to?"

"Open your eyes, son. Move on. Some things

aren't meant to be."

"Some things are. Like you and dad."

He glanced sidelong in time to see the smile fade to a frown. What was that about?

His mom was probably right. Amy may never accept his advances, but there was no doubt she needed him now more than ever before. He'd give it one more go. One more try at being the person she wanted hanging around instead of that Jack character. Humph. Jack had ruined his chances now anyway, kidnapping little Mattie. Amy would have to see Hank's truest intentions hiding beneath his occasionally not-so-humble surface. Wouldn't she?

Daybreak. Amy paced the path near the woods as Canine Officer Debby and her German Shepherd Cosmo prepared to enter the same location as the night prior.

Debby pulled Cosmo to a stop at the forest's edge. "Sich sitzen." Again the handler presented Mattie's nightgown.

Cosmo sniffed it and wagged his tail.

They had to have better luck today. The search grid could already be more miles than Amy cared to calculate. When Debby and Hank had returned the night before empty-handed, Amy's stomach had lurched and stayed upside down all night. Sleep had not come. Instead Amy had watched the night sky fade to dawn from the front porch, wondering what Mattie was experiencing. Imagining how terrified she must be.

Debby scratched Cosmo's ear and spoke in a low tone words only the anxious dog could understand.

Amy touched Debby's shoulder. "Please, find my sweet girl."

"We'll do our best." Debby smiled. "Voran, Cosmo." She unclipped his leash.

Cosmo pinned his nose to the ground and beelined into the woods.

Wainwright approached with a tight-lipped smile. "Morning."

Amy drew in a sharp breath. "You're not going with them?"

"I figured I'd stay here with you today."

"I don't need you to stay with me. I need you to find Mattie." Amy spun away from him and stomped into the trees. Being nice to him was backfiring. He was misinterpreting her congeniality for needing him near. Footsteps crunched in the leaf litter behind her. "Go away, Wainwright."

"Not Wainwright." Sam looped her arm around Amy's shoulders.

"What if they don't find her?"

"I don't know."

Amy's chin dropped. "You're supposed to tell me they will."

"I'm human too."

Amy flung Sam's arm away. "No, you're supposed to stay positive. Make me feel better." She swiped at a tear trickling down her cheek. If Sam didn't believe anymore, why should she? They wouldn't find Mattie. Department of Children's Services would show up and scold her. Maybe even file charges for being an irresponsible foster parent. And the chance to have a child without a man involved would vanish. The chance to help an innocent child avoid Amy's fate would evaporate.

Sam called after her retreating back.

Amy didn't stop to listen. She darted deeper into the forest and scanned the ground for signs the police had missed. There was nothing but forest debris. Any tracks that may have been there were covered over by new ones left by the searchers. Amy flung her hands up and plopped onto a log. Hopeless like everything else in life.

Time passed while she sat, but it was as if her internal clock had jammed. The sun's rays piercing the canopy changed angles, yet her thoughts remained stagnated in one place. Mattie was gone. Reality asserted itself as real.

"Amy?"

She jumped.

Wainwright approached with downcast eyes.

"What?"

"They found something."

Amy shot up from the dead tree.

"It's not good news."

She covered her mouth with a clammy hand and searched his eyes for answers.

"Debby and Cosmo found a large amount of blood. She believes this is now a recovery effort."

Recovery? “No, she can’t be dead.”

He strode to her side and gazed down at her. “I’m sorry.”

“They’re just giving up?”

“They are going to continue looking for the body.”

Amy gasped. Body. No. It couldn’t happen this way. Mattie was fine. They just had to keep looking. Her fingers clawed at her forearm, digging with minds of their own.

Wainwright gripped her hands in his. She pulled away and tucked her hands in her pockets. “I want to see.”

“They marked the location with the GPS and are bringing more men to scour the area.”

“Take me to it.”

He shook his head. “I don’t think that’s a good idea.”

“I said, take me to it. Now.”

He studied her face for a long moment. “There’s no talking you out of it?”

“I’ll get the horses saddled.”

Amy rode Cobalt and led R.C. to Wainwright.

He hesitated with his boot in the stirrup. “Are you sure you want to see this? Ready for the emotional toil?”

“Don’t worry about my emotions.” She squeezed her thighs and clicked her tongue.

Cobalt strode into the woods, his head swaying side-to-side as he gnawed at the copper bit.

Wainwright skirted around her on R.C. and led the way silently through the forest. Several miles later, he held up his hand and halted them. He swung off the horse with rigid posture.

They must be there. Amy looped the reins around the saddle horn and dismounted. Her legs wobbled under her, but she forced them forward.

Wainwright stepped to the side to reveal a ghastly scene. Her pulse thrummed in her ears as she took it all in.

Debby and Cosmo waited on the outskirts of a small clearing. The two officers from yesterday stared at the ground where a large dark spot discolored the lush grass. Blood spattered the blades in a five-foot radius, trailing down the tendrils and mixing in the soil.

Bile rose into Amy's throat. "Are you sure Mattie was here?"

Debby's gaze whipped toward her, and her face blanched. She nodded once, twice, then looked away.

Amy charged toward the clearing, but Wainwright grabbed her by the shoulders and held her back.

"You can't go in there, Amy."

She struggled against his iron grip. "Lemme go." Amy's spirit weakened. She collapsed into his arms. With a quick intake of breath, he wrapped her in a bear hug. "How do you know that's Mattie's blood?"

"We don't yet. But Cosmo tracked her scent

here. We gathered a sample and are sending it to be analyzed."

Amy jerked back, and Wainwright flinched. "Then it might not be hers."

Wainwright chewed on the corner of his lip. "Don't get your hopes up. Cosmo is a good scent dog. One of the best we've got."

"But just because she was here doesn't mean," she spread her shaking arms wide to encompass the grotesque field, "this is hers."

"I'm sorry. I told you it might be hard to see. Let's head back." He placed his hand on the small of her back and attempted to steer her toward Cobalt.

She slapped his hand away. "Let me see the whole scene. I don't need to be coddled."

"Fine. Help yourself. Just don't touch anything."

"And keep your hands off me." She tossed the words over her shoulder, hoping they stung. Hoping he would get the point. Her weakness a moment ago was not an invitation for him to fondle her.

Amy strode to the edge of the magenta pool and knelt. So much blood. How could one little girl have so much in her body? It couldn't possibly be hers. The metallic smell burned her nostrils. Horseshoe prints stood out like half-moons drawn on a canvas of red paint. She recognized the imprint of Vasper's small stride. Red did have Vasper.

Where was Jack then? He must've decided to hike out after all.

She rose, feeling four sets of eyes glaring at her, and circled the site in ever-widening arcs. A trick Aunt

Zena had taught her long ago. She picked up Vasper's prints in a muddy patch several yards away. They headed northwest, deeper into the vast wilderness known as Royal Blue. Unless some random four-wheeler rider spotted them, there were few chances Red would be discovered any time soon. No houses, towns, or roads for miles.

Amy returned to Wainwright and the others and put her hands on her hips. "What's the plan?"

Debby looked at the ground, and the two officers shifted on their feet.

Wainwright broke the silence. "The search is officially going to be considered a . . . recovery from this point."

"What? Mattie isn't dead. She's out there somewhere. And you all have a responsibility to find her."

"You . . . we have no proof of that. Who's to say Mattie didn't wander away on her own. Maybe she had an accident."

"An accident? Then where's her body?"

"Even if Jack —"

"It wasn't Jack! How many times have I got to tell you that?"

Wainwright's red face and bulging eyes looked ready to explode, like purple grapes squeezed by cruel fingers. "Okay, fine. Whoever took Mattie then. Obviously we are chasing a murderer now. Here's your proof." He swept his right arm in a dramatic arc.

Amy took a deep breath and studied his face. There was no point in arguing. "If you won't look for her, I will."

"You can't just take off into the mountains on a feeling or whatever it is you are having."

"Watch me."

Chapter 8

How dare Wainwright try to tell her what to do! If he wouldn't keep looking for Mattie, she would. Mattie was alive. She felt it. Red had been a monster, but surely he wouldn't resort to murdering an innocent child. Though, there were worse things than murder. Amy knew that from experience.

She bit her cheek. There was no room for thoughts like that.

Cobalt loped back to the barn.

"Sorry, bud, I don't have time to brush you out right now."

She tucked him into his stall and threw a few extra flakes of hay into the rack, then speed-walked to the house.

Sam met her in the kitchen with a cup of coffee. "What's the news?"

"They found some blood, and they think it's

Mattie's. They're downgrading the search to a recovery."

Sam's eyes grew wide. "Why aren't you more upset?"

"Because I don't believe them, that's why." She slammed the mug onto the countertop. It cracked up both sides, and hot coffee spilled out. She yanked her hand back and blew on the red welt forming on her palm.

"Let me see." Sam gently took her hand and inspected the burn.

"I'm fine."

Sam searched her face. "You're not fine. And I'm talking about more than your hand."

"I can't believe she's dead. I won't let myself. I can try to find her." Amy jerked her hand away and stuck it in her pocket. The jean scratched against the burn, but she didn't pull it back. "Remember all the stuff you and Aunt Zena taught me about tracking and trapping? I can do this."

"It's been a long time since you did any of that stuff, Amy. Let the police do their job."

"They aren't moving fast enough."

"Give them another day. If they still haven't found a bod. . . found Mattie, then I won't stop you from going."

"One more day gives Red an even bigger head start."

"Red?" Sam squinted. "Please, Amy."

Amy dropped her chin to her chest. "Fine. One more day."

Amy stared at her bed covered with articles of clothing and first aid supplies. How was she supposed to know what to pack when she had no idea how long she would be out in the boonies?

She sank amid the pile and closed her eyes. How could her heart feel so broken when Mattie wasn't even her child? She didn't know how to be a mom, how to raise a child. Was this what it felt like? This horrible, aching hollow spot inside? This relentless, gnawing fear? She'd had Mattie less than six weeks and already lost her. Turned out, she was a horrible parent.

Amy swallowed and took a deep breath, stilling her fingers grasping the comforter. She had to find Mattie. To bring her back and save her from whatever it was Red had in mind. No matter how poor a mom she would be, it was better than a lifetime with that awful ogre.

Summers spent with the foster kids in camp taught her a few things, but nothing like this ordeal was teaching her. She had come to love Mattie with a fullness, a passion, she had never known before. In a few short weeks, Mattie had stolen her heart. And for once, Amy didn't want it back.

But what if she found Mattie and then Amy turned out like her own mother? Selfish and incompetent. A pitiful excuse for a loving parent.

Jewel didn't know about Mattie, about Amy

becoming a foster mom. No doubt she would scoff and tell Amy of her shortcomings. *You? A mother? Ha!*

The sudden urge to visit Jewel struck her. Amy needed to remind herself she wasn't like her mom. To be reminded that in her mother's weaknesses, Amy had found her own strength long ago.

She could make a quick trip into town, see her mother, and get back before dark to finish packing. Maybe by then she'd have the mental list tidied.

Twenty minutes later, she drove the camp van down their long driveway. She wiped each hand in turn on her pants. Would going into town always elicit this fear response? She raised her right eyebrow. Probably.

Maybe the visit with her mother would give her the courage to do something brave.

The closer she got to the jail, the more her heart skipped. She parked out front and took a deep breath. How long since she had last seen her mother?

The officer at the reception desk didn't recognize her. No surprise, but heat burned her face nonetheless. No matter how terribly inept Jewel's parenting had been, Amy's gut told her she should've visited more often.

"Follow me," the officer said from the doorway.

Amy jumped and skipped to get through before the door closed.

Jewel waited at a metal table and stared out the high, barred window toward the sky.

"Hi, Jewel." Amy sat across from her.

"You know I hate it when you call me that. Mom sounds much nicer."

Amy knew, but still she couldn't bring herself to use the endearing term. Not in years had she said that word out loud. Maybe in her mind occasionally when good memories managed to find their way to the surface.

Jewel's gaze fell upon her only daughter. "My beautiful Amy." She reached both cuffed hands across the table.

Amy took her mother's cold hands and attempted to smile. Jewel looked older, thinner. Her eyes held less light. "Sorry it's been so long."

"I was getting worried. Thought maybe you'd abandoned me for good this time."

Ouch. "No. I've just been busy."

"Too busy to drive down here?"

Amy pulled her hands free and placed them in her lap. "I'm a foster mom now. I have . . . had a beautiful little girl."

Jewel looked to the window again. "That's nice. I'm sure you'll be a better mom than I was."

Wow. That was actually somewhat kind. Amy frowned. "We've talked about this before. You did your best in some bad situations." Why was Amy always trying to soothe her mother's guilt? Jewel was right. She had been a terrible mother, but Amy still loved her. She supposed she always would. Funny how a child's love didn't really have to be earned. It was a law of nature, like gravity or decay.

A smile spread over Jewel's face as she gazed back into Amy's eyes. "Let's talk about something else."

Amy reapplied her smile and nodded. “Her name is Mattie.”

Jewel’s lips twitched. “It looks hot out there. It’s been a while since I’ve been outside.”

Amy creased her brows together. Talking about Mattie was out of the question? “It is.” A long pause settled between them. Amy forgot why she had come. Talking to Jewel about anything helpful was pointless.

“Did you bring me anything?”

Like money? “Not this time. Sorry.”

Jewel’s sigh filled the room.

“Mattie’s been kidnapped.”

Jewel tipped back into her chair and huffed.

“I’m going to look for her myself.”

“That’s stupid.” She chuckled. “Ain’t that what police are for? They found me when I didn’t want to be found. Look at me.” She held up her wrists and jangled the cuffs.

How typical for Jewel to make this about herself. “Coming here was a bad idea.” Amy shoved her chair back and signaled to the jailer.

As anger bubbled through her, her resolve locked into place. Jewel wouldn’t save Amy and look where she was now. A past so painful Amy had blocked out as much of it as possible. Never talked about it. Thanks to a mother who refused to protect her. Amy would never stoop to that level. Whether from bravery or a desire to be different than Jewel, Amy didn’t know. But she would try to find Mattie, no matter how long it took or how many demons she had to face.

Sam paced along the western end of Amy's porch. Her feet and legs needed to move as much as her mind raced. When Amy first came to Camp Hope to live with her Aunt Zena, Sam had been Zena's shoulder to cry on when Amy's nightmares became too much to bear. Zena had relied on Sam to be strong and to keep praying. Sam felt helpless then. She couldn't stop Amy's nightmares. She couldn't stop Zena's worry. But she had been the strength Zena needed when she was weak.

This time, though, with Mattie's disappearance, Sam's helpless feeling reached new levels. Never had she felt so powerless, so utterly confused and uncertain of how to proceed. She needed to do something, for Heaven's sake. But what? Her heart ached, sending up wordless prayers.

What if they were right and Mattie was already dead?

A car crunched on the gravel driveway. Oh, what now? As the visitors creeped toward the house, the sign on the passenger door came into view. Department of Children's Services. Sam's pulse kicked into fourth gear. What was she supposed to tell them?

A prim brunette stepped from the car. "Ma'am, is Amy here?"

She was sure the wobble in her voice was audible when she responded. "Not just yet. Should be back soon. Did we forget about a visit or something?"

The look on the woman's face spoke volumes. She knew the truth of the situation, and she was ready to call the firing squad. “You know why we’re here, don’t you?”

What could Sam do but nod and wring her hands?

“We’ll wait in the car until Ms. Dawson returns.” Without waiting for her reply, the brunette sank into the driver’s seat and slammed the door.

Harder than necessary, if you asked Sam. It was like the exclamation point to the brunette’s anger. Sam couldn’t just wait under the scrutiny of those irritated gazes. She made sure the house was locked and strode to the field where Cosmo and Debby had disappeared into the forest. If she willed Mattie’s presence hard enough, maybe the little one would magically appear?

Sam resumed her pacing at the tree line. Squirrels chattered and barked overhead as if nothing amiss was happening underfoot. Birds chirped and flitted about. Oh, to be a bird and search the forest from the sky. To dart into the branches and witness the trail the kidnapper had taken.

That was it. An air search. Why hadn’t Wainwright thought of that yet?

She dug her phone from her blue jeans and dialed the number Kat Jenkins had given her. “It’s Sam. Is your offer still good to see if your husband can help search for Mattie?”

“Of course, Sam. What do you have in mind?”

“Does TWRA have the resources to mount an air search?”

“I’m not sure. Let me call Ryan and check.”

“Call me back as soon as you can. Please.” Sam

pushed the red button to end the call. This had to work.

Twenty minutes later her phone jingled. "Kat. Tell me you have good news."

"Not ideal, but it's something. He said they aren't allowed to do an airborne search and rescue without directives from the higher ups. But they are dropping powder on a small forest fire nearby. He thinks he can get the pilot to 'take the long way home.' It's the best he can do without an order. I'm sorry."

"I'll take it. Tell them to look for a man and girl on an old horse. Vasper is chestnut, so he'll probably blend in with the forest well. And thanks."

Hope burbled in her heart, like a spring of water spilling from the earth. *God, please help that pilot. Help him find our little girl.*

The white car parked in front of her house made Amy's stomach plummet to her toes. The gold medallion sticker on the driver's side door read Department of Children's Services. Had she forgotten about a home visit? Today was only the sixteenth. Their monthly check-in wasn't until the twenty-first. She had five days to find Mattie. What were they doing here?

Wainwright stepped from the shadow of the porch and waved to her.

She yanked the door open, jumped out, and marched toward him. "You called them?" She spoke through gritted teeth and then threw a glance toward the two ladies waiting in the car.

"I'm sorry, Amy. I have to do my job."

"You spiteful jerk. You could've waited. Could've given me a heads-up at least."

"Calm down. I'm simply doing what needs to be done. Mattie is a child of the state. They had to be notified." He licked his lips. "Besides, I tried to call you. It went straight to voicemail."

Some of her spitfire evaporated. Right. She had turned her phone off to visit with Jewel.

The doors on the car behind her opened simultaneously.

She plastered a neutral look on her face and spun to face them. Neither was her usual DCS worker. A flitter of fear chased through her.

"My name is Faith, and this is Grace. We are with the Department of Children's Services."

Amy shook each of their hands. Faith and Grace. Really?

"We need to talk."

She shot Wainwright a look that said, "Stay out here or I'll kill you," and led the two grim-faced ladies inside. "Would you like some coffee?"

Grace sat at the table. "No, thank you."

Faith pulled out the chair next to Grace and shook her head. "Tell us what happened."

Okay, diving right in. She shoved her shaking hands under her thighs. "I went to wake Mattie up yesterday morning, and she was gone."

Faith took the lead. "And you have no idea when or how she disappeared?"

"Well, at first I thought she snuck out."

"Was that common for her since she came to you?"

"No. Yes. I mean sometimes she wandered. And it was hard to find her because of the whole nonverbal thing." Amy fisted her hands together in her lap.

"Was there something else occupying your mind that morning?"

How much had Wainwright told them already? She dropped her gaze to the salt and pepper shakers in the middle of the table. "Yes. Some campers had taken a few horses and decided to go on a ride the night before."

"Did you check on Mattie during all this?"

"I . . . I didn't want to wake her up."

Faith and Grace exchanged knowing glances.

"You don't understand. Mattie is an amazing child. I love her. I would never do anything to put her in jeopardy."

"It seems," Grace said, "that is exactly what's happened here. Sheriff Wainwright tells us that he believes we are on a recovery mission now."

Amy shook her head. "But—"

Faith's voice softened marginally. "This type of thing has never happened within our region. We are not quite sure how to proceed."

Grace looked over Amy's shoulder. "We've been advised criminal charges may arise."

"Of course. Once they catch the kidnapper, he deserves—"

"Against you," Grace said.

“Me? For what?”

Faith rose from the table and hovered in the doorway. “Neglect. If you had paid better attention, put Mattie’s safety first during the nighttime debacle, she may still be here with you.”

Her worst fear had been spoken aloud. The ceiling hovered over her, heavy, threatening to implode with each shallow breath Amy took. “I . . . I—”

“We’re sorry. Sheriff Wainwright is to keep us apprised of the situation. Now would be a good time to pray she returns in one piece.” Grace pressed her hands together and laced her fingers. “We’ll be in touch.”

Amy didn’t walk them out. She couldn’t move. Her legs were mush. Her heart rate uncountable. Her fear like a scorpion in her throat. Did they think she’d done this on purpose? If anyone was to blame, it was Red. Not her. She loved Mattie. Cared for the sweet child like she would’ve her own.

Pray? What good would that do? This situation called for action. Not prayer. God stopped listening to her pleas when she was a little girl. Neither He nor Jewel bothered to keep her from the men that abused her. Why bother God’s ear now?

No, she wouldn’t pray. She would find Mattie. And punish Red.

Chapter 9

Amy grabbed a bag of trail mix, a dozen water bottles, a container of beef jerky, and a handful of granola bars and stuffed them into her backpack beside the other supplies. She slipped it on her shoulders and raced back upstairs. She crammed a sweater in the front zipper and tied a light sleeping bag onto the front. "There." She was ready.

She spun around and slammed into Sam. Her mouth gaped open.

"I'm not here to stop you. I see the fire in your eyes. No one could derail you. But here, take this." Sam pulled a revolver from her waistband and held it out.

Amy touched the silver curve of the trigger guard and snapped her hand back. "No. I can't."

"You're going up against a kidnapper. Possibly a

murderer. And you don't want a gun?"

"I've got a knife." Amy bit her lip.

"What about food? You can't hunt with a knife."

"Got wire for a snare."

"Amy, I know you want to find Mattie, but you aren't thinking this through. You need a gun."

"I won't . . . I can't." Her mother's boyfriend, Lionel, pointed a gun at her one too many times as a little girl to force her to do as he wished. She wouldn't touch one now. Not ever. "Is Wainwright still here?"

"Staring down the driveway after those DCS ladies. What did they say anyway?"

Amy darted her gaze to the hallway behind Sam. What should she admit? It hurt too much to say it out loud again. "Nothing."

Sam's gaze bored into her. "Fine. Don't tell me." She pulled Amy into a bear hug. "You'd better sneak out the kitchen if you want to avoid Wainwright."

Amy pecked Sam on the cheek. "Thanks. I'll be home soon. With Mattie."

"Be careful."

"I will. I just can't sit around here and do nothing. It makes sense to at least try since Debby and her dog aren't getting anywhere." Was she trying to convince Sam or herself?

She crept downstairs and peeked out the kitchen exit. No sign of Wainwright. If she circled around behind the oak tree, she could skirt the hill and get to the barn without him spotting her. If she was lucky. She made it to the tree in a sort of bent-over, side-stepped gait and peeped out from behind it.

Wainwright paced the front porch, muttering and gesturing with both hands.

The last thing she needed was for him to try and stop her. But waiting for him to do his job was so far off the back burner, it wasn't even on the stove anymore. She waited until he turned his back and ran down the hill. Once the grassy slope hid him from her view, she slowed to a walk. The closer she got to the barn the louder her heart pulsed in her ears. Was she completely crazy?

Cobalt whinnied from his stall and stuck his nose over the half-wall.

Pooh. She'd need to pack grain for him too. She flung open the tack-room door and dug through a pile in the corner. She uncovered large, leather saddle bags at the very bottom and pulled them out. "Perfect."

With Cobalt brushed, saddled, and bridled, she swung her leg over the horn and slipped her feet into the snug stirrups. Taking one last deep sigh, she rode from the barn and aimed for the lower pasture.

"Amy?"

Her shoulders stiffened. She pulled back on Cobalt's reins and froze in her seat.

"What are you doing?"

"I need to clear my head."

Wainwright stepped beside her and placed his hand on her knee. "Awful lot of stuff for a clearing head kind of ride."

Amy jerked her knee upward and nudged Cobalt to the left. "Don't touch me."

"I thought we were making progress. You've

been so nice to me the last few days."

"There's nothing to progress, Wainwright."

"Too bad." He spat into the dirt next to his boot. His voice softened. "You know how I feel for you."

"And you know how I feel."

He took a deep breath. "Debby and Cosmo just left. She said they'd be back tomorrow to resume the recovery. But if it rains like it's supposed to, it'll slow them down considerable."

"Rain?"

"Ain't you seen the forecast? Been predicting a terrible line of storms to move in early tomorrow morning."

Great. "I've been a little preoccupied to watch TV." She squeezed Cobalt's sides, and he took a step forward.

Wainwright grabbed the rein under Cobalt's neck and pulled him to a stop. "You wouldn't be planning on doing something a little crazy, would you?"

Couldn't he just let her leave already? Amy ground her teeth together. "Wouldn't think of it."

"I don't need to remind you that DCS is already considering charges against you. You wouldn't want to add obstruction to that list." He slipped his fingers into his gun belt and whistled.

Amy thumped Cobalt's sides with the heels of her boots.

He jumped and shot away from the barn in an easy run.

Obstruction? No, she wouldn't think of doing

anything crazy. What she set out to do seemed perfectly logical. Almost.

Jack tossed the cigarette butt to the side of the trail. Humph. Trail. That was a funny word. He'd been picking his way for two days through undergrowth so thick he couldn't see how the horse made it through. How would he explain this to Amy? Jumping up and disappearing in the middle of the night wasn't exactly what he'd planned. But circumstances changed so fast he was still catching his breath. He'd seen an opportunity, and he'd taken it. Explanation would just have to come later.

If he hadn't gone off all half-cocked, he'd be better prepared. A mandolin didn't exactly provide cover from the elements. But oh well. How long had he been surviving, in all types of places, on his own? More years than he cared to count.

There had been no cries for help from the little girl. Shouldn't surprise him too much, he guessed, with what Amy had told him.

He refocused his eyes on the lay of the land before him. He needed to watch for snakes. This bushy, shady landscape would be the perfect place for a copperhead or rattler to hide. His stomach growled. Too bad he couldn't find a lazy one and eat it. Snake would be fine right about now. Anything would be fine, for that matter. He'd heard it tasted just like chicken.

At least he'd had enough common sense to bring a canteen full of fresh water. It was a good thing, too, since he hadn't seen a drop of water since he left Amy's garage apartment. Too bad he hadn't managed to pilfer more food. One snack-size bag of beef jerky wouldn't last very long, even on the most meager of rations.

He descended a steep hill, slid the last half-way on his behind, and glanced back up its steep face. Would Amy follow? No doubt she would. If she was anything like the girl he'd known fifteen summers ago, she'd be hot on his trail. She'd taught him everything he knew of tracking. Funny how it was helping him now in connection to her again.

Claw-like branches tore at her hair, but she didn't slow. If she slowed down, she might turn around. One particularly nasty branch grabbed her neck and sliced. Hot blood trickled down her neck and under her shirt. It didn't matter. All that mattered was getting to the field and picking up Mattie's trail.

Cobalt's sides heaved with the unexpected exertion.

"Just a little farther, boy." He probably couldn't hear her over the whoosh of the wind. She could barely hear herself. It was like the forest stole the words from her mouth and carried them into the dusky twilight. Kidnapping them and dragging them into an abyss of worry and uncertainty. Shadows danced beneath the trees, each blurry movement in her peripheral vision making her heart skip a beat. Stop it, Amy. Wainwright couldn't have caught up that quickly.

Her sides burned from the beat of Cobalt's run. Breaths came in shallow gulps, hers and his. She had to make it to the clearing before dark. Mattie had camped there just a few nights prior. If she could make it to that little fire circle, she could make it to Mattie.

She yanked on Cobalt's reins so hard his rear feet slid to a stop. When she looked around, deep horseshoe-shaped rivets marred the path. "Sorry, boy."

Directly below her left foot lay the bloody patch on the ground. She had missed it by a grass blades' width. Whew. Wainwright would hang her if she tampered with evidence. She kicked her foot loose and flung her leg over Cobalt's back. She slid to the ground and laid her head on his sweaty shoulder. What was she doing? Tearing away from Wainwright like that, chasing after a ghost from her past like she was sane. Wasn't it all a fool's errand? The investigation team had already searched this area and come up without any further clues. Why did she think she would find something?

The wind kicked a strand of loose hair and tossed it over her neck. It pasted to the blood trickle. With it came the scent of dusty rain. She'd better hurry. Amy knelt to inspect the ground. So many footprints. How would she sort them out? She left Cobalt's reins dragging the ground and again walked in growing circles, fanning out from the bloody patch. Nothing had changed, minus the few added pockmarks of investigators' boot prints. She ended at the same location as the prior day. A northwest-heading trail with one horse's steps. That had to be it. She pushed aside drooping plant stalks. A set of prints left by cowboy boots glared up at her.

She wrinkled her brow. Why would Red walk the horse when he could easily have ridden with Mattie? Ugh. With Mattie. She shivered. Poor little girl to be subjected to that man's body clinging to her so she wouldn't fall off. To the smell of artificial grape that seemed to waft out of his skin, as if his obsession with the gum were literally a part of his cells. She hated grape.

Amy pulled her cell phone from her back pocket. Where had the time gone? The sun sank over the horizon like it couldn't wait to see the other hemisphere. Clouds lit up briefly bright red then faded to dark blue and finally black. She clicked on her flashlight and fumbled in the dark for the lighter. One quick touch to a small pile of sticks she gathered and a fire was blazing in the middle of the clearing. As far away from the blood as she could be without lighting the entire forest on fire.

A flash of light brightened the clouds in the distance, but no rumble followed. Could she be lucky enough to avoid the rain? Doubtful. Amy dug into her pack and pulled out a small tarpaulin. Better prepare just in case. Four large sticks jammed into the ground provided a base to tie the tarp over. She unrolled her sleeping bag and laid it under the tarp. Then she set out to gather more firewood.

It had been a long time since she spent the night outdoors under the vast sky. Maybe she should have brought Sam's gun after all.

Settling in under the tarp, she leaned against Cobalt's saddle and took a deep breath. Clouds closed in the gaps of free sky and covered the stars. Was the entire universe against her plan? Rain would eliminate the prints necessary to trail Mattie.

The night grew darker, broken only by the flickering of the orange campfire. Quivering shadows played at the edges of its light, casting haunting shapes onto the tree trunks. Red's face taunted her, laughing at her on the darkened leaves shaking in the coming wind. He had her little one. She'd never find him. More likely, she'd die out here of stubbornness.

How long until Wainwright followed her? Probably first thing in the morning. And no doubt about it, he would be mad.

The sky lit up like a slow strobe light, eerie in its sizzling intensity. Thunder boomed over the next ridge. Amy jumped and pulled the sleeping bag tighter around her shoulders.

Cobalt nickered and edged closer to her shelter.

"It's okay, boy. Just a little rain coming."

But it wasn't okay. Rain would wash away Red's tracks. And Amy would have no way to follow. She'd have to go back to relying on Cosmo, whose nose apparently wasn't as keen as it should be. If it was, they would've already found Mattie. And that dog handler, Debby, had already given Mattie up for dead. No one believed Mattie could be alive.

Except her.

The blood results weren't back yet. They would prove it wasn't Mattie's. They had to.

Why did she feel so strongly Mattie was alive? It wasn't like Amy to hold hope. Maybe it wasn't hope at all. Denial. Guilt. Anger. Yes, those sounded more likely.

God still didn't hear the longing of her heart. If He did, He would've held the rain at bay. Lightning split the sky, and thunder splintered the air. She curled into a ball and pictured Mattie's sweet face. The first drops of rain thudded into the tarp.

A short smattering of raindrops bounced into the dusty earth around Amy. The wind gusted, and suddenly the sky opened up once more. The clouds raced away over the horizon like they were being pulled on an excited fisherman's line. Stars peeked from behind the tendrils of the leftover clouds. The thunder and lightning faded behind the distant mountains.

Amy peeked at Cobalt from under the tarp. He stood sleeping with one rear leg under him and the hoof resting on its front.

She crawled into her sleeping bag and munched on half a granola bar. She never would've thought sleep would come, but the sounds of nature lulled her eyelids closed.

The storm had jumped clean over them. Interesting. Was God possibly, maybe listening after all?

Chapter 10

From her front porch, Sam surveyed the sky. Thick, gray clouds darted past, congealing on the horizon. Last night's short spit of rain wasn't the end of the bad weather, from the look of it. She swallowed two ibuprofens with the last swig of her coffee. *Lord, let today be the day they find Mattie. Please.*

Wainwright and Debby were holding a tense conversation at the edge of the forest when Sam approached. As soon as she was within earshot, their lips sealed tighter than zippers on a banker's deposit bag. "What? What is it?"

He hoisted his bulging utility belt higher on his waist. "I know Amy wasn't 'clearing her head.' Where is she, Sam?"

Her stomach churned. "What do you mean?"

"Do not lie to me. You're terrible at it."

"Have you checked the barn?"

Wainwright's face passed red and went straight to purple. The veins in his neck threatened to leap out and accost anyone nearby. "Do. Not. Play. Dumb."

"Fine, Hank. She couldn't just sit here on her behind doing nothing. It was eating her from the inside out not being able to help."

Without a word, Wainwright pushed past her and strode to the barn.

Debby fingered Cosmo's leash and looked anywhere but Sam's eyes.

"Please find her today, Officer Debby."

"I'll do my best." With those four mumbled words, she and Cosmo entered the forest and soon faded from view.

A hand clamped her shoulder, and she nearly collapsed. What in the world? She spun around. "Tom? Are you trying to kill me?"

"Sorry." He cleared his throat. "I came up with Hank. Is there anything I can do?"

"I feel so helpless."

"I know."

She knew she shouldn't ask. Being near him was inviting troublesome feelings. "Stay with me today? It's awful being alone with my worry."

"Sure."

His sturdy presence at her side both calmed and agitated her, but it was much better than pacing alone. The sounds of the meadow and nearby trees filled the air, but her mind followed Cosmo's occasional yips farther and farther away until she could no longer find them among the other noises. "What if they don't find her?"

Tom wrapped his arms around her.

Her heart fluttered even as tears for Mattie and Amy leaked from her eyes.

"Evangeline left me."

Sam jerked back. "What?"

"She's gone. Said she needed to find that part of herself she'd been missing. Plans to travel the world. See new places. Meet new people." He paused and sighed. "She didn't invite me."

"Does Hank know?"

"No."

"Oh, Tom. I'm so sorry." And she truly was. She'd never in a million years have wished this kind of pain on the man she loved. Even if it meant she couldn't be with him, she'd always wanted his happiness.

The morning sun warmed Amy's feet and dragged her from her nightmare. Only to awake to the real one. She peeled her eyes open but still felt the sensation of the prickly splinters poking through her shirt. She jumped up, packed her things, and saddled Cobalt.

The tracks had circular muddy splotches inside them, but as far as she could tell they were still useful in leading the direction. With a furtive glance at the trail entering the glade, Amy mounted and set on a course to follow Red's prints. Tracking from Cobalt's back would be difficult, but she didn't have the time to walk. Red already had a two-day head start. Her only chance at catching him was Cobalt's faster gait and better endurance.

Besides, Wainwright was no doubt headed her way. She needed to hurry.

Jack's face, his full lips, flashed into her mind. She had pushed thoughts of him aside to follow Mattie. But where had he gone? She could've used his help right about now. She had spent weeks teaching him about tracking that summer, but it only took him a few tries to pass up the teacher in his ability. She'd been both jealous and admiring of his talent. Too bad she'd probably never see him again. Again. Why had she let even the slightest sliver of him sneak back into her heart? It was like a tiny, irritating cactus prickle jabbing from the inside.

Cobalt bounced down a slight incline.

Amy gripped the saddle horn with her left hand and massaged the cramp under her right ribs. The cowboy boot prints gathered together in a jumble. She stopped Cobalt and dismounted. Something had caused the man wearing these boots to stop and thoroughly inspect this area. Amy kicked aside sticks and lifted branches of small bushes. Under the fourth raspberry vine, she spotted a cigarette butt. She lifted it gently and brought it under her nose. The faint scent of grape lingered with the tobacco smell. Red. She tucked the butt into a side pocket on her pack. Maybe once she returned to civilization, they could test it and match Red's DNA.

Amy straightened and stilled her movements. A very faint sound reached her ears. Cosmo's bark? Maybe. She couldn't be sure, but if Debby had resumed the search, Wainwright was in the forest already too.

Her cell phone vibrated in her back pocket. She pulled it out and looked at the screen. Not enough bars for a phone call, but apparently Sam's texts could come through.

Wainwright's coming. He's madder'n a hot hornet. Better put some distance between you.

Great. She'd thought she'd have more time. Whatever positive thinking she'd held about Wainwright letting her go out of the decency of his heart evaporated. At least Sam had the forethought to warn her.

A shout that sounded vaguely like "Aaaa-meee" echoed down the hill behind her.

Oh no. Wainwright would be on top of her and force her back home in no time. With one step, she sprang into the saddle and charged deeper into the dense brush ahead. Thorny vines and dried out branches tore at her pants legs and arms.

Poor Cobalt's tough skin welted up and blood trickled from dozens of small abrasions on his neck and hips.

"I'm so sorry, boy. We can't slow down just yet."

Cobalt flicked his ears back but then perked them toward the trail ahead.

How in the world did Red get Vasper through? At least beneath the shelter of the plants, the tracks stood out bold and easy to follow. They broke free from the tangle of overgrown weeds. The tracks shot to the left, on a clearer path through old-growth forest. Amy nudged Cobalt into a trot, which did nothing to soothe the cramp in her side. She hadn't spent nearly enough time in the saddle lately.

The tracks weren't as clear under the trees, but at least the shouting had faded. She needed to slow down or risk losing the trail altogether. Should she risk getting caught by Wainwright? Could his grudge for her disinterest in a romantic relationship make him mad enough to really press charges?

Cobalt trotted deeper into the cover of trees. The light grew dimmer. The pain in Amy's side stole her breath.

She glanced over her shoulder. There was nothing but trees behind her. As she turned her gaze forward, Cobalt lunged to the right. Amy grabbed for the horn, but it was already out of reach. Her feet flipped from the stirrups, and she crashed to the ground. Her elbow took the brunt of the landing. For a moment she lay in a heap, staring at the treetops swaying in a light breeze that didn't reach the forest floor. Sunshine shimmied through the leaves. She closed her eyes and watched the gold and black pattern play on her eyelids.

She flexed her fingers. A burst of pain stampeded through her arm. Her eyes snapped open. She gritted her teeth and sat up slowly. A second, slicing pain ripped through her left elbow into her shoulder.

"Cobalt, boy, what happened?"

The quaking horse waited several feet away with the reins dangling to the ground. His nostrils flared. He stamped his left front hoof on the ground.

Amy turned her head in the direction he watched. From a low branch hung a dead turkey, dangling upside down by its feet. Its feathers and tail splayed out. Its head missing. A chill swept over her. The forest felt darker as goose-pimples crept up her extremities.

She rose to her feet and placed a gentle hand on Cobalt's neck. "It's okay. Just a careless hunter who forgot where he hung his kill, I'm sure." She attempted to extend her left arm and again breath-stealing pain jabbed at her. "Okay, mount with one arm. I can do that."

At least she could wiggle her fingers this time without pain, as long as she kept her arm bent. That meant it wasn't broken. Probably.

She'd wager to guess they were only two or three miles from the blood camp. Not far enough to outrun Wainwright if he had borrowed one of her horses. Which he no doubt did. She had to keep moving, but Cobalt's every step sent a throb through her arm. Amy squeezed her eyes shut and pictured Mattie's face for several long minutes. Cobalt trembled and picked his way through the trees. She couldn't give up because of a little pain.

When her eyes opened, she looked to the ground

for the tracks in front of her. She would follow them. She would find Red. Decision made. She could ride with one arm as long as it took.

Wait. She slapped the saddle horn with her good arm. Where were the tracks? In her haste to get away and the confusion of the fall, she had drifted from them somehow. She would have to circle back and pick up the trail. Wasting more time she didn't have. She yanked Cobalt's reins more roughly than she intended.

He snorted and tossed his head.

"Sorry, boy. I'm . . ." Just scared. Maybe she couldn't find Mattie. What if she didn't? Maybe Cosmo's nose was right and Mattie was dead already. Tightness gripped her chest and squeezed. She pressed her eyelids closed to stop the tears that threatened. What was she supposed to do? She halted Cobalt and leaned over to scratch his neck. Maybe Wainwright was right. Maybe she was crazy to take off on her own, following her gut and a sporadic trail of cigarettes and bubble gum wrappers. And her arm needed a doctor. It didn't feel broken, but something was definitely wrong.

She took a deep breath, patted Cobalt's neck one last time, and whispered, "Let's go home."

She turned Cobalt around and followed their prints back toward the tree. Cobalt shied away from the dead turkey, but this time Amy was ready if he reacted.

Ah. That's where she went astray. The tracks cut right just past the turkey tree and she had continued straight. Several feet past the dead bird, Amy stopped

Cobalt and climbed off. One more look at the trail and then she'd make a decision.

A thick layer of past years' leaves made individual tracks difficult to decipher. Was her mind playing tricks on her, or did she really see what she thought she saw? She knelt and brushed aside a few damp leaves. Another cigarette butt. It, too, smelled like grape. She tucked it into her pack with the other one. Red had been here.

There in the recess between two gnarly roots was a singular footprint. A tiny tennis shoe just the right size for Mattie. She recognized the imprint of the flower from Mattie's sole. She'd followed it so many times down to the barn. Amy's heart danced a jig. Mattie hadn't died in the clearing. She had made it this far. With Red. But at least she was alive. Amy had been right.

"Amy, stop." Wainwright's deep voice exploded behind her.

She whipped around and backed into the trunk of the tree. "I can explain."

"I don't want to hear it." He gritted his teeth, and the muscles in his cheeks bulged.

"You don't understand. I found evidence. Mattie's alive." She pointed at the ground beneath her. Her stomach plummeted. She had scuffled the ground when Wainwright surprised her.

"I don't see anything."

"There was a footprint. A little one."

"All I see is a woman trying to interfere with an ongoing investigation."

Wainwright closed the gap between them and grabbed her left wrist.

"Come on, Amy. This is ridiculous."

"I can't give up on her. If you're not going to find her, I will." Amy winced as he straightened her arm. He pulled her away from the tree. Stars of pain clouded her peripheral vision. She had to get to Mattie. She pulled back on her arm with all the might she could muster. Her elbow popped, the sound reverberating in her ears. Everything went black. She felt her head hit the ground and heard Wainwright's worried voice from far away. A vision of Mattie swam under her closed eyelids. Sweet, little, silent Mattie.

Amy forced herself to climb through the cloud of pain and open her eyes.

Concern marred Wainwright's handsome face.

She struggled to sit upright. "You . . . you have to let me go. Please, Wainwright. I need to do this. To find her." She had to make him understand.

He hung his head. "You're hurt."

"I'm tough." She held her breath and sat upright, cradling her arm against her chest. "Besides, I think you helped me set my dislocation, so thanks."

A smile tugged on the corner of his mouth.

"I'm sorry I don't care for you like you want me to. But if you care for me at all, please let me go find my sweet little girl." Please. She could handle the pain in her arm as long as he let her continue.

Wainwright rose to his feet and nodded with a frown on his face. "You know how stubborn you are?"

"Yes."

"Be careful."

Her spirit buoyed. She wanted to hug him, but she couldn't bring herself to allow that intimate contact. "Thank you, Wainwright. Really. Here, take these." Amy dug the cigarette butts and bubble gum wrappers from her pack and put them in his hand. "It's not Jack. You'll see." She hid the wince from him as she mounted Cobalt, hugged her arm to her chest, and smiled at him. "Thank you."

"If you aren't back in two days, I'm sending the search party for you instead of Mattie. Understand?"

Amy nodded.

He tipped his hat and strode in the direction of the blood camp.

Hank's steps carried him away from Amy without conscious action on his part.

He had done it. He'd broken Amy. Quite literally. Not the way he'd intended. He hadn't wanted to hurt her. He'd wanted to break through the walls. When her arm popped in his hand, a wave of sickening heat had washed over him. And when her eyes fluttered open, like a newborn kitten, instead of panic and pain, he'd read fear. His position hovering over her, with his worry practically dripping with each drop of sweat, hadn't comforted her. It had terrified her.

He punched his thigh. What had he been thinking all these years? Yes, Amy was broken. But no, he wasn't the one who could put those pieces back into place. He'd driven a wedge between them in his carelessness, his lack of finesse. He was foolish to think his charms would sway her. After all the rumors he'd heard about her terrible childhood. She'd been just a kid, six years younger than he was, when he first met her. And she'd been through more than a nightmare. He hadn't truly believed the terrible atrocities she'd undergone. Until now. In her pain and complete vulnerability just now, he'd seen into that frightening window. And he repulsed. Not because of her past, but because of how he'd treated her. Like a prize to be won. Like a broken vase to be glued back together in his capable hands. He was an idiot. Amy didn't need a romantic relationship. She needed a friend.

That was what he'd be.

And he'd start by letting her go. The investigative part of his brain argued against it. But his heart told him it was what she needed to do.

Lord, she's hurt. Please help her. Protect her where I can't.

He made it back to where he'd left R.C., mounted silently, and rode back toward the clearing. He dismounted at the blood camp and squatted near the prints exiting. He brushed aside damaged grass and leaned closer. Amy was right. Someone on horseback had left this camp. The tiny shoeprints at the tree where he'd accosted Amy proved that Mattie had made it past this point alive. So where did the blood come from? A deer? Maybe. If only the blood sample results could move more quickly through the bogged-down system.

He pulled his cell phone from his pocket and dialed. When the dispatcher answered, he knew what he needed to add to their hunt. “We need to line up an aerial search. When can we get one in the air?”

As soon as he was out of sight, Amy shivered and shook off the feeling his closeness had evoked. The fear, the memories, the helplessness. She returned her eyes to the ground and followed Vasper’s prints. Every few hundred yards a white cigarette butt dotted the brown leaves and powdery dirt. She didn’t take the time to retrieve them.

At dusk, she reached a campsite hidden among fallen trees. She dismounted and inspected the ground. Little flowered footprints dotted the ground around a charred place on the ground. Red was smart. He’d only lit a small fire and apparently kept Mattie close.

The sky still held a faint glow, enough light for Amy to keep riding. She climbed into the saddle and plodded along.

Red had to have been planning this for days, maybe weeks. The supplies she grabbed would keep her for a few days on meager rations, but the farther she rode into the wilderness, the more she realized this was not some spur of the moment decision on his part. The cigarette butts didn’t cease, no matter how far she followed. How many cartons did that man have? And the turkey. It was probably his. He clearly came prepared to hunt for game. He must have Vasper loaded down. That was a good thing, though. It would slow the old horse even more. It seemed the one thing Red hadn't taken into consideration was which mount he chose. Luckily for Amy.

Amy pulled her flashlight out and shone it at the ground before them as darkness settled in. She knew she shouldn't press on and risk losing the trail again, but something inside wouldn't let her stop.

Cobalt's ears drooped, and his steps faltered.

Poor thing. She had pushed him so hard. It wasn't fair to him to keep going. After all, he'd been a pasture ornament for long years. Never doing hard work and conditioning.

"I'm sorry, Cobalt."

She pulled him to a stop and climbed off. She traded the bridle for a halter and pulled the saddle and blanket to the ground. If she exhausted her mount on the first day, her search would be over before it could truly begin. A dark rim of sweat on his sides gleamed in the pale starlight. She scooped some grain into a small pan and held it to his nose. "You're such a good boy. Thank you."

Cobalt finished eating, paced a few feet away, and dropped with a groan to his knees and rolled. When he finished, he stood up, shook the dust off his back, and munched on the fallen leaves at his feet. Every part of him drooped. She'd be more careful tomorrow.

No fire tonight. She didn't need it anyway. It was warm and dry, and she had granola bars and a bottle of water. She tied Cobalt to a branch nearby, filled his pan with one of her bottles of water, and backed against a tree with the saddle for a pillow. As soon as she pulled the sleeping bag around her shoulders and lay her head down, her body cried with exhaustion. How many years had it been since she rode more than a few minutes at a time? Somewhere in the chaos of running the camp, she had forgotten how much she loved it, and traded riding for a clipboard and rigid schedule.

Her eyes slid closed to the sound of a soft wind in the trees above and a screech owl whinnying somewhere nearby.

Amy opened her eyes to darkness she hadn't experienced in long years. At home there was always a light. The pole in the drive, the microwave blinking green, or the night light in Mattie's room. She groped for the flashlight she had tucked in the sleeping bag beside her legs.

Cobalt didn't stir.

What had pulled her from sleep? She lay motionless, listening for several minutes, but heard nothing. She needed to go to the bathroom. Maybe that was what had awakened her?

She slid from her sleeping bag and clicked on the flashlight. A bush rustled behind her. She spun to face it and caught the green glow of a set of eyes in the beam of her light. Her breath stuck in her throat. Too tall for a raccoon or skunk. Too short for a deer. Her hand shook, but the eyes didn't waver. Their intense gaze held her like a statue. To her left, a coyote yipped and broke the eerie silence. Amy jumped and turned the beam. A second set of green eyes met her and inched closer. The dog scented the air and licked its nose.

Cobalt snorted and stamped his hoof. The coyote's call must've awakened him.

The second coyote turned its head and disappeared into the dark trees.

She swung the beam to the first and found its spot empty. Amy exhaled. "Thank you, Cobalt. Again."

Amy pulled her cell phone from her pocket and powered it on. Only two bars of battery left. Dawn would light the eastern horizon in thirty minutes. Already the sky held a tinge of gray. Her stomach growled, but she refused its plea. Instead she drank a half a bottle of water and gave the rest to Cobalt. He sucked it loudly from his dish. She had nine bottles left. If today was as hot as yesterday, she needed to find a water source soon.

When the sky turned rosy, Amy was in the saddle with her gaze glued to the ground. The trail climbed higher, and the trees began to change. By noon, the ratio of oaks waned until only evergreen trees scaled the mountain.

Cobalt's breaths came in shallower heaves.

Amy couldn't keep pushing at the same pace. As much as Mattie's image called to her from ahead, riding Cobalt to death would do no one any good. The tracks faded into the squishy bed of needles beneath the pines and hemlocks. Better to walk and take it slowly anyway. If she got turned around in this deeply bedded glade, she might never find the trail again. She halted Cobalt, dismounted, and gave him a long drink of water. Six bottles left. Her stomach felt as if it might eat her backbone for nourishment soon.

She took the reins in her right hand and walked west after Red's trail. Individual hoof prints no longer waited for her. With the thick cushion of needles, Amy had to work hard to find divots from Vasper's hooves. An hour later, Amy guessed they had only traveled a mile. She stopped to rest on a rock and took a small sip of water. Just enough to wash the dust from her mouth. Why had the cigarette butts stopped? Maybe Red finally ran out.

"C'mon, boy. We can't stop now."

Cobalt lifted his weary eyelids and swished his tail.

"No time for naps."

At the crest of the mountain, Amy paused and took in the view below her. Nothing but waves and waves of different shades of green. A person could get lost out there forever and no one would find their bones. She pushed the melancholy thought aside.

Cobalt nickered as she scooped out a small handful of grain and placed it on the ground for him.

While he munched, Amy checked the rocky ridge top ten feet in both directions. There was not a single sign of Vasper's prints. No manure. No butts.

Nothing. She put her hands on her hips and glared back down the mountain. Had she lost the trail again?

A cloud passed over the sun, bringing welcome relief from its scorching rays. But the wind kicked up and dragged the cloud with it. Amy shielded her eyes and peered north, along the top of the mountain. Something sparkly lay on the ground about fifteen feet away.

Cobalt followed her with his reins dragging the ground as she made her way to the small piece.

She knelt down and picked it up. A sequin. A bright pink sequin. Why did it look so familiar?

The dragon she gave Mattie. Its wings held these same sequins.

"Oh, Mattie, you brilliant child." A smile spread over Amy's face. "You left me a trail to follow."

The sparse covering of stunted trees did not shield Amy and Cobalt from the beating summer sun. Amy picked their way through loose, rocky soil, gathering sequins every twenty to thirty feet and tucking them in her pocket. Her mouth felt like a glue trap and the back of her neck like a skillet. Sweat drained in steady drips off Cobalt's back.

The sun disappeared behind another cloud, casting grayish-blue shadows on the ground. A chill crept up Amy's back. Her eyes felt heavy. She needed to sit before she collapsed.

Amy pulled Cobalt to the closest tree with a smidgen of shade beneath and sank onto her bottom. Though she and Cobalt had drank half the water, the pack felt like it weighed double.

Cobalt slurped down another entire bottle and looked at her as if to say, "That's all?"

She wanted to answer him, but the words stuck in her throat. She took a few small swigs of water and tucked the bottle carefully into the bag. Four and a half bottles left.

Amy took her cell phone out and powered it on. A text from Sam awaited her.

Wainwright back. What did you do to that man? Officer Debby thinks Cosmo picked up on Mattie's scent.

Good. Maybe some backup would be on its way soon. **Send water please. Not emergency. Yet.**

Her phone beeped three times and died. Her last line to civilization. The grandness of the empty mountains pressed in around her. She needed to keep moving, or her body and mind might give up on her. The sequins in her pocket jingled as she rose to her feet and stumbled farther along.

Chapter 11

The end of the ridge sloped downward, bringing with it a much-welcomed full cover of shade. Amy stopped against a tree and sighed. Cobalt looked about ready to collapse. She wasn't far from it herself. She let him drink two more bottles of water while she finished the half bottle and chewed on some beef jerky. Every article of clothing, soaked with sweat, clung to her body. Her hands and legs shook. How much more of this could her out-of-shape body take? How much more could Cobalt?

A grove of tall oaks and pines stood proud amid a field of green grass untouched by a blade. In the center, a flattened section of grass and a cold fire pit stood out like a sticker on a blank page. She stumbled to it and plopped onto the cushion of grass. If she could close her eyes and rest for a minute, her thoughts would stop drowning in thick gravy.

Cobalt tore off mouthfuls of the luscious grass faster than he could chew and swallow it all. She needed to stop him before he foundered. But her arms and legs were too heavy. Rolling over, something scratched her cheek. She reached around with her good arm and pulled a red pick from under a clump of grass. She caressed the smooth plastic. “Jack.”

What if she was wrong? What if Jack really did take Mattie like Wainwright believed? But Jack didn’t smoke, did he? She really didn’t know him at all anymore. The teenager she knew clearly had changed. Where had he been? A vagabond wandering the country, thieving? Kidnapping? Murdering? Her stomach churned at the possibilities.

He knew her history with Red and all about Red’s obsession with grape gum and cigarettes. Had Jack planted those clues just in case someone was able to follow? Stupid of her to think he came back for her. He had a much more devious plan all along, didn’t he? Figured. Every man in Amy’s life had betrayed her. Why should she dream Jack would be any different? When she saw him, gun or no gun, she would wallop him a good one. And yell all the thoughts she’d kept pinned up for too many years. Then she’d take Mattie and Vasper from him and leave him for the coyotes.

Could that sweet, chivalrous young friend really have changed so much?

Amy squirmed as Red’s lips pulled closer once

more. Bile rose into her throat.

"Let her go." Jack's voice rang out from the doorway of the barn.

Red's hands loosened on her upper arms, and Amy took the chance to slip away from him. She backed toward the far end of the barn as Jack stepped in front of Red.

He threw his head back and laughed. "What're you going to do about it, boy?"

Jack's hands balled into fists.

She could see the muscles in his jaw working. The splinters from the barn wall irritated her back. She reached around and pulled them out one by one. Time stopped. Jack stared into Red's eyes. Red snarled. None of it felt real. She was supposed to be safe here. Aunt Zena had promised.

"Not worth it anyway." Red spat on Jack's boot, pushed the younger boy out of the way, and stormed from the barn.

Jack's hands uncurled, but he didn't turn to face her. It was like he forgot she was even there until she touched his shoulder and he jumped.

"Thank you," she whispered.

He grabbed the bill of his cap and nodded once.

She took his hand in hers and stopped him from leaving. "No, I really mean it. You're a good friend."

Jack looked at the floor. "I couldn't let him hurt you."

"You're the first one who's ever stood up for me."

He kicked at the floor with the toe of his boot.

She realized she was still holding his hand and released it. “Sorry.”

“Can I kiss you?”

No one had ever asked her that before. Amy wrinkled her brow. The men that abused her took what they wanted, when they wanted, and she had no say in the matter. Kissing Jack of her own free will was a novel idea. And one that suddenly seemed tempting. “Yes,” she said, with the formality of a business transaction or a handshake.

She closed her eyes and felt his warm, minty breath on her cheek moments before his full lips brushed against hers. He didn’t raise his arms to embrace her. Or step closer so that their bodies touched. Just a quick, sweet peck, and he was gone. She liked to imagine that was her first kiss ever. It was certainly the first kiss she welcomed. When Amy opened her eyes, she was alone with the horses and the hay. And the fluttering of her heart.

Amy peeled open molasses-lined eyelids. A dream? A memory? A mix of both. She hadn’t meant to drift into a hazy sleep. She nudged a grasshopper from the back of her hand, slipped the pick still hiding in her closed fist into her pocket, and stretched. “Cobalt?”

His heavy steps plodded closer, and his long face appeared in her line of sight. He nudged the top of her head, green drool foaming the corners of his mouth.

She smiled and raised a heavy arm to stroke his long-whiskered chin. “Hey, bud. Ready to get going again?” The image of Jack’s smile flashed through her mind. How could he? Who did he think he was, marching into her life again only to steal the one thing that made her feel normal? The one part of her life who had nuzzled into her heart and found a home?

Anger made her head feel clearer. New fire to find Mattie and Jack ignited in her.

She left Cobalt munching on the grass and scoured the perimeter of the clearing for footprints or sequins. In the thick grass, it was impossible to follow the trail. But at the edges, dirt reclaimed the landscape. They had come into the glade from the south and left to the northwest.

Cobalt’s belly, fat and round, gurgled as he approached.

“Bloated from all that fresh grass, eh? Please, don’t get sick on me. Not out here. Not now.”

He lifted his head and stared at her with a tendril of green hanging from his mouth.

“Well, it’s time to go, mister. Enough lollygagging on both our parts. If we can keep up this pace, we’ll close in on them tomorrow.”

Amy climbed back into the saddle. Her elbow, the size of a doorknob, was slowly regaining some flexibility. Her quick rest refreshed her weary mind, but they would need a water source very soon, or her eyes might close permanently.

Cobalt walked with a lighter step, renewed from the grass.

Her tongue still felt tacky, but the swimmy-head had retreated. She scratched her neck and winced. Her skin must be charred. Why hadn't she thought to bring sunscreen? She longed to guzzle more water, but it was far more important to conserve it for Cobalt. If he went down, she'd never catch Mattie. And never give Jack the beating he so deserved.

Chapter 12

The sun rimmed the horizon in red as Sam followed the path from her cabin toward the barn. She pulled her phone from her pocket for the hundredth time. Still no return text from Amy. What if she was in trouble? Maybe Amy's phone was just off to conserve battery? It had taken her almost a day to respond with the request for water. Sam just needed to wait a bit longer. Everything was fine. Right?

Alone on the huge farm, shadows at the fringes of her sight took on new forms. Creatures moving in the waving grass. Stalking her in the dusky twilight. She was letting her nerves get the better of her. She forced her focus on the prior day's events. Wainwright had returned and silently motioned for Tom it was time to go. They'd left while Sam's mouth still hung open, she was pretty sure. Evangeline had left. Sam suspected Wainwright had encountered Amy, though he wouldn't speak when he returned. She had never seen him so despondent. Debby, with a permanent frown on her face, had taken Cosmo home with no new leads on Mattie's whereabouts, even after a temporary excitement when Cosmo had seemingly picked up on the scent only for the trail to go cold. Nothing normal seemed to be happening anywhere in Sam's world. The stitches of the sky itself were likely to rip apart with dawn.

The horses whinnied at her presence. "Sorry, everybody, no more hay today. You had flakes at breakfast." She talked to them as if they understood every word. Who knew? Maybe they did. "It's too wet and the grass ain't drying out. I promise I'll finish as soon as the weather allows." With no campers needing the horses, she should turn them out to pasture. "That's what we'll do, okay? First thing in the morning, to the near pasture with all of you." She stroked Moonpie's forelock as she talked. "Oh, bud, your little girl's gone. I sure miss her. Amy too."

Moonpie nickered between bites of grain.

"Thanks for understanding. It's awful lonesome 'round here, ain't it?"

Strange that a woman who had chosen never to marry hated being alone. She'd never really had to be, though. Even though her cabin was all hers, the farm was constantly populated with friends. More like family, really.

Her thoughts drifted back to Tom. It had been so many years since they were sweethearts. Too many to bother with counting. They were just twenty-three when she'd broken his heart and told him she needed space. What had she been thinking? That conversation was the exact thing that drove him to Evangeline's arms. And left her pining after her stupid words.

Sure, she was an independent woman. She liked being that way. Why had she convinced herself that loving and marrying a man meant betraying her ideals? She'd regretted it every moment since. The love she held for Tom didn't die through the years. How was it that it grew stronger despite his marriage to another and children? Love was an awfully strange beast.

Maybe Evangeline's departure was Sam's chance at happiness. After all, Sam had respected their marriage all these years. Never mentioned a word about how she still felt for Tom. Never dreamed he could be hers. And Evangeline had left of her own accord. And Tom was heartbroken.

No. She couldn't step in now like some long-lost lover reclaiming her ground. It would be un-Christian-like, sinful. Wrong.

Lord, help Tom heal his marriage. And please, I beg you, help me keep my mouth shut and my feelings hid. Forgive me for the sinful lusts of the flesh and mind. She paused and tilted her head. *You know what, Lord, not just hid. Make these feelings completely disappear. I beg you.*

Sam slid the barn door closed, closing the door on her emotions at the same time. Now was not the time to let them go all willy-nilly free. She spun on her heels and aimed for her lonely cabin, eyes on the ground, emotions close-fisted in her chest.

A sharp snort of breath stopped her dead in her tracks. Her gaze crept upward and scanned the now dark path. Why hadn't she brought a flashlight? A large animal stamped a hoof on the ground ahead and snorted again. She struggled to find her shaky voice. "Get on out of here," sounded much weaker than she'd intended. She slipped her phone out and touched the screen. Its bluish light pierced the darkness ahead and illuminated an elk cow. "Go on. I won't hurt you." Her voice didn't quiver as much with the second instruction, but her insides quaked. If there was a calf nearby, this momma could trample Sam with surprising speed.

She and the elk gazed at each other a moment more. Then the elk kicked up her rear feet and raced into the night beyond the light of Sam's phone. Sam exhaled and pressed a hand to her chest. "That was fun." Adrenaline coursed through her body and made her legs shake. The empty farm haunted her with its silence. Though she'd never felt the need before, a flashlight would definitely become part of her outfit from now on.

As the afternoon sun traveled farther west, Amy covered a lot of easy ground with the topography remaining unchanged. Gradual climbs and descents, old growth trees with a litter of leaves, and summer-dried earth provided the perfect opportunity to make up lost time. By nightfall, Amy's back and calves ached from the ride. She halted Cobalt at the base of another near-vertical mountain and fed and watered him. The last bottle. Amy sipped the remnant trickles from the bottom and stuffed the crinkly plastic into her backpack. Tomorrow would be miserable and dangerous for both of them if something didn't lead them to a water source.

Cobalt was too tired to do much more than eat. His eyes slipped closed while Amy finished setting up her bed. Another dark camp closed in around her. She climbed into her sleeping bag and instantly fell asleep.

It felt like a matter of minutes, but when she opened her eyes the sky had clouded over so thick not the slightest sparkle of starlight shone through. She could just make out Cobalt's shadow at her feet and recognized the jangle of his halter.

He nudged her foot a second time.

"What is it, boy?"

The white flash of lightning lit up the trees. A distant rumble followed.

"Oh, bud, I'm sorry. I know you don't like thunder. It'll pass soon." She sat up and patted his nose, which was now trying to get into the short tent with her. She giggled and gently pushed him back. "You don't fit."

Her body longed for more rest, but if her horse stepped on her trying to squeeze into her sleeping bag, she'd need more than rest. She climbed out of the bag, rolled it up, and tucked it under the tarp. Maybe it would have a chance of staying dry under there.

"Okay. I'm up." Amy rubbed Cobalt's ears and

looped an arm around his neck. His trembling magnified when another bolt illuminated their surroundings. A crack of thunder jolted the air. The storm must've been moving at lightning speed. She chuckled at her accidental pun. Lack of sleep and water were making her brain think such clever things.

A gust of wind brought the sounds of the first raindrops. They crept across the leaves in a line from the west, a pleasant tiptoeing on the thirsty earth. Amy closed her eyes and remembered the sound of summer rain on the tin barn roof. Or in the tree house with the steady drip-drip falling onto the wood overhead. Sitting next to Jack in silence. Words not needed. They understood each other. Understood the pain of their pasts. The fists and the invasion of someone else's forced will. The pieces of the soul that had been ripped from them, broken like a glass jar filled with frozen rainwater. Expanded. Shattered.

The rain came, soldiers marching in form, and soaked her again. Refreshing relief from her sticky clothes.

Cobalt shook with each blast of thunder.

Rain poured from her head down her nose, off her shoulders in rivulets down her arms. Running from Cobalt's neck, it filled her boots.

Rain. Fresh water.

She licked it from her arms, made salty as it mixed with sweat, but her tongue craved more. If only she could soak it through her skin like a frog and remain wet and glistening. Carry it with her tomorrow when the storm had passed.

Duh. The bottles. She quickly dug them from her pack and uncapped them. Feeling with her feet and stumbling in the dark, she managed to prop them against logs and rocks. But the openings were too small. They would never fill before the quick-moving clouds raced away to bless the next county.

She loosened the ropes on the taught tarp and let the water pool in the middle. The next lightning bolt flared like a flashlight, and she hurried to set the pan under a low-hanging bough of the large-leafed magnolia she had spied next to camp before dark. She returned to Cobalt's side. The satisfying sound of water plinking in metal and plastic made her lick her lips. She had never been so thirsty in all her life. The ground was lucky it could drink by soaking the rain as it fell, pulling it deep into its core. With her face upturned, she opened her mouth and caught the fat drops like snowflakes on her tongue. Warm, wonderful, dusty-tasting drops.

Dawn crawled into the clouds and changed them from black to dark gray. With enough light to see, Amy rushed to fill the bottles from the tarp that looked like a toad's belly ready to burst at the midline.

She pulled Cobalt's lead rope and guided his nose to the pool. "C'mon, Cobalt. Drink up."

Cobalt slurped and sloshed until the puddle in the blue tarp was reduced to a thin layer.

Amy retrieved the pan and drank it greedily. Her stomach ached, but she drank it all.

The rain slowed and then stopped as it marched onward, but the clouds hovered. Amy inspected her gear. Nothing had been spared from the downpour. She couldn't ride Cobalt with a soaking wet saddle blanket. He'd have sores the size of oak leaves by sundown. What were the chances of finding enough dry wood to build a fire?

She pulled her sleeping bag out from under the tarp. It was still somewhat dry. Using her pocketknife, she cut a small slit in one of the squares at the bottom and pulled out the fluffy white stuffing. Perfectly dry.

Amy broke off branches and gathered fallen limbs. She piled them in teepee fashion and stuffed the sleeping bag guts into the middle. The matches were soaked, but the lighter flared on the first try. The stuffing took the fire as if it were hungry for it, blazed up, and boiled the water out of the small sticks. They, too, caught the fire and sizzled like bacon as they dried out and burned. She gathered more limbs and found the insides dry as she split them with the hatchet.

The rope from her bed cover stretched between two trees made a makeshift clothesline. She hung the saddle blanket, fluffy side out, next to the fire. Steam wafted from it in thick waves. Her wet blue jeans clung to her legs, rubbing sore spots on her thighs. She longed to dry them before the fire with the rest of her gear. What was she so afraid of? It wasn't like anyone would see. She peeled off the layers of sticky clothes and hung them with Cobalt's blanket. A strange, self-conscious sensation stole over her. She was half-bare in the middle of the forest. Was this what it was like in settler times? They didn't have infinite changes of clothes either. If it was, it sure felt weird.

Without the sun or her cell phone, she had no way to know the time. No way to know how long she spent recuperating and regrouping. It felt like every moment, Mattie slipped farther away.

Where were they headed? It wasn't like one could live off the land forever out here. Royal Blue was surrounded on all sides by some sort of civilization. Not like the wilderness she'd read about in Alaska or Canada. There had to be a destination, an ultimate plan of escape somehow. But what?

The wet morning air tingled her skin. She was thankful for the cooler temperature, but with her sunburned neck it felt downright chilly. She shivered and pulled her stiff shirt from the line. The warmth it absorbed from the fire seeped into her back.

Maybe the plan wasn't escape at all. Amy shuddered. She knew well enough there were men that wanted more sinister things.

Chapter 13

The rain drenched Jack, and all he could think was that he wished he had something more to catch it in than leaves. He'd managed to find a couple springs along the path the last few days, but looking for them had slowed his progress. He was slipping farther and farther behind. If only he'd secured more provisions before setting out.

He carefully poured the small rain puddles into the canteen. They barely filled it halfway, but it would have to do. He slung the mandolin and small wet bag onto his shoulders. The downpour had wiped away all traces of prints, and the little girl had stopped dropping sequins. He had to trust Red would continue in the direction he hadn't wavered from since that first night.

Jack's stomach growled. Clearly, the beef jerky he'd managed to find in the apartment cupboards was not satisfying his appetite. But he'd been hungry before, and he knew how to push food thoughts aside. He took a cleansing breath and pictured Amy's little girl.

Was it his imagination, or did he smell smoke? He took another deep sniff and was certain of it. This was it. Red had messed up. He'd lit a campfire. If Jack could smell it, it meant Red must be close. Smoke wouldn't travel too far in the dense forest before dissipating. And all Jack needed to do was find a high spot to locate it.

Tall trees with branches out of reach surrounded him. If he could find one with a low enough branch to get a start, he could climb. He paced northwest several hundred yards and finally spied one. Dropping his mandolin and pack to the ground, he grabbed the rough pine branch and ascended. Halfway up the thinning trunk, the tree began to sway, but he pressed upward until the sticky branches grew too small to support him. The low-hanging clouds made it impossible to see the horizon. A slow mist rose from the trees. Great. How was he supposed to see a trail of smoke in all that?

He scrutinized the landscape in a full circle around him. There. Directly to the southeast a tendril of smoke curled among oak and pine branches. Southeast? Jack had to assume Red had no clue he was being followed, so why would he attempt to circle back and throw Jack off the trail? Unless the vile man's plans had changed. Or he was lost.

Jack descended and scooped up his belongings. A half-mile southeast, he paused to listen. The popping of burning wood and the jangle of metal on a horse halter echoed through the otherwise quiet forest. He stole closer, walking flat-footed, careful to place his feet just so. A glimpse of what he was up against should help him formulate a plan for stopping Red and taking Mattie home. He touched the guns tucked in his belt, one on each hip. They were two things he hadn't let out of his sight since he nabbed them from his uncle fifteen years ago.

His breath caught in his throat. Amy stood not a hundred paces away, her torso hidden behind a horse's saddle blanket. Her bare shoulders and ivory legs were all he could see of her. A pair of jeans and her t-shirt hung on the makeshift clothesline. Long brown hair draped down her slender neck. With his heart pounding in his chest and a stirring in his abdomen, he turned his eyes and waited until she dressed. It would be years before he forgot this particular image. Who was he kidding? He'd never be able to put it aside. Not that he wanted to.

Over the last few days, he'd wondered if Amy would follow. There shouldn't have been a question in his mind. He smiled but let out a sigh. He hadn't found Red at all. Maybe he and Amy could join forces and use both their skills to catch up. He waited several minutes after she'd redressed to approach. A stick snapped under his right foot. Amy's appearance when he'd arrived had broken his concentration completely in two. He froze.

Amy spun toward him with a pale face that quickly flashed to red. "You. Where's Mattie?"

He took a step closer.

Amy grabbed a log from the fire pit. Its end glowed red like a hot poker. "Where is she?"

"I . . . I don't have her."

"Liar!"

"You think I kidnapped her?"

The stick in her hand lowered a few inches and doubt crossed her eyes.

"It was Red."

"I knew it," she said almost to herself. She tossed the log back into the fire. "Sorry."

Her assumption was a nail being driven into a board already filled with them. She, too, believed the worst in him. What a surprise. His fingers grazed over the scar. Maybe he should turn around and go home. After all, the only reason he was out here was to help her. Her doubt, like alcohol poured into a gaping wound, was a painful reminder that time had changed both of them.

"Want some water?" She held a bottle out for him.

Did he ever. No sense in turning down fresh water. He could drink it and then go home. "Thanks."

"Do you know where they are?"

The hiccup in her voice made him cringe. "Northwest somewhere."

Her voice dropped. "I thought you left."

"I did." He elbowed her and smiled. He never could stand to see her sad.

"You know what I mean."

He nodded. "I couldn't sleep. I never even tried,

actually. I had been sitting in the dark for hours thinking about leaving the next day. All that thinking made me thirsty, so I got up to get a drink of water and looked out the window. Red was getting on a horse with your little one. I couldn't just let him get away."

"Why didn't you come tell me?"

"There wasn't time. He raced out of the yard and I thought I could intercept him. I grabbed my stuff and that pack of jerky from the cupboard and flew out the door. By the time I realized he was too far ahead, it would've been a waste of time to come back for you."

There was a long pause in which his heart thudded in his ears. He hung his head. He'd screwed up again.

"Thank you."

Wait. What? She wasn't going to yell at him, berate him for such a stupid plan?

"We're wasting time now." She pulled the saddle blanket from the line.

Sure, her doubt hurt, but he couldn't leave her here to fight this battle alone. "Can I help?"

"Put out the fire?"

Jack used a long stick to throw wet leaves and mud onto the fire. It sizzled, fighting for air, but then faded under the weight of the damp cover. He poked it a couple times with the stick. Smothering puffs of hopeful smoke escaped. Curling upward, rising. Awakening with new purpose.

Cobalt was saddled and eager to set out. He seemed fully recharged and refreshed after the ample water and a night's and morning's rest.

But how were she and Jack both going to ride him? It would take too much time to let Jack walk. But Cobalt couldn't possibly carry them both at the speed he'd carried her for two days. Not to mention Jack riding double with her appealed to her senses. She wanted to have his arms wrapped around her waist, their bodies so close they shared heat. The fact that she wanted it made her hands shake and her mind go dark.

He would have to walk.

How much had he glimpsed of her while she dried her clothes? The thought brought a deep heat searing up her neck. He'd been a perfect gentleman about it all, but he'd yet to look her in the eye. She glanced at him squatted next to the fire, his back to her. Her hands longed to smooth the wrinkle from his shirt where it peaked at his spine. To ruffle his hair, longer than she remembered it being as a boy. To run her fingers over the puckered, whitened skin of his cheek and smooth the pain of the past away.

He spun on his heels.

She jumped, and the blush deepened. He'd caught her staring. What must he be thinking of her? She shook her head and returned her attention to Cobalt's girth strap.

"Fire's out."

"Okay."

It would be a slow day trying to decipher which direction to go in the muddy ground. The tracks had washed away like a clean blackboard the teacher had erased before the students finished copying the notes.

She sighed and mounted Cobalt. “Ready?”

Jack touched the bill of his hat and nodded. “Lead the way.”

They picked their way through trees and thorny undergrowth, past where Jack camped the night prior, in what they thought was a straight northwest bearing. Amy led the way, twisting in the saddle often to check Jack’s progress. He followed diligently with his gaze focused on the ground.

Amy studied the forest floor, but the rain had left them little to follow. Even the sky was being difficult with no sun to guide them.

After an hour of riding, frustration mounting in her breast like a stubborn fist refusing to open and yield its prize, she halted Cobalt and stepped to the ground. She paced several hundred feet to the left then back past Cobalt’s watchful nose and a hundred feet to the right. Not a single sign they were headed in the right direction. The forest floor remained covered in years’ worth of leaves and downed trees grown spongy with time. No one had disturbed it since the mountains sprang up from the turbulent plates.

Jack stopped next to the horse and took a swig of water.

Amy waved her arms. “This is pointless.”

“I’ll admit it’s been right difficult.” Jack removed his hat and wiped his head with his shirtsleeve.

“Why did you come back?”

Jack drew a sharp breath. "I wanted to see you. Been praying about coming back for a long time."

Amy's muscles tensed. He prayed about coming to see her? When had he become a believer? She couldn't bear the intense scrutiny of his gaze for one more second. With one fluid motion, she mounted Cobalt and looked down at Jack. "I was fine, you know. Before you came back."

Jack dropped his head, and his shoulders slouched.

"Which way is northwest?"

He cleared his throat. "It's been awful hard to tell with the sun hiding like it is. Maybe we should make a wide circle here and see if we can pick up on anything."

"We are taking too long as it is." She could feel the bite of her words as soon as they sliced off her tongue. It wasn't Jack's fault, but he was the only one to take it out on.

"You have a better idea?"

Get off this horse and wrap her arms around his waist. Thank him for thinking about her as much as she thought about him. She dropped her stony gaze. "No."

"I'll circle to the left and forward in a hundred-yard radius. You circle to the right and behind. We will meet back at Cobalt. Just holler if you get turned around."

Amy nodded. Good idea to put some distance between them. Once again she stepped to the ground and tethered Cobalt to a sapling.

Jack had already started on his course.

She stared at his strong back for a few moments. She had grown lonely the past two days with no one to talk to, but now was not the time to discuss all the questions running through her mind. Not the time to fling accusations at his retreating back. Accusations that would be laced with longing. All the doubts and fears no one had been able to drag from her.

The circle she walked held on a level plane and provided no clues. Not a single print, human, animal, or bird, dotted the ground. Just pine needles, leaves, mud, and more needles. She arrived at Cobalt's side before Jack. What was keeping him? Maybe he found something. She wouldn't be that lucky, though. They were lost and Mattie was gone forever.

The back of Jack's neck burned as he turned and walked from Amy. In her agonized state, he caught a glimpse of the frightened girl he knew. The one who used snippy comments and a wall of rage to squelch her fears. Her words stung. Delivered without an eye bat, he knew she meant them. He never should've come back. One more failure to chock up in the long column of past losses. After, no, if they found Mattie, he would be road-bound and out of her life again. Forever.

Cobalt disappeared from view as Jack delved farther into the forest. He stepped over a fallen log and froze. Soaked ashes lay in a heap surrounded by stirred up muddy ground. Two sets of footprints, one large, one small, pockmarked the reddish earth. He'd done it. He'd found their camp and the heading in which to bear. Red and Mattie had clearly packed in a hurry. A sliver of plastic from a food container and several matches were left behind.

Ten feet away, horse prints gashed the ground. From the looks of it, Amy's stolen horse had bolted from camp and torn through the trees sometime after the rain. The footprints ended where the hurried horse tracks began. Lying in the trail, a child's stuffed animal. Only two pink sequins clung to the little dragon, with torn strings protruding from its wings like flimsy white hairs. Amy's little one was a smart child leaving the sequins for them to follow. He picked up the dragon and retraced his steps to Amy.

"You found something," she called when he was still several yards away. Her eyes sparkled.

He held the dragon up to her, and she took it with gentle hands. "Their camp is just a little way ahead. We've been on the right track all morning, and we are catching up." Should he tell her about his suspicions that Red knew he was being followed and picked up the pace early this morning?

"She loved this dragon."

Amy's voice was but a whisper. He longed to take her hand, but instead he patted Cobalt's neck. "We can find her, you know."

She took a deep breath and let it out slowly. "Let's get on with it then."

As she rode Cobalt into the forest ahead, he barely heard her thank him. Again. Pride swelled like a baking biscuit rising in his chest. Warm and satisfying. Something he hadn't felt in a very long time.

Chapter 14

Hank grabbed the handle of the door. "Good morning," he called through the screen. There was no response. He slipped into the kitchen. The screen door banged shut, loud in the empty room. What in the world? Where was everybody?

He turned toward the living room to find it empty. "Dad?" No answer. He pulled the lacy curtain aside and gazed toward the barn. Sure enough, his dad strode in that direction, shaking his head. His lips moved, but Hank couldn't make out the mumbled words. Something strange was definitely going on.

In the kitchen, he searched the pages held by an assortment of cow magnets to the fridge until he found the church directory. His mom wouldn't mind if he lifted a number. In fact, she'd be thrilled to know he might finally call Mary Beth.

Hank pulled his patrol car around to the barn and

rolled down the window.

His dad leaned into the passenger side. "Morning, son."

"Where's Mom?"

"Not here."

Well, that much was obvious. The look on his dad's face warned him not to press. "Want to ride with me up to the farm? I've got to search a few more places."

"Still no sign of the girl?"

Hank shook his head as hope faded lower in his chest. "Hop in."

Sam swung the pasture gate open. "Go on, y'all."

The horses didn't need her encouragement. They dashed through the gate with R.C. in the lead. He elevated to a full out sprint and let loose a happy whinny. The rest followed suit.

She probably wouldn't see them again for days.

Around the corner of the barn, she patted the tractor's front fender. "Morning, Rosy."

Dawn broke in layers of colored clouds. Purple, blue, orange, and pink, like a stacked Jell-O cake in the sky. Faithful old Rosy started right up. Sam puttered to the hayfield and pulled the lever to drop the hay fluffer to the ground. The rhythmic whirl of the tined wheels and gentle purr of the tractor lulled her mind to thoughts of the task at hand, thankfully droning out the worries that plagued her night and day.

East to west, back and forth across the neat rows she and Rosy traveled until the sun baked her skin. A fine mist trailed upward into the midmorning air. A good sign that she'd have dry grass before too long. It was a good cutting this go around. Their wet, muddy spring, though hard to deal with during chores, had enticed a plentiful grass crop. Good for the horses. Good for the farm. Maybe they'd even have a few bales to sell this year.

Sam cut the engine. The blades slowed to a stop. The silence that ensued felt so complete, so oppressive she was tempted to keep pushing, but her parched mouth argued for a break. She strolled up to her cabin and prepared a turkey sandwich lunch and tall glass of ice water. Her phone beeped, alerting her of a new voicemail. Maybe it was Amy.

"Hey, Sam. It's Kat Jenkins. I'm sorry to leave this on a voicemail, but the pilot looked today. No sign of Mattie or the horse or anything. He said he wouldn't be able to sneak any extra flight time again without being caught. I wish it had worked. Let me know if there's anything else we might be able to do."

The spring of hope evaporated.

She hung her head. *Lord, I need you. I've lost confidence. Amy was wrong. Mattie's dead. Amy's lost. I'm alone and I'm scared, Lord.*

As if on cue, the sun's rays burst through her kitchen window and shone a warm beam directly on her. His presence filled her like an embrace. She opened her Bible and flipped the pages. Her gaze fell on Romans 15:13. "Now the God of hope fill you with all joy and peace in believing, that ye may abound in hope, through the power of the Holy Ghost."

She needed that hope now. To cling to the slim chance that things would work out well. That Amy would return with a healthy, happy Mattie. But it was so hard. The odds weren't in their favor, and each lonely moment she spent added to her worry.

In a whispered voice, Sam repeated the verse aloud. This time allowing each word to fill her mouth before she spoke it, savoring the Word of God, and committing them to heart. *Thank you, Lord. I will try.*

She closed her Bible, ran a loving hand over the spine, and turned to face her work and the heat of the midday sun. She stuffed two bottles of water into her back pockets and sighed. "Rosy awaits."

Sam touched Rosy's black seat andyanked her hand away. The sun should definitely have dried the grass by the end of the day, as hot as it was. She started the engine once more. A loud pop made her jump. Oh brother, what now? She peered over her shoulder. The blades weren't turning. The belt wasn't driving the gears. Instead it hung limply from its position. "Great. Hang on, Rosy. I'll go see if I've got another."

Sam dug through the pile of spare parts in the corner of the barn. At the very bottom of the bin, still in its packaging, lay a brand new belt. "Perfect." She grabbed the wrench and a rag and returned to the field. "Here we go, Rosy. Let's get you all fixed up." If she kept talking to her tractor, someone would have her admitted. She snorted. Who would notice? The emptiness of the home place threatened to crash down again. Work. Work kept her mind occupied.

She pulled the broken belt free and inspected the housing. The rusty bolts didn't budge under the pull of the wrench. She gave one last hard yank when she heard another pop. This one internal. She dropped the wrench and grabbed her spasming back. Doubled over, sparkling dots flashed before her eyes as the throbbing climbed up her spine and down her legs. She attempted to straighten, but needle-like pain stopped her. "This ain't good, Rosy."

She shuffled all the way back to her cabin, with one hand on her low back and one hand out for balance. With an ice pack and four ibuprofens, she managed to maneuver onto her bed. If she lay perfectly still, it subsided. But with every small adjustment of her legs or hips, excruciating, hot pain stabbed her spine.

The door creaked. Sam's eyes flew open. Had she really managed to sleep?

"Hello?"

"Tom?"

She struggled to sit upright but gave up and flopped back onto her pillow. How embarrassing that he would see her in bed. At least she was dressed.

Tom entered her small bedroom with his cap in his hand. "Are you all right?" His eyebrows knitted together.

She wanted to paste on a smile and say yes. "No, not really. I've hurt my back."

"What can I do to help?"

“I don’t want to impose. What are you doing here?”

“Hank is hiking out and looking at some things today.” He refused to meet her gaze. “The canine lady said she lost the trail, and there isn’t anything else she can do.”

All hope hinged on the long-shot Amy was taking, then.

“Let me help. Need medicine or something?”

“I think what I really need,” she hated asking for help, “is a doctor.”

Through stabbing pain, Tom helped her walk to her truck and drove her into town. Normally in such close quarters, she’d feel overwhelmed by his presence. But the bumps and jolts of the road kept her mind occupied with the pain coursing through her. The hour and forty-five-minute drive to Knoxville seemed to take much, much longer.

Tom pulled into the parking lot and parked in a handicap spot. He trotted around the truck and opened her door, offering his arm to assist her down. Moving her legs in any kind of coherent fashion hurt. A lot. Bending, twisting, lifting, all were off the table of possible movements.

Tom hovered next to her while she signed in, his cologne stirring familiar old sensations within her.

“You might as well wait in the truck.” She patted his hand. “I’ll be a while. And I’d hate for you to get a ticket parked in the handicap spot.”

“Sure thing.”

“Thanks. I’ll be out in a bit.”

She waited with a frown that threatened to be her new, permanent expression.

After he adjusted Sam and helped her sit upright, her chiropractor grimaced. “You need surgery, Sam. Now, don’t give me that look. You needed surgery last time. I can’t imagine your MRI will look any better this time, considering the pain you’re in.”

“I know, doc. But it’s terrible timin’.”

“You said that last time.”

“It’s worse now.” Images of Amy lost in the mountains and poor Mattie being held captive flashed across her mind. “Much worse.”

“Well, I can’t make you. But this is just going to keep progressing until you either get it fixed or stop working like you do.”

“Amy’s depending on me. Neither of those options sounds very good.”

“Maybe not, but it’s the way it is.”

“I don’t like it.”

Dr. Emert chuckled. “No, I imagine not.” He gave her a sympathetic smile. “I’ll send you for another imaging test and make a referral to the surgeon.” He squeezed her hand. “Please, Sam, get it taken care of before that disc ruptures. You’ll really be in trouble then.”

She’d known Dr. Emert since he was a child. He had her best interests at heart, but it was a hard horse-pill to swallow. Either way she went, she’d be completely useless for months. When Amy came back, she’d deal with it. Until then, the back brace and Advil and ice packs would have to suffice.

The drive home was awkward. Sam felt a margin of relief with the adjustment, massage, and traction table treatment. But she still braced with her elbows against the door and middle console, keeping her back straight and minimizing movement. Tom parked the truck at her cabin and helped her out of the cab.

"Thanks again, Tom. Really, I appreciate it."

"You and me go way back. I couldn't just leave you here like this. I'll stay a while and make sure you don't need anything."

"No." She responded a bit too quickly. She was supposed to be working on expelling her feelings for him. The warmth of his strong hands on her waist and arm guiding her up the steps weren't helping at all. She couldn't spend the rest of the day alone in her tiny cabin with him. "I mean, no, I couldn't impose any more on you. I'm sure Hank is ready to get out of here. You go on home. I'll be fine."

At the door, she shrugged away from his hands and smoothed her t-shirt. "Really, I'm fine."

Tom's happy expression fell.

She hadn't meant to hurt his feelings. She couldn't control her emotions around him, though. Not yet anyway. He needed to go before she forgot again that he was still married. And that she was praying for his marriage to heal.

"I'll check on you tomorrow." He flashed a weak smile and turned to leave.

As soon as he was out of sight, she sank into the cushioned rocking chair. She wasn't okay, but she wouldn't let anyone else know that. Gathering her resolve by the belt loops, she vowed to cinch it up and not let her weakness show again. Her problems were nothing compared to the events with Mattie.

About midday the sun broke free from its cloud prison and beat down on the forest. Wisps of evaporating rain were like specters all around, rising from each surface. Amy halted Cobalt and waited for Jack to catch up. She'd lost track of him a while back but been unable to make herself rein Cobalt in slower. There was a chance they'd find Mattie today. If only she'd pushed a little harder before the rain storm, she might've found Red's camp and taken Mattie back already.

She peered into the woods around her. There was a clear patch ahead. She urged Cobalt into it. Not a clearing, but a bumpy, rutted trail cutting perpendicular to her current direction. Jack's voice behind her made her jump.

"Four-wheeler trail, I'd say. They're spread all over up here."

"Doesn't that mean we're near civilization?"

He shook his head. "Not necessarily."

She knew that but wanted to believe otherwise. "Could you follow it out and bring more help?"

"No telling where this trail leads. It could take days for me to hike out and then back in. I'd better stick with you."

Amy nodded. At least they still had plenty of

rainwater in their bottles, enough to last another day or so.

"I'm going to look around a bit."

Jack disappeared around a bend in the four-wheeler trail as Amy dismounted and stretched her legs and back. The soreness wasn't as bad today, and for that she was grateful. She prodded the muscles between her ribs with an index finger and grimaced. Okay, parts weren't as sore. Ribs still stung like they were full of bees. She paced a few feet back and forth in the mud. It was quickly drying up in the intense rays, already a thin layer of goop atop hardened and caked clumps.

"Amy!" Jack's voice sailed through the forest.

Her heart leaped. Had he found something else? She grabbed Cobalt's reins and jogged in the direction Jack had traveled. She rounded the bend and found Jack kneeling in the middle of the trail.

"Look at this," he said.

Amy stepped to his side. The area Jack pointed to was filled with tracks. Three sets of shoe prints, fresh Vasper tracks, and four-wheeler tire marks. "Someone's helping him."

"It would appear so."

"But why not just leave Vasper here and ride out on the four-wheeler? That would be a much faster get away."

"Maybe they don't want to be back on the main roads yet?"

Amy pursed her lips and nodded. That made sense. She scooped up a cigarette butt and tucked it in her pocket. Whoever was aiding Red had delivered fresh supplies. Too bad they couldn't get in on that delivery service. Her stomach had stopped growling hours ago.

Jack picked up a purple bubble gum wrapper and handed it to her.

She tucked it in her other pocket. "When do you think this exchange happened?"

"These tracks are fresh. Maybe a few hours ago."

"We can catch them, then. Let's go."

"You go on ahead. Just be careful. I'll follow your trail and catch up when I can."

Amy held her breath for a moment. "No. We'll both ride." She mounted Cobalt and kicked her foot from the left stirrup. "C'mon." She held out her left hand and helped Jack mount behind her. "Hold on."

He placed his hands on her waist and leaned close to her back.

A tingle sparked out from his fingertips and electrified her. She squeezed Cobalt's sides and set him in an easy, quick gait. Jack's breath on her neck brought heat to her face and a flutter to her pulse.

Chapter 15

Riding double at such a quick pace and trying to keep to Red's dim trail through the trees left no energy for talking. Her breath remained caught in her throat, and a strange exhilaration grabbed hold of her. Amy pressed thoughts of Jack's close presence aside and concentrated on keeping them both on Cobalt. And willing Cobalt to remain strong with double the weight. It was a good thing he had draft horse blood in him.

By dusk, though, Amy's spirits were sinking. They had ridden for hours, pressed Cobalt to his breaking point, and still it felt Mattie must be worlds away. Red's tracks told her that he had pressed Vasper too. The elder animal showed signs of stumbling in the kicked-up places every so often. If Red continued at his breakneck pace, he'd kill the poor horse. Even though Cobalt was faster with a solo rider, Vasper held the lead carrying only one grownup and an underweight child.

Amy halted Cobalt at the foot of the next mountain.

Jack slid off. He looked stiff and cramped as he attempted to gather firewood.

She managed to get her numb feet from the stirrups and made it to the ground some minutes later. Jack wasn't the only stiff one. Amy's legs felt like they weren't even her own. Like someone else was trying to command them, and they were not obeying. She threw Cobalt's saddle and blanket to the ground and haltered him with no rope. He was far too exhausted to wander.

Cobalt moved to a tree and rubbed his back against a low-hanging limb.

She fed and watered him, then dug through her pack for some nourishment for herself and Jack. Their supplies were dwindling. The trail mix was gone, as were the granola bars, except for the one she'd stashed in the saddle bags. And she wouldn't touch it until they were desperate. A few strips of chewy jerky remained, but it wouldn't last them much longer.

Jack disappeared into the forest, and when he reappeared moments later he wore a grin. "I found water."

"Great. Here, take my bottles and refill them. It's clean water?"

"Straight from a spring. God's looking out for us today."

She didn't know about that, but fresh water was a relief. "Hurry back. We need to get moving. If we can ride another hour, it'll put us that much closer." She picked up the saddle and moved toward Cobalt.

Jack grabbed her arm. "Amy, wait. You can't push him any farther today. I mean, look at the way his back's sagging. He's exhausted."

She ripped her arm from his grasp. "I know!" Amy turned her back to him and dropped the saddle. "But we're so close."

"Red's horse will be exhausted too. We will close the gap tomorrow."

Amy resigned and plopped down next to the saddle, tears pulling at her eyes. She needed to string the tarp, but her arms felt full of water, heavy and useless. She finally prodded herself onto her feet and set up a nighttime area. Where would Jack sleep? The tarp wasn't wide enough for both of them side by side without being too close. She could still feel the sensation of his arms around her waist. A blush flashed to her cheeks. She'd definitely liked it a little too much having him so near.

Jack returned with the full bottles as the sun set orange through the trees. He set them at her feet. "I'm starving."

"Me too." Sam was right about the wire she'd brought. Why hadn't it occurred to Amy that she wouldn't be in one area long enough to set up a trap? She handed Jack a strip of jerky, and they chewed in silence for a long while. Her thoughts turned to the years they'd been apart. She'd gotten used to the scar, but what had caused it? "What happened to you?" She felt his arm jerk.

He let out a loud sigh.

Jack's feet dangled over the edge of the barn loft. He didn't dare glance at Amy while his lips still sparkled with the taste of her lip gloss. He had kissed another girl once. It hadn't made him feel like this. Like anything he could imagine might be possible. Any dream he wished could come true. "Your past sounds awful, Amy. I mean, I know you told me about that one guy, but I didn't know all this. I'm sorry." Tears glistened in streaks on her cheeks. He wanted to swipe them away. Or throw his arm around her shoulder and hold her until the pain faded.

She wiped them with her sleeve and gave him a half-smile. "Thanks. Not much I can do about it now, though."

"Men like that Red make me sick."

"Me too. Thanks again for stopping him." She pushed her glasses up her nose and gazed toward the main house. "So, what's your story?"

"Oh, it's been a downright fairy tale." He snickered.

"I told you mine. Your turn." She elbowed him in the side.

"I had life good with my mom and stepdad. You know, with both of them alcoholics and all. A few months ago they both got drunk and ended up in a brawl in the front yard. Neighbors called the police and they took me. Said it wasn't safe for a fifteen-year-old boy to live with them anymore. My real dad didn't want me, so I ended up in the system."

"Do you like your foster family?"

"They're all right, I suppose."

"That's good."

The hard scrutiny she passed over his face made him squirm.

"You miss your parents."

Her assumption was a statement rather than a question. How was it that this new girl could read him so easily? Jack dropped his chin to his chest. "It's dumb, I know."

"It's not dumb. I miss my mom too. Doesn't matter how awful they treated you, there's always this gnawing beast in my heart that misses her, even though I don't want to."

He nodded and fought the emotions threatening steady speech. "Here comes your Aunt Zena."

Amy's gaze whipped over the field where Jack pointed. "Shoot. We've been gone a long time, ain't we? I'd better meet her halfway. You circle around while she's distracted with me and get on back to your cabin, or wherever it is you're supposed to be right about now."

He climbed down the ladder first and exited the back while Amy walked out the front, but he paused, pressing his back to the outside wall of the barn.

Aunt Zena's voice rang clearly through the hall. "Where've you been?"

"I just needed some alone time."

"I was worried about you. Hey, listen, I have

news for one of the campers. Jack Evans. You seen him?"

Jack held his breath. What news?

"He must be with the campers. Want me to go find him?"

"You know him?"

"Yeah. What do you need to tell him?"

"Don't say anything to the other campers, okay? DCS just called. They are coming to pick him up this evening. They found a relative who's willing to take him up in Ohio. His dad's brother, I think they said."

The barn rocked behind his back, threatening to send him to his knees. He tilted his head back too quickly and rubbed the tender spot that banged against the wall. Not his uncle Pete. Didn't DCS know anything? Jack Sr. came from a whole family of drunks, and Pete was the worst of them all. His pulse beat a thunderous melody in his neck.

No. No way would he be sent to Ohio to live with someone he barely knew. And what he did know wasn't good. He slammed his curled fist into the open palm of his other hand.

But what could he do? He was stuck on this mountain. In this camp with a bunch of kids and no way out.

He had to run. It was the only thing left. If he stole some food from the kitchen and a horse from the barn, he could make it. Live off the land like Davy Crockett, deep in the woods away from everything and everyone.

Amy appeared in the doorway and jumped when

she saw him. “I thought you were going back to your cabin.”

“Didn’t make it that far. I heard what your aunt said. I won’t go. Not to him.”

“He’s an alcoholic too?”

“The worst. I’ve got to get away before they come.”

“Running won’t fix it. But I won’t stop you.” She turned her back and walked away.

He stared after her, watching the way her hips swayed in her jeans. Her long hair bounced against her back. It’d probably be the last time he’d ever see her, and he wanted to remember everything.

Jack retrieved his meager things from the cabin, snagged a few muffins and granola bars from the bowl on the kitchen porch, and snuck back to the barn. He’d borrow a horse, ride it to the nearest bus station or place he could hitch a ride, and leave the animal. It wasn’t stealing if you didn’t keep it. Right?

He opened the stall marked Wrangler and saddled him the best he remembered from the previous day’s lesson. Once in the seat, he realized how poor of a job he’d done. No matter how he tried to stay balanced, he slid farther down the horse’s sides and had to lean heavy in one or the other stirrup to right himself. Was it his imagination or did he hear footsteps behind him? He pulled Wrangler to a halt.

Amy came through the trees on her horse and bore a hole through his heart with her gaze. How could he run away from her? Facing life with Uncle Pete was a nightmare of a future, but leaving the only girl who ever believed in him was a nightmare of a past.

He turned Wrangler around and followed Amy back to Camp Hope.

Jack waited on the top step next to Amy. He heard the phone ring through the screen windows, Aunt Zena's murmured voice, and then her footsteps headed his way.

"Well, Jack, it seems you are staying with us a bit longer. Your uncle needed a little time to get your room ready, so you can finish what's left of your two weeks' camp."

Amy's smile radiated, but he couldn't quite catch it. Ten more days at camp just meant more time to dread living with Uncle Pete. DCS would be back, and his time here would come to an end. Then what?

Jack spent every free moment with Amy. Time he should've been doing the camp activities, he slipped away and found her. She taught him everything she knew about tracking and horseback riding, and he was a quick learner. Their ten days together evaporated like the morning fog burned away under the intense gaze of the sun.

The night before DCS was due to arrive, Jack could stand the thought of Uncle Pete no longer. Once again he saddled Wrangler, this time making sure he cinched it up tightly, and crept from the barn. His heart tugged at him, longed to stay with Amy. He glanced at her darkened bedroom window as he snuck past. "I'm sorry, Amy."

He couldn't let them take him to Ohio. He'd never survive the brutality he was sure came barreling at him in the fists of his uncle.

Once past the porch lights and away from the barn, the darkness swaddled him in a warm embrace. Comforted him. Pushed the future away with its thick air and the soft buzzing of cicadas. He was the only one on the road. Maybe the only one left in the world. Invisible in the thick layer of night where no one could harm him.

For an hour Wrangler carried him down the winding gravel road in a bubble of contentment he was sure would never encircle him again. He was tempted over and over again to veer off the road and wander into the vast forest surrounding them. He wouldn't last long with absolutely no supplies, though, so he forced himself onward.

He had to reach Briceville, leave Wrangler, and hitch a ride far, far away. Someday he could return for Amy. When he was grown and living life his way. No more adults using him as a punching bag.

The lights of the little store at the town center made him squint after the pure darkness on the road. The streetlamp in front would be a safe place to leave Wrangler. He would tie the reins around it and Wrangler could wait on the sidewalk, out of the way of any passing traffic. Surely the locals all knew where his home would have to have been. And they'd return him safe and sound.

Jack dismounted and looped the leather around the light pole. Twinkling flashes of red and blue reflected off the pole from behind him. What in the world?

The realization dawned on him too late to run. He spun slowly.

Hidden around the corner, a police cruiser was parked. Its lights now flashing and a serious-looking cop exiting the driver's side.

Jack hung his head. He failed. Again.

It took three months for the newness and excitement of having a teenage boy living with him for Uncle Pete to reveal his real nature. The one Jack had heard about all his life. The one Jack knew existed and would tear them both to pieces. Just before Christmas, Pete came home with a case of beer.

"Want one?"

Jack shook his head.

"Come on, be a real man. My brother never amounted to nothing neither. Don't you want to be better than him?"

Of course Jack did. But beer wasn't the way to do it. Jack retreated to his room and listened as his uncle's stumbling footsteps grew heavier.

"Get in here, boy."

Jack searched his room. There was nowhere to hide that Pete wouldn't find him. He puffed out his chest and held his chin high. Better to face him now anyway. He cautiously entered the living room.

Pete waved him over to his chair. "Set down and have a talk."

Jack did as instructed, but the warning sirens blared in his mind, as loud as the ones warning fishermen the river was rising beneath the dam back in East Tennessee.

"You are about growed up now. Getting good grades in school. How many girls you been with?"

"None."

"None, sir."

"Sir."

"That won't do. You ain't a man until you been with a couple, ya know."

The drool sliding from the corner of Pete's sagging lip repulsed Jack. How would Pete know? He was so disgusting, Jack doubted a woman ever glanced his way.

"What was that girl's name from camp you told me about?"

Jack knew letting that information slip right after his arrival would come back to bite him. He lowered his gaze to the ratty carpet.

"Oh, right. Amy. I bet she was a pretty young thing, wasn't she?"

Not pretty. Beautiful. But that was none of Pete's business. Jack gritted his teeth. "You leave her out of this."

"I'll talk about whatever I please in my house. You may live here, but you ain't worth nothing. The least you can do is give this old man something to remember. Come on and tell me. How was she?"

Jack's clenched fists shook at his sides. "Nothing to tell."

"You expect me to believe that? I know what kind of boy you are, though. Maybe you weren't man enough."

If his trembling legs would have held him, he

would have bolted through the front door.

“Get me another beer, useless.”

Just what Pete needed. More alcohol. “I won’t.”

Pete’s face flushed red. In his anger, entire words wouldn’t form. Pieces of them flew out with spittle.

In slow motion, Pete raised the empty beer bottle. Jack saw it all as if it were happening to someone else. In another time altogether. The glass crashed against the side of Jack’s face. But it was like he wasn’t in his body. There wasn’t immediate pain. Someone else was being screamed at, being beaten. His vision blurred. He fell. The nasty carpet scratched his face. Tacky, warm blood trickled down his cheek. He tried to rise, but his brain no longer seemed connected to his limbs. He lay there staring at the ceiling until the emptiness was broken by someone crashing through the front door. A man in uniform with the Star of Life emblazoned on his shirt knelt and spoke, but the mute button was on. Why couldn’t Jack hear him? Why couldn’t he lift his arms or nod his head? Or breathe out of his nose like normal? A hazy fog settled at the periphery of his vision, dimming the corners of the world.

He was being lifted, placed onto something hard, strapped to a stretcher. Leaping up toward the ceiling as the stretcher was raised. Everything in silence thicker than a sound-proofing layer of new snow.

Sounds returned slowly at first. The nurses shouting from far away even though they were in the same hallway with him. The wheels of the stretcher whisking along on the linoleum floor. Then, all at once, life was on high volume. Every scrape and cough amplified until they drilled through his ears into his mind. Threatening to burst his eardrums.

His head ached, burned like maybe his brain was trying to break loose. Trying to escape the pounding pain. And flee somewhere no one knew him. The nurses told him to lie still, and they gave him some medicine in an IV he didn't remember them placing. The room grew fuzzy. If only he had a volume button and could turn it all down. Why did it seem he was looking at everything through a sheet of thin water or cellophane? Or maybe one of those fancy silk skirts he'd seen on television. A dark blue one that would look fantastic flowing around Amy's tanned ankles, playing against skin he longed to feel himself. His eyes closed with heavy lids.

When he woke, the room was dark and empty but for the sound of a heart monitor beeping angrily at his side. The door cracked open, allowing a slit of white to slip in. He squeezed his eyes shut against the dagger-throwing neon light.

"You're awake," a nurse with gray hair said. "Need to check your vitals, young man."

Jack struggled to scoot up in the bed. His tongue clove to the roof of his mouth.

"You've been through quite an ordeal tonight, haven't you?"

He didn't know. What happened? He wrinkled his brow, the movement causing pins to stab his cheek.

Oh, right. Beer bottle to the side of his face.

The nurse gently lifted his arm and wrapped the

blood pressure cuff around it. "The stitches will itch in a few days. You'll have quite a scar, but you're still a handsome young thing."

Scar?

"Forty-three stitches and a fractured cheek bone."

No wonder it felt like his cheek was imploding. He wanted to ask about Pete, but all that escaped his lips was a pitiful moan.

"Nope. Don't try to talk just yet. You'll stretch the wound and make it bleed. Besides, it's going to hurt to move your jaw. Take a sip of water if you can manage and try to get some rest." The nurse handed him an insulated cup and pointed the straw to his mouth.

She was right. It did hurt to move his mouth. Agonizing points of pressure seared through his face. But the water was delightful, cleansing his mouth and refreshing his tongue. He turned his head and refused any more drink.

Where was Pete? He needed to get out of here before he showed up and tried to apologize. Jack wouldn't allow himself to go home with Pete ever again.

Chapter 16

Jack's painful story slept with Amy. Each time she woke with a rock or stick irritating a sore place on her side, she looked toward him. Though Jack had fallen asleep at the base of a tree nearby, leaning awkwardly against it in a seated position, she couldn't see him through the inky night. He'd wanted to come back for her?

The morning after Jack's disappearance, the camp had been virtually shaking with the news as it flew from mouth to mouth. Leaves on trees before a storm, whipped into a frenzy with the wind. Jack was missing. DCS had come, and he wasn't there. The excitement grew until at breakfast time Aunt Zena had to call a special meeting and address the entire host of campers.

Amy had listened from the edge of the group with her pulse pounding in her throat. Aunt Zena told them Jack had borrowed Wrangler and tried to get into town, but a police officer had taken him into custody where DCS would be picking him up shortly to deliver him to his waiting family. The foster parents had been informed. All was well. Jack was safe.

Amy knew that was a lie. Jack had confided in her the truth. Her heart plummeted to her ankles. She had raced to the tree house and spent the afternoon crying alone. Then she'd spent the next fifteen years trying to forget that pain. How could a teenager love someone so completely, so deeply that it hurt even now to recall the loss she felt back then?

She shook her head and forced her gaze to the sky. The moon rose and shone weakly through a hazy sky. The night air was no cooler than the prior day's and sat heavy in her lungs. Yet, she trembled. Jack's presence, a little unsure, yet so wholly masculine filled the night air. His arms, the ones that held her waist most of the afternoon, were only a few feet away. She could call out to him and there would be no doubt he'd wake and come to her. Warmth spread through her, tingling her insides, hovering in the pit of her stomach. She swallowed. Hard. And pressed her fingers to her lips. No. Her thoughts shouldn't be traveling down that rutted-out road. Jack wasn't the same boy she fell in love with.

Rolling to her left side, away from Jack, she pulled her sleeping bag tighter around her shoulders. It would have to hold her in place.

Mattie, where are you? She ached to hold the girl's thin frame in her arms. To stroke her soft hair and whisper that everything would be all right. Amy couldn't keep chasing her tail, stopping to find the trail and losing precious time. If only she could deduce Red's final destination, they could intercept him. She couldn't keep riding double with Jack either. It was too close. Too intimate. Too enjoyable. This was life or death. Her life was serious. No room for mistakes. No room for romance. That's the way it had to stay if she had any chance of finding Mattie. She could never truly trust Jack again, could she? Somehow, with swirling thoughts muddling her mind and pricking at her heart, she managed to drift back into fitful sleep.

Jack stirring awoke her. She peeled her eyelids open and rubbed the sleepy dirt from them. The dawn sky had just begun to color pink and violet. She uncurled her stiff limbs and massaged life back into them.

They gathered their belongings, packed the saddle bags, and each drank a bottle of water. With Cobalt taken care of, Amy mounted. "I have a new idea today, but it could backfire."

Jack stopped packing and looked up at her.

In the dim light, his features were dark, save for the scar which stood out starkly white. Now more than ever she longed to smooth away the wrinkles. "You keep tracking them on foot. I will attempt to intercept them. Red hasn't left a northwest bearing the entire time. Maybe I can circle around and head him off."

He shook his head. "Too dangerous. You could get lost out here forever and never find him."

She jutted out her chin. "It's worth the risk, in

my book."

"I don't suppose I could change your mind?"

Amy shook her head.

His shoulders slumped. "Never could."

She caught a glimpse of his pale, toned stomach as he lifted his shirt. Her heart skipped a beat.

"Here take this." Jack produced a handgun from his waistband. "Don't shoot it unless you find Red and are forced to. Don't try to get meat with it. The sound will echo and it'll tip him off like our fires did yesterday."

When she didn't move to take the gun, he slid it into her lap. She stared at it as if it had fangs but then picked it up and stuck it in her belt. "Thanks."

"We need meat soon, though."

"That we do."

Jack's gaze lingered on her face.

"What?"

"Just getting a good look at you before you disappear."

A shiver crept up her spine, sent sparks whizzing around in her abdomen. She looked away.

As soon as she left Jack, heaviness filled her gut. Maybe splitting up was a bad idea after all. She squared her shoulders west and urged Cobalt into a trot. Guess she'd find out. The forest ahead posed an easy ride, and she covered what she guessed to be ten miles easily. From the peak of the next mountain, she spotted a deep valley gorged by a river. "The shortest distance between two points is a straight line," Aunt Zena used to say. If only she had wings and could skip right over. Her thoughts drifted to Jack. Where was he? What was he seeing? Was he making more progress than she?

Amy dismounted and held Cobalt's reins loosely in her hand. She let him pick the path for both of them.

His knees crackled and popped as he descended the steep mountain.

At times they both slid on the loose shale and dried clay until their feet hit something solid enough to stop them. Once at the base, they rested side by side, both covered in dust and sweat. They'd left the cover of trees and entered a breezy open space.

Cobalt practically dove into the lush grass nose-first. He nickered happily as he filled his belly.

Too bad she couldn't linger in this beautiful oasis. It would make the perfect homestead. A house back against the tree line. The barn over toward the east. A field full of light-stepping horses and energetic calves. Jack would like the peaceful isolation of it all. It was easy to picture him walking at her side, maybe holding her hand. Fishing in the river. Hunting in the forest. Mattie skipping between them, chattering away like a happy squirrel.

She shook her head before her daydreams carried her any further. Nonsense. He wasn't that boy she adored anymore. And she wasn't the open-book girl either. He'd assured that when he left and failed to keep his promise to stay in touch.

Amy tugged Cobalt's nose away from the grass and strode to the river's edge. It was deeper than it had appeared from above. At least it wasn't winter. The chance to plunge into the clear water was actually appealing. Of all Cobalt's wonderful traits, swimming with a rider wasn't one of them. Amy changed his bridle for the halter, cinched it a notch tighter, and led him in.

He reared hard on the rope. His nostrils flared and the whites of his eyes flashed.

"It's okay, boy. I know it's not your favorite. But please, we've got to get through."

With an iron arm, she heaved on his rope. She clucked her tongue and babbled soothing words. Holding the lead rope firmly, she backed into the water. Cobalt entered the river with baby steps. A few more and the squishy ground beneath her boots gave way. She swam into the refreshing water.

Once his feet were moving, Cobalt pulled her along like a bobber.

"Slow down. I can't . . . keep up." She spluttered water and released the rope.

He was too scared to worry about her.

The current in the middle was far stronger than she would've estimated. It ripped her downstream and pinned her feet to each other. She flopped like a mermaid on land might have, and pulled with all her strength. Her arms cut through the water like butter knives, catching nothing and making no headway toward land. Her head plunged under. The current pressed in on her, sucked her to the murky bottom. Her arm brushed a sunken log, and she was suddenly suspended in motion. Caught by her backpack on the mangled limbs. It was as if she were in a snow globe.

The water swirled around her with bits of leaves and clouds of dirt instead of fake snow. The silent world of fish and river otters sped by, pulled at her clothing, tore at her hair. Yanked thoughts from her mind and washed away her purpose. Why was she here anyway? Where was here? Tiny air bubbles escaped her nose and tickled her cheek as they rose heavenward.

Mattie. She had to get to Mattie.

Her thoughts congealed and turned into a cloud of clarity. She wriggled from her pack, shoved off the log with her legs, and popped to the surface. Was it her imagination, or was the summer air much sweeter when she gulped it down than it had been before? Burning lungs and an acrid-tasting mouth gasped for air between attempts to swim to the shore. Her arms and legs were giving out, but she was lighter without the backpack and its contents. She pulled herself through the current and several hard strokes later, her feet touched ground on the far bank. She crawled onto the shore and lay in the warm sun until her heart rate returned to normal. That was too close. When had she allowed herself to get so out of shape?

Once she caught her breath, she found Cobalt half a mile upstream, munching in a patch of purple clover. Drool streamed from the corners of his mouth, but the swim didn't seem to have fazed him.

"Thanks for your help." Amy petted the lock of hair between his ears.

At this rate, she was losing time, not gaining it like she had planned. Jack was right. Separating herself from the trail and from him was a terrible idea.

As big as the river seemed, Jack would have to cross it at some point too. She would gather what was left of her pride and follow it downstream until she found where Red and Mattie had crossed. If Jack's footprints didn't show this side of the river, she'd wait for him.

What was left of her supplies had been drowned at the bottom of the river. The few pieces of jerky and all her water bottles. Somehow the gun was still plastered to her hip. She had the bedroll tied to the saddle, as well as a small amount of grain for Cobalt and the tin pan. But not much else remained.

Cobalt did not want to leave the clover patch. He planted his feet stubbornly and refused to walk even an inch in the direction Amy desired.

"Oh, come on." She didn't have enough feed to use it for enticement. He just needed to stop being stubborn and move. She climbed back out of the saddle, stood in front of him with her hands on her hips, and glared deep into his soft brown eyes. "We have to find Mattie. Remember?"

He flicked a fly from his ear and clanked the bit against his teeth.

A bouncing hot ball ricocheted around in her chest. With each bounce, it climbed higher and threatened to break free in a string of blazing words and flying fists. Nothing was going like it was supposed to. The full gravity of Mattie's kidnapping pounded against her, aggravating the volatile emotions she needed to release.

"Move, you stupid horse!" As soon as the words

left her mouth, she regretted them. It wasn't Cobalt's fault he was tired and worn. She was the one who dragged him on a wild Red chase. And now she had no food, no fresh water, and no idea where she was. She'd spent so many years trying to control every single aspect of life that she didn't know how to let anyone else affect her anymore. Until Jack resurfaced. Every word he spoke kept her off-kilter, as if she was balancing on a wobbly plank board across the creek like when she was a child trying to run away from her mom's boyfriend and his cronies. Staying on the board required concentration and skill she no longer possessed. Falling off meant trusting another human being. Terrifying either way.

She pressed her forehead to Cobalt's soft neck. "I'm sorry. Can we please go now?"

Her hands shook as she returned to the saddle. So much unknown lay ahead. She'd better find Jack fast and get back on the right trail. Before her resolve and common sense ended up at the bottom of the river with her gear.

Cobalt stepped out in his familiar trot with light pressure of her knees. She sighed, wiped her eyes, and gritted her teeth. No more fool's errands.

Sam awoke before dawn but didn't jump out of bed like usual. Instead, she carefully rolled onto her left side and readjusted the myriad of pillows to support her lower back and legs. Each movement brought fresh stabs of pain but not as intense as the day prior. To the touch, her low back felt puffy and hot. Her eyes slid closed and didn't reopen until the rays of hot sun pierced the window above her bed. She checked her phone for the time. Was it really eight-thirty? She hadn't slept this late in decades.

She struggled to sit upright and scuffled into the kitchen for coffee. The sound of Rosy starting in the field raised the hairs on her arms. What in the world?

Sam shuffled to the porch and gazed out over the field where tidy rows of cut hay lay waiting to be baled. Sure enough, Tom sat in the driver's seat, cowboy hat pulled low over his eyes. Sam chuckled. "Stubborn old man." She hated to be a burden, but she was surely thankful for him.

Once dressed, she retrieved her Thermos of coffee and a mug and made her way back to the rocker on the porch. The morning passed quickly as she watched him methodically pass up and down the rows. Neat square bales of hay bound with bright green twine popped free of the baler every few hundred feet and thudded to the ground. It was thoughtful of Tom to help out, but she wished she was in the driver's seat. She enjoyed the rhythmic sounds and sweet smells of the baling process and especially the feeling of knowing she had accomplished something that would help the whole farm.

Around lunchtime, Sam hobbled inside and fixed sandwiches, barbecue chips, and coleslaw on plates and filled tall blue tumblers with sweet iced tea. She met Tom on the front porch as he approached. "Got lunch ready."

"Thanks."

"It's the least I could do. You have no idea how big a help this is."

Tom blushed as he took the plate she offered and sank into the rocker next to hers. Sweat ringed his neck and trailed down his back in a wide, dark streak on the denim. He drained his first cup of tea before he took a bite.

Sam refilled it before he could ask for more. They always had an easy rhythm between them, like the tractor and the baler. She'd known Tom a long time, but the ease with which their actions synced up never seemed to dissipate.

Tom crunched his last chip and handed the plate back to her. His hand lingered on hers.

A shiver crept up her arm. She yanked her hand away too fast and dropped the paper plates. "Sorry. I'll get those." She reached down for them, and her back caught.

"Let me." Tom leaned over and froze.

She felt his warm breath on the back of her neck and then his hot lips. His mustache tickled her skin. She couldn't move. Her mind knew it was wrong, but her heart yearned for the way things used to be when they were young and in love. Before she'd made the biggest mistake of her life.

"Tom," Sam whispered, "you're a good friend, and I appreciate your help. But we . . . this can't happen. Not even a little bit. You're still married, and Evangeline is my friend."

Tom's lips slowly lifted, like a Band-Aid peeling away. It hurt to lose the feeling of his passion against her skin. And the wound underneath was still painful and raw.

She sat up and swiped a hand across her neck. He wouldn't meet her eyes.

"Better get back to work." His heavy steps—was it her imagination or were they heavier than when he approached?—clunked down the stairs before she could even try to form more words.

Chapter 17

For the most part, riding alongside the river was easy. Four or five miles downstream, Amy spotted clear tracks in the gravelly mud ahead. Vasper's shod feet had passed, and the sun had not had time to dry the prints out. There was no sign of Jack.

Again she was torn. Follow Red and close the gap or wait for Jack to arrive? She could leave him a signal. Something he would recognize as hers.

No. Separating from him this morning was what caused her to lose over half their supplies and nearly drown. It would be better to be patient and wait. Maybe she could find something for them to eat while she did. Besides, charging into a camp with Red was a crazy notion without some backup.

A faint hum fell from the sky. Amy cocked her head and stopped to listen. What was that? The sound grew closer and closer. Her eyes snapped open.

A plane. Her two days were up.

She caught a glimpse of a small, low-flying fixed wing. It buzzed overhead. One pass. A second. An angry hornet waiting to swoop in and steal her back home.

Amy ran for the cover of trees, dragging on Cobalt's reins until she felt guilty about the bit clanking against his teeth. But she couldn't let the pilot see them. She laid a calming hand on his neck and pressed her back against a full-leafed oak tree. *Please, don't spot us or Jack.* Would he have the sense to hide? Or would he try to flag them down? She hadn't mentioned the threat of the sheriff's department potentially scouting for them too. Wainwright still considered Jack a suspect. What would he do to Jack if he found him?

They'd been in the air for forty-seven minutes. At first, Hank had strained his eyes peering into the dense summer foliage that resembled crowns of broccoli below. But the vibration and the constant ear-pounding drone were drilling into his brain, wearying his eyes. His head ached, and his back grew stiffer each moment.

What was his mom seeing from her seat thousands of feet above the level he glided at now?

He was a grown man, but it didn't matter. When his mom used the word "separation" and then informed him of her plans to travel, his heart felt like it had been punctured. His parents' marriage seemed so strong. So sure. It rocked the ideals they'd instilled in him all his life to think of them divorcing. It wasn't right. It couldn't be happening.

But Mom had left. And Dad was acting like he'd forgotten how to speak.

Hank tapped the pilot on the shoulder and motioned for him to head back to the airport. There was no point in continuing. He couldn't see a thing past the treetops. He fixed his gaze again on the undulating canopy. Where are you, Amy?

The pilot turned the plane into a wide arc.

Shades of green earth swirled beneath them. Wait, what was that? Hank picked up the binoculars and adjusted them to focus on a slip of bright blue color shining near the edge of the river. The singular area clear enough of vegetation that he could actually see the ground for a couple miles.

A tarp snagged on a log rippled in the current of deep, greenish water. His stomach lurched. Was it Amy's? Or some old remnant of a hunter's camp? He pulled out the GPS and marked the coordinates. He needed to get the four-wheeler and investigate once they landed. His heart hammered against his ribs. Was Amy lying beneath that tarp, blue lips and lifeless eyes? He shuddered. The plane couldn't get on the ground fast enough.

How could a plane fly so slowly without falling

from the sky? The minutes crept by and Amy didn't dare breathe. Finally, the vibrating drone trailed over the trees out of sight into the empty sky.

She exhaled. Wainwright was serious in his threat to find her, wasn't he? She waited a few more minutes and then stepped away from the trunk and let Cobalt resume grazing on the ample greenery underfoot.

What if the plane found Mattie already and had news that would end this terrible search? What if they found her after they passed and Amy wandered the forest purposelessly for another week? And why hadn't Wainwright dispatched aerial support sooner? Was he more concerned about her getting in the way of the investigation than he was with finding Mattie?

So many angry, anguishing questions surged within her that her head ached. There were no ready answers.

She left Cobalt in a small patch of stunted grass sheltered from the afternoon sun by tall trees and set out to explore the bank of the river, careful to stick to the cover near the water. If the plane returned, she didn't want to make it easy on them. If she was lucky, something edible might just surface. She grabbed a handful of chickweed and several small dandelion flowers. Maybe not the finest salad in all the world, but it would provide some vitamins and something in their stomachs. It was a shame she'd lost the wire in the backpack. Tiny critter footprints dotted the shoreline. She didn't enjoy killing anything, but she and Jack both could use a hot meal and fresh meat.

From a patch of marshy weeds ahead, a river otter darted into the water when it spotted her. Its sleek brown body disappeared beneath the surface, silently, as if it had never been there at all. She stepped over a fallen log and searched the area the otter had occupied. With the toe of her boot, she pushed aside plants and finally found what she sought. A large, headless fish.

"Sorry to steal your lunch, little guy. Or gal. But thank you."

The fish's tail still twitched, and it smelled like the river. She was fortunate to have startled the otter so soon after a new kill. The trout's rainbow side glittered in the sunlight. It would provide a full meal for both of them. Of course, they'd need to build a small fire, and her lighter and matches were at the bottom of the river. She gutted the fish and made her way back to Cobalt.

Jack sat on a rock nearby, tapping his heel in a quiet rhythm on the ground.

Amy's heart fluttered at the sight of him. Muscular and tan. Kind and gentle.

He looked up and waved.

She returned the wave by holding the fish high for him to see. His laughter brought a smile to her face. "Any chance you can start a fire without matches or a lighter?"

His brow wrinkled. "What happened to yours?"

"I kind of, might have almost drowned myself and lost my pack in the river."

The color drained from his face. "What?"

"I'm okay. I just lost most of my supplies. Cobalt is afraid of water and the crossing didn't go so well."

He closed the gap between them and wrapped his arms around her.

The unexpected embrace drove all thoughts from her mind. She couldn't protest, and for a moment she let her forehead rest on his strong shoulder and enjoyed the hug. Her eyes fluttered open, and she remembered where they were. "We should cook this fish before it spoils. Any suggestions?"

"I have a lighter." He dropped his arms and fumbled in his pockets. "Here. I'll find some dry leaves and sticks." Jack paced into the woods with his head bowed.

Amy sighed. She was glad to have a few minutes to compose herself. How was it that she felt so comfortable in his arms? She broke a thin branch from a beech tree and speared the fish on it. Then she gathered rocks and made a fire ring on the muddy ground between the river and forest, under the boughs of a cedar.

Jack silently reappeared and started a small fire. He cooked the fish, rotating it on the stick until it sizzled.

"That smells wonderful," Amy said over his shoulder. He hadn't spoken since his return.

He grunted and pinched off a piece of steaming white meat. "It's ready."

They sat knee to knee and ate with their fingers like starving cave men.

Nothing had ever tasted as amazing as the sweet, flaky meat and the fresh, crisp improvised salad. Amy could never remember a time in her life when she had been as hungry or appreciated a hot meal more. But every moment they lingered, lolling in the fullness of their bellies, was another minute Red pulled farther away. Amy licked her fingers and tossed the scraps into the river. “Ready?”

Jack nodded and put his bag on his shoulders. “Did you see the plane?”

“Yes.” And she’d hidden from it too.

“Think they were looking for us or Mattie?”

She hesitated. “Both.”

He arched his eyebrows.

“Remember Wainwright? He warned me not to come out here. He thinks you kidnapped Mattie, and I’m ashamed to say, almost had me convinced of it too. I really didn’t believe him until I found your pick, then I started questioning my gut. I’m sorry.”

“We haven’t seen each other in a long time. And then I show up here broke and unexpected. It’s understandable that you would doubt my intentions.”

“Wainwright gave me two days to find Mattie. Promised he would come looking for me if I wasn’t back by then. He’s threatened to nail me with obstruction of an active investigation.” She expected more questions or at least some sort of frustration on Jack’s part. She hadn’t exactly been forthcoming before.

Instead, he tipped his hat and strode after Red’s trail.

Two hours later, Hank stopped the four-wheeler fifty yards from the GPS point at the river and dismounted. The bright blue tarp waved at him from the shore. His heart sank. The plastic looked brand-new, hardly used. It wasn't some old hunter's gear. But he didn't know it was Amy's either. Calm down. Investigate and don't jump to conclusions. Yet.

He knelt and lifted the edge. Relief flooded him like the ebbing water pulsing against the shore. There was no body beneath. He pulled the tarp free from the water and inspected it. No name label or other indicatory marks. Squeezing the water from it as he folded it, he placed it on the rear rack of the ATV and returned to the river's edge.

Though the clean water appeared clear at the edges, the depth a few short feet out made it impossible to see through to the bottom. He paced left several hundred feet and found nothing but thick grass that caught his boots. Good. No signs that Amy had been here and had an accident. No signs of her whereabouts, either. But at least there was nothing to point to foul play.

The silence of the short valley sank into him. What if Amy never emerged from this vastness? What if he never got a chance to make up for the way he'd treated her all these years? He shook his head. Not the time to lose hope. *Lord, I'm counting on you to help her. To bring her home.*

He retraced his steps and proceeded right several hundred feet. At a gentle curve, with the earth and grasses squishing beneath his boots and mud oozing around each step, he paused. Something hard clicked against the toe of his boot. He pried the grasses apart. A yellow lighter reflected the sunlight. He scooped it up and slipped it into his pocket. Maybe he could pull some prints from it later and compare them to Amy's. Then, at least, he'd have a direction. He wanted to refuse to let himself wander to the negative, but it was hard. It felt like every second or two, he had to force his mind to detour away from morbid thoughts. If this was Amy's stuff, her body could be floating downstream . . . No. He had to cling to the hope she was okay.

She was convinced Jack was not the kidnapper. Should Hank believe her instincts? What if she was wrong, had caught up to Jack, and now he held both Amy and Mattie captive? Or had gotten rid of Amy altogether? A weight began crushing his chest so heavily his breath came in short gasps.

This wasn't like him at all. He'd seen every kind of case imaginable through the years. Why was he so emotional over this situation? He didn't love Amy. Not like he'd thought he could. Yes, he cared for her as a friend. Felt for her current situation. He didn't even know Mattie. Yet the weight of it tugged on his conscience. If he'd been faster to believe Amy, to get onto the kidnapper's trail, would he have caught up to them? What if the blood was Mattie's, and this whole charade was pointless?

That wouldn't explain those petite footprints at the tree where Amy's arm had nearly broken in his grasp.

He drew a deep, calming breath and climbed back onto the four-wheeler. He headed back to the main road, lining out a mental map of next steps. If the fingerprints came back consistent with Amy, he would plot the coordinates of this site and the house and map out a trajectory. As long as he kept his focus on logical planning, and off the situation with his parents, he'd be all right.

Amy was alive, and he would find her. Wouldn't he?

Chapter 18

The muscles in the backs of her calves protested, but Amy swung onto Cobalt's back. They resumed a northwest bearing, following the intermittent prints.

This time Jack led, with his nose aimed at the ground. He walked at a quick pace several hundred feet ahead.

Cobalt seemed content to mope along. No doubt he didn't want to leave the valley and the riverside full of greens.

They began to ascend and descend a series of small hills, each gradually growing taller until they were faced with another near-vertical mountain.

Jack stopped near a rock face and waited for her. "I hate to tell you this, but I'm pretty sure Red knows he's being followed."

She'd been watching Jack, not the tracks, and she hadn't noticed. Her face grew hot. "How do you know?"

"He's stepping on every hard surface available. Ain't you seen the way the legible tracks have grown far apart?"

No. She'd seen the way Jack moved, firm steps but somehow still unsure of himself. Absorbed in his own world, yet somehow still self-conscious. Muscular, strong. Handsome. Her blush deepened. "Sure. Yeah. You're right. Guess I'm just tired."

"And worried." The left edge of his lips curled upward.

It was the first hint of a smile she'd seen since before lunch. "Is there something else?"

He refused to meet her gaze.

"What is it? You found something while we were split up?"

"Blood. Drops on the trail. They've stopped now, but the whole morning it dotted the path."

Her throat constricted. Whose blood?

Jack read the look on her face. "I don't know whose. It could be an animal he killed. But either way, it unnerved me."

It bothered her too. It couldn't be Mattie's, though. It just couldn't. There was another explanation. Had to be.

They followed the impassable ridge southward for many miles. There was no way over. The rock face went on forever, it seemed. But if they couldn't find a way over, Red couldn't either.

Finally, Jack stopped moving ahead and again waited for her to catch up.

"Ain't going to be easy." He pointed at a steep, leaf-strewn trail between the rocks.

It was as if the front half of the mountain had broken free, slid forward, and left a secret passageway behind it. The only foreseeable ascent anywhere. She'd have to walk Cobalt and hope none of them fell. Red's tracks weren't hidden well in the break between the mountain and were easy to follow. But the terrain made it treacherous. She placed her feet in the faint imprints of Jack's larger ones and climbed, arduous step by arduous step. Cobalt followed without a fuss, thank goodness. She planted a hand on her hip and arched her brow. "As long as water's not involved, you'll pretty much do any crazy thing? Hey, old boy?"

Cobalt blinked and continued to plod upward and onward.

Amy chuckled and paused, panting, to glance at their progress. Her head swam dizzily. A terrible fall awaited any misstep. Straight down onto the tops of boulders ready to smash a person or horse should they be so misfortunate. The leaves made the ground slippery and unclear. They hid pockets and stones that caught Amy's feet and tripped Cobalt. Horrible images of watching Cobalt stumble and fall to his bloody, broken death flashed through her mind.

She reached a narrow ledge where Jack waited.

"Let's take a breather."

Amy nodded and squatted against a boulder. Her burning thighs trembled.

Cobalt nudged her shoulder.

"It's okay, bud. It'll be over before you know it."

A sound, like the swish of a large insect passing in a hurry, pinged in Amy's ears. Somewhere below, the report of a gun banged off the cliff side. Amy and Cobalt flinched in the same instant. Another bullet zinged past her head and thunked into the rock behind her. "Jack?"

"Get down!" Jack dove behind the boulder and pulled her with him. Cobalt was left unprotected as another shot flew into the stone wall.

Amy's ears rang with the concussion. "Do you see anyone?"

He peeked over the top and yanked back as another bullet zipped by mere inches over his head. "Would Wainwright shoot at us?"

"No. He wouldn't. I don't think."

Jack raised his left eyebrow, the scar wrinkling like a white caterpillar.

"He might shoot at you. He is convinced you kidnapped Mattie."

Another shot showered them with pebbles and rock shards.

"We have to move." Jack paused. "That makes five shots, right?"

"Right."

"One more and we make a mad dash for the next hideout."

"How do you know they only have six shots?"

"I don't."

Another bullet thudded into the boulder.

Before Amy could argue, Jack sprinted up the narrow path. She grabbed Cobalt's shaking reins and raced after him.

Cobalt nearly overran Amy, but they both managed to make it to the next place that afforded protection. Jack waved his hands and motioned for her to hurry.

"We're almost to the top. If we can make it, we can get to a spot and be on the offensive if he follows."

Six more shots in rapid succession pinged off the rock faces all around them. Amy didn't know what it was like to be in a war zone, but she imagined it must be something like this. Her stomach tied in knots, her breathing ragged, and her thoughts fuzzy. Her ears bursting. Buzzing drilling into her mind, chasing logic away.

Cobalt pranced in place, ready to move away from the thunderous noise of the gunfire catapulting off the cliff.

"Let's go."

Jack took her hand in his and dragged her over the tip of the ridge point.

One glance at the downward side and Amy's stomach fell even further into the pit of her abdomen. This side proved equally steep and even narrower. "Great."

"At least Red did the hard work of blazing the trail for us, right?"

He had an interesting take on their situation. She wasn't so amused. She pursed her lips. "Lead the way."

Jack picked the way down carefully but quickly. They weaved through sharp rock spires and crumbling ledges until Amy thought her nerves would send her flying off the cliff whether she wanted to or not. When her feet hit level ground at the base and she turned to look at what they had accomplished, her jaw dropped. From below there was no visible path, not a single flat surface for which four people and two horses should have been able to climb.

The forest ahead opened in a scattering of trees with high branches that blotted out the sky. Brown, yellow, and copper leaves tinted the ground in a crunchy carpet. Each time a breeze blew in, the top leaves moved and danced in the air to land in a new place. There was no undergrowth to speak of at all. Just trees and leaves as far as she could see. Lichen-covered rocks that had broken free from the mountain and rolled away speckled the area. Their escapes stopped by gravity and friction. A strange quiet filled the air with no bird songs or angry chipmunk chatter.

"No time to stop. Let's find some cover then I'll backtrack a bit and see if we were followed."

He pulled her to a gathering of trees squished close enough together to form a semi-circular kind of fence.

"Stay here."

"Jack, wait." She grabbed his shirtsleeve. What was she supposed to say? Certainly not what she was thinking as she gazed into his eyes. "Be careful."

Jack flashed a smile. He turned and ran back toward the wall.

Amy paced the length of the nature-made corral while Cobalt ate the leaves from the area. What was taking Jack so long?

"No sign of 'em."

Amy jumped and spun to face Jack. "You about gave me a heart attack."

He chuckled. "Sorry. I think they left."

"Good. Maybe we can concentrate on Red now."

Jack wrinkled his nose. "Do you smell something?"

"Smoke."

Their gazes met, and Amy's heart fluttered. Her eyes grew wide.

"He must be close. Come on." Jack strode into the forest ahead.

Amy followed, leading Cobalt as quietly as possible on all the crackly leaves. She had no idea who shot at them, but this could be it. They may have caught up with Red. She took a deep breath and pulled the gun from her waistband. Hopefully the dive in the river hadn't messed up its functions. Her hand shook as she pressed memories aside. It was not the time to picture the last time a gun had been aimed at her head and she'd been forced to stand as payment for her mother's and her boyfriend's spending habits.

Jack held up a hand.

She froze.

He studied the land ahead over the crest of a short hill.

What did he see? She tiptoed to his side and peered over the hill. The breath flew from her lungs. She grasped Jack's arm.

He turned to her with a sheet-white face and

mouthed one word, "Run!" He grasped her hand in his and pulled.

Amy broke free from her trance. As she turned, she blinked and pictured the line of fire racing up the hill. It strangled the tree trunks and consumed the dead leaves in a hissing, spitting band of red. The sound of the fire chased them, along with another new sound. Laughter. The deep, booming cackle of a man.

This forest fire was no accident. Her blood boiled, spurned even hotter by the fire closing in at their backs. Why was she still running on foot? She pulled Cobalt to a stop and placed her foot in the stirrup. A gust of wind stirred Cobalt's mane and the fire crackled and popped. She glanced over her shoulder. The fire topped the hill and edged closer. Her throat threatened to close off. They weren't going to make it.

Cobalt pranced sideways as she pulled on the horn and tried to mount. "Steady, boy."

His sides heaved. He let out a frightened whistle and bolted sideways.

Her body jerked. There was a tug on her lower leg, and she was staring at the sky and trees overhead, being dragged over the rough ground. Rocks scraped her back. She flailed her arms and tried to grab hold of something substantial. A tree sliced open her right palm as it whipped by her bouncing head. "Cobalt, stop!" His pace slowed for a moment, and Amy was finally able to kick her foot free. Her leg slapped to the ground, and she lay breathless, her gaze fixed on the thickening white smoke.

Cobalt's hoof beats vibrated through the ground as he dashed away.

Amy struggled to sit upright and suck air into her startled lungs at the same time. Strong hands gripped her waist, and again she was being carried away with the sky shining down on her. This time cradled in gentle arms. Jack's heavy breaths and quick footsteps sounded in her ears. The warmth of his chest pressed against her cheek. Each step he took bounced her tattered body. Blood dripped off her hand in warm streaks. She nuzzled her face into his smoky-smelling shirt and closed her eyes.

Wait. The fire. Cobalt. Mattie.

"Put me down. I can walk."

Jack complied and gripped her shoulders. "You okay?"

"I'll survive."

The roar of the fire gaining tinder came on the next gust of wind. Jack had carried her back to the bluff. She stared up its vertical sides and then whipped her gaze left and right. There was nowhere else to run. It was either up or dead. And up might be dead, too, if the shooter was still waiting. She'd rather be shot than burned alive. Up it was.

"Can you climb?"

She nodded.

He ripped a sleeve from his T-shirt and wrapped it around her hand. "That's the best I can do right now." He used his teeth to tie a knot in the ends. His lips brushed her knuckles.

Amy shivered, though the fire pressed closer and

heat radiated in waves around them. Walls of flames paraded nearer, sucking the oxygen from the air.

Jack scrambled up the first part of the trail they had descended and waited for her on a rocky ledge. “Come on, Amy!”

She ignored the pain piercing her hand and crawled on all fours until she reached Jack’s side.

He jackrabbited to the next stopping point, waiting again for her.

When she reached his side, he took the next section until they made it high enough that the air thinned out. It didn’t escape her that he stopped short of the crest in an area well protected by rocks.

Amy collapsed at his side and pressed her fingers against the wound in her palm. From their higher vantage point, it was evident how quickly the fire had demolished the forest. The line of red was highlighted by a thick border of smoking black, like too-heavy eye makeup.

“The fire will go out. Nothing on this bluff to burn. Too steep anyway.”

“This is crazy.” Amy glanced behind them. “Are you sure the shooter is gone?”

“Can’t be positive, I suppose. But I think if they were going to follow, they’d have done so by now.”

She nodded, but the hairs on the back of her neck refused to relax. Seated rather comfortably in a divot on a rock, Amy leaned into the one behind her and took a deep breath. Her lungs burned from the smoke. She coughed hard enough to see stars. When the fit had passed, sudden exhaustion stole into every part of her.

In the span of hours, they'd been searched for by officers in a plane, shot at by a ghost of a person who may or may not be the sheriff, and tried to be baked alive by a sadistic kidnapper. Not to mention her near-drowning.

Regret, like a hot knife, seared down to her bones. Her body ached, but her mind and heart pained her more. "Red's getting away again."

The sound of Jack's teeth grinding together made Amy cringe. But she understood exactly what he meant. They'd catch Red again, and next time he wouldn't escape.

Chapter 19

The fire crept to the edge of the rocks below, scorching everything in its path until there was nothing left to burn. Its fingers licked the walls as if trying to climb up to them, or to drag them down, but then it sputtered and died. Tendrils of acrid smoke climbed into the air from smoldering piles of leaves and bases of saplings.

"I thought you didn't like guns," Jack said.

"I don't."

"Then I guess you could put that thing away now."

Amy looked at her hand as if it belonged to someone else. How had she clung to the gun through everything that happened? And crawled without noticing it in her palm?

"Here's your glasses." Jack reached into his back pocket and handed the bent frame and cracked lenses to her.

"Everything is a bit fuzzy." She straightened them as best she could and slipped them on her nose. The crack in the left side would irritate her, but it would have to do for now.

"Found them behind you when Cobalt first took off."

"Thanks." She tweaked the lenses one last time and resigned herself to them being lopsided. "It'll be dark soon. I hope Cobalt made it away from the flames. He could be halfway home by now the way he ran off."

"He was as scared as I've ever seen a horse."

Poor Cobalt. He could've hurt himself in his frantic run or be so lost they'd never find him. How could they devote time to tracking him and Red at the same time in two different directions? Amy winced. Cobalt would have to fend for himself until after they found Mattie.

"What if he gets the reins caught on something or the saddle?"

"It's a possibility, I suppose."

"That doesn't make me feel better."

Jack's voice rose. "What? You want me to lie to you?"

"You've done enough of it. Why not now?"

"That is low. I didn't want to leave. But once I was gone, I realized you were better off without me." The rock wall surrounding them echoed his words. They bounced angrily to the ground and rolled around in the ashes for a long while.

"That wasn't your decision to make," Amy whispered through clenched teeth.

"You want me to say you were right?" Jack raised his eyebrows. "Fine. You were right. Running from my problems never solved them. But hiding from them doesn't either. You've put yourself up on that stupid mountain and hidden from all men—from life—for how long now?" The veins in his neck bulged as he rose to his feet and paced away. He couldn't go far because of the terrain.

Amy needed to put more space between them. His words stung. What did he know? He left and never looked back. The one person who knew all her deepest secrets. The one person she trusted when she never trusted anyone, and he'd smashed that trust. He'd carried her secrets out into the world where they had the potential to be exposed and left her raw and scared. She may have only been fifteen when they met, but she had loved him like she'd never loved anyone, not even her mother.

She still loved him.

The realization pummeled her. She had to get away from him. She couldn't love him. Wouldn't love him.

Sliding on her rear, she managed to descend the trail once more. Her feet hit the blackened earth, and puffs of ash floated into the air. Her nose tingled with an oncoming sneeze. Her feet carried her in a line following the bluff southeast. Between the broken glasses and the tears, she could hardly see what lay right in front of her. Her hand and head throbbed, splintering pain shooting from temple to temple with each hard footfall. A dark crevice opened in the side of the bluff. She slid into it and pressed her back against the cool rock. Quiet tears flowed down her face as her breathing slowed to normal.

Jack's shouts reached her ears, but she couldn't face him in her current state. She stepped deeper into the darkness and tried to blend in with the shadows.

He passed before the opening of her hiding spot and continued walking.

Amy exhaled and adjusted her feet, planting them farther from the wall. Something squished beneath her boot. A faint shaking, like beads in a rain stick, sounded. Her heart plummeted.

Jack was right. Hiding was dangerous. She didn't dare move. The snake's straining muscles brushed against her calf. Why hadn't it bitten her yet? Either it was stunned or she had managed to land directly on its head. If she lifted her foot a fraction, it would coil and strike before she could squeeze out. Would she be lucky enough that it would strike her boot? She needed help.

"Jack!" Dust sprinkled down from the crevice with her scream. She counted to ten and then shouted again.

The snake still struggled under the weight of her foot. She could feel the dirt slipping from underneath it. Jack didn't appear. She couldn't see well enough to try to shoot it and miss her own foot. And what if the bullet ricocheted off the stone? The rattling stopped as the snake fought for freedom. Amy took a deep breath, squeezed her eyes shut, and pictured her plan. It would have to be quick, before the animal had a chance to compose its own.

"One, two, three." She jerked her foot up and jumped away. Sucked in her stomach and squeezed into the narrow place between her and the exit. A thump bumped her calf above the level of her boot. She hadn't been fast enough.

Amy pushed her way into the waning day and collapsed on the ground in front the rock slit. She grabbed her pants leg and yanked it up to her knee.

Jack approached from behind. "There you are."

She ripped off her boot and searched her leg. No blood. No trace whatsoever of a bite. Her insides quivered with each breath. "That was too close."

"What happened?"

"Snake."

"Where?"

Amy pointed to the crevice. She took one look at his face and frowned. "Don't say it."

He shook his head and fought the smile at the corners of his lips. "Wasn't going to say a word." He held out his hand and helped her to her feet. "What kind of snake?"

"It rattled."

"I'll go have a look."

"What? No." Before she could grab his arm, he walked to the opening, dropped his things, and slipped in. She cupped her hands around her mouth. "Are you crazy?"

"Yes." The word filtered from the rocks.

Amy paced back and forth. What was taking him so long? "You okay?" She leaned into the edge of the darkness.

He bumped into her as he backed out, holding a long, black snake in his hands.

She leapt back three feet in one step. "You are crazy."

"Did you know rat snakes will shake their tails in loose leaves to scare predators?"

"Rat snake?"

"Yep, I'd say his little trick worked on you, you big, bad predator. That's why there wasn't a bite. Their tiny teeth can't usually pierce blue jean. Want to touch him?" Jack extended the hand holding the snake's tail.

"I'll pass." A shiver shook Amy's shoulders. "Technically, I've already touched it."

Jack laughed. He put the snake down outside the crevice.

It slithered back into the shady, cool den.

He turned to her with a grin. "We'd better find a place to camp. We might as well have a fire so we can see. Hopefully Red will just think it's his lovely attempt on our lives still burning. He already knows we're here anyway."

Amy stooped and picked up a charred stick. "Not much here that isn't already burned."

Jack turned in a semi-circle, inspecting the ground. "Good point."

Amy's stomach growled. "Maybe we should eat the snake?"

"I'll break some branches off and we'll see if we

can get a fire going. Want me to catch it again?"

"Nah, I guess we shouldn't since he had the courtesy to be non-venomous when he tried to bite me."

Jack chuckled. "I sure am hungry, though." He swiped his hands on his grimy pants. "Let me see what I can come up with for wood. It's going to be a messy camp with all this ash."

"Maybe there won't be any mosquitoes that way." She joked, but the truth was she was filled with worry. They had virtually no supplies left now that Cobalt had disappeared. What were they going to do?

Jack searched the ground for any sticks with viable wood left on them, but, finding none, he raised his gaze to the trees. Several of them still smoldered, their trunks tinged black waist-high. Red had some nerve. And no conscience whatsoever. He could've lit thousands of acres on fire. Idiot.

As he reached for another branch, he realized his hands still trembled from Amy's run-in with the snake. If she'd been envenomed . . . He didn't know what he would have done. There was no hope of getting her to a hospital in time. The thought made his insides quake.

Jack broke a brittle branch from a beech tree and slapped it into the crook of his arm. Amy risked her life to save Mattie. Jack understood that. He risked his life to protect Amy, and she didn't even realize it. He'd almost lost her three times in one day.

Why did he care so much? Amy had always occupied a special place in his mind. She was the one beacon of light in a lifetime of gray. But his shaking fingers told him it was more than that.

Jack returned with a light armful of branches. Their fire wouldn't last long, but for some reason he craved the comfort of its flicker. Maybe the light while he fell asleep would chase away the dreams that left him sorrowful when he had to wake. Dreams of happiness and love that were unattainable in his life. No, he was destined to be alone. Amy was the only one who ever believed in him and, clearly, that faith ended long ago. *Lord, help me accept her avoidance of me after this. I know she will return to her hidden mountain, tucked away from life, and I will have to walk away. Give me the strength, please.*

"You okay?" Amy had cleared a small area using a pine branch to sweep away the ash and sat cross-legged in the middle.

"Fine. Just hungry and tired." And heartsick.

"Maybe we should eat the snake."

"Nah, you were right. He was such a gentleman and all."

The sky faded from navy to black as Jack bent to light the fire. The dry sticks engulfed quickly. He settled onto his elbows, stretching his sore feet toward the fire. Stars dotted the sky through the gaps in the leafy canopy. Awkward silence hovered between them, daring one of them to speak first. He didn't know what he could say that wouldn't betray his emotions. It had been a hard few days and the end would be even harder. Red was obviously willing to do whatever it took to hang on to Mattie.

Amy tossed a stick onto the small fire. “What’s the plan?”

She was asking him? So far on their little adventure, she’d pretty much led the way. He chewed on his bottom lip. “We are going to have to find water tomorrow.” He shook a half-empty bottle. “This is all I have left. But I doubt Red made it very far before sunset. That horse he’s riding stumbled a lot today. It’s tired.”

“He waited on us too. With that fire. He waited to make sure we were in the middle of this area before he left.”

“You saw him?”

“I heard him laughing.”

Jack’s eyes snapped fully open. “He’s more deranged than I thought.”

Amy’s chin dropped.

“Sorry. I know you’re worried about Mattie and what he has done. I would be.”

She nodded.

“But we have to stay positive. It’s the only thing we can do.”

“It’s so hard.”

“Your childhood primed you for thinking the worst in men, I know.”

Again, she merely nodded.

“I haven’t forgotten everything you confided in me.”

“How could you?” Sarcasm laced her words.

"It wasn't right what they did to you. No child should be forced to pay their parent's debts like that."

A tear glistened in the corner of each eye, like little beads of glass.

He balled his fists. It wasn't right how they'd used her body. Ruined her childhood. Her life. He took a deep breath and forced his fingers to unfold. "You know, when you told me that, I wished for a long time I could hurt your mom and her boyfriend. Atone for what they did. For years after I left, I imagined the punches I could land. The pain I could inflict."

Amy's eyebrows rose.

"I would've done it. For you."

"For me?" Her whispered words faded into the night. A faraway look glossed her eyes.

"God knows about your pain, you know. Your past. You have no reason to be ashamed. He loves you. There's always hope in Him."

Her eyelids narrowed to slits. She tossed another stick into the fire. "If God loved me, He would have protected me from them."

What could he say to that? Nothing that would make her feel better. He took a deep breath. "After I ran away from Uncle Pete, I hitchhiked as far west as I could get. I finally landed in California and started playing my mandolin on street corners. People tossed coins into my case because they felt sorry for me, I think, not because of my talent. One of the corners I played a lot was in front of this little café. The owners were a young couple then, maybe in their late twenties. They had a little boy who would come out and sit with me. He jabbered on and on every time I came about the people that came to the shop. He was fascinated by all the different stories. And I was fascinated by him." He paused.

A smile tilted Amy's mouth.

"I was sixteen, and this little boy had the perfect life. The parents I never had. The cozy home, the school, the easy life I dreamed about. Somehow in his innocent little way, he understood me. He brought me food and tea and told me I played good. Eventually his parents hired me. I think Cody had something to do with that." He laughed. "Imagine a little eight-year-old getting me a job. But those people changed my life in the short time I stayed there."

"How?"

"They invited me to church. Introduced me to God."

"Why'd you leave?"

"One day I came to work. I'd slept in an abandoned house with another teenager. He was a druggie, but he left me alone. A plain clothes police officer showed up and started asking questions. I ran out the back door and never looked back. I didn't say goodbye or anything. I thought Uncle Pete had found me and would drag me back to Ohio. Or maybe Cody's parents had called DCS, and they would take me back."

"That was a long time ago. Where've you been since then?"

"All over. I've walked thousands of miles. Worked so many different jobs, I couldn't even name them all."

Amy clasped her fingers together and expelled a slow breath. "You've never . . . never been a criminal?"

Ah, there it was. The suspicion everyone held about him. "Never stolen as much as a doughnut. And I've been hungry a lot in my life."

"Sorry. It's just so hard to believe you've lived all these years an honest vagabond."

His shoulders slumped. Why could no one understand that just because he had no home, no family, he wasn't some pilfering low-life? He'd only done what it took to survive.

"Lesser men would have stooped to crime long ago."

Her smile lifted his spirits. "Was that a compliment?"

Pink tinged her cheeks. "Take it however you like."

"Thank you. You have something else you want to ask. It's fine. Ask it."

"Wainwright said you had a rap sheet. Theft, evading arrest, and assault."

Jack clenched his jaw and drew a breath. "It was my uncle. His attempt to find me was to file a report that said I attacked him and it was self-defense. That I stole two of his guns, which I did, but only to protect myself from him. When I was released from the hospital, I went back to his house. Waited until I was sure he was gone and snuck in to retrieve some of my stuff. It was the scariest moment of my life. Even worse than when he hit me. Knowing if he found me in the house then I'd never be able to leave again. Anyway, I almost left without them, but I knew he had guns. I was just a kid. A scared kid. And I thought if I had them he'd never be able to hurt me again. I have no idea where the evading arrest part came from." He met her gaze.

Amy studied him, chewing on her bottom lip for a full minute before she responded. "Okay." She paused and threw a pebble into the fire. "Thank you for helping me with all this. Now, seriously, what's the plan?"

He sighed. Amy believed him. Was counting on him. "We close the gap. Move as quickly as we can and get into his camp. He thinks his plan stopped us, and we will use that to our advantage."

Chapter 20

Amy awoke to a dull gray sky after an uncomfortable night. Hunger, thirst, and worry dug their sharp nails into her mind. She'd guess she had about two hours of good sleep. The rest of the night had been filled with morbid thoughts. As they had nothing to pack and the fire had gone out long ago, they rose in silence and plodded into the forest. Though Amy had swept their camp area, Jack's face and arms were smudged with soot. She must be a mess. Her hair was crinkly and her clothes stiff and heavy. A hot shower would be the most blissful extravagance. And a cheeseburger and sweet tea and fries with loads of ketchup. Her watering mouth told her to stop dreaming or she'd be plagued with even harsher stomach pains.

She followed Jack down the hill to where Red's fire had begun. He paused and inspected the ground.

Amy knew she should be looking for clues, but her eyes wouldn't focus well through her damaged glasses.

"Here," Jack said, pointing to the ground. "Blood again. And mostly hoof prints. See, each step the horse takes, there's a few drops of blood."

"Vasper's injured." Guilt filled her for being happy that her horse was injured. But it would slow him down even more, and Mattie was the priority.

"I betcha he has a leg wound and that's the blood we saw before. It tries to heal and stops bleeding, but when Red pushes him too hard, it pops open again."

"What are we waiting for?" That same sense of urgency pressed in her chest again, driving her forward at a jog. Her lungs burned from the smoke in the air, but she wouldn't slow down. Not until she laid eyes on Mattie.

Jack, too, seemed to feel the pressure to find Mattie today, before sundown. His footsteps thudded the ground behind her.

He had her back. Just like old times. Red must've thought he had finished them off, for he took no care to hide his path today. It stood out like highlighter on blank paper. In his frenzied dash toward his destination—wherever it may be—Amy also read desperation. He knew the tables were turning. Amy smiled and steeled her tired body to finish the sprint for the finish line.

Today, Vasper's blood didn't cease to shimmer magenta in the fallen leaves. He stumbled often, evidenced by elongated hoof marks and close-together prints where he caught himself. Red was killing the poor horse with each step he forced him to take. A pang shot through Amy's chest. Vasper had been a part of her life for fifteen years. He was loyal and mild mannered and willing. A good horse and she loved him, but if he died or went down, Red would be on an equal plane as they.

Thank you, Vasper. I'm sorry it's like this. Maybe I can save you yet, but if I can't, thank you.

Amy pressed the grief aside and glanced over her shoulder. Sweat poured from Jack's brow, but he managed a weak smile.

"We need water. Soon. Let's keep our eyes peeled."

Her mouth wholly agreed. So much so that she couldn't respond. They slowed to a fast walk as they ascended the next hill. At its peak, she paused for a moment to catch her breath.

Jack stepped to her side and placed his hand on her elbow. "Let me see your hand."

Amy had forgotten about the injury, still wrapped in Jack's shirt piece. It throbbed, but she had blocked it out in her intense fixation on Mattie. Now that she thought about it, pain ebbed into her wrist. It itched and burned under the wrapping and felt damp. It was bleeding again, or oozing, and likely becoming infected. She couldn't see it, but she knew. He started to untie the knot, but Amy jerked her hand away. There was nothing he could do, so why show him something else to worry about? "It's fine. Come on."

She picked their way down the opposite side, cutting a diagonal slice out of the mountainside. The drops of Vasper's blood increased to a thin line. The downhill effort must have put greater pressure on his wound. How many of Mattie's tears were mixed in with that red stream? Surely the child must be scared, must be hungry and lonesome. Amy quickened her step, though her aching body protested.

The sound of trickling water reached her ears at the next bend and dip in the trail. A small stream bisected the path. She knelt, more quickly than she had planned, and became aware of the queasiness in her stomach and trembling in her thighs. How much longer could she keep this pace?

Jack was at her side, splashing water on his face and slurping it from his cupped hands. "Hope we don't get sick."

"Me too. But this will be over soon, and we can get treatment if we need to."

"True." He tilted his cap with two fingers and gulped another handful.

When he excused himself to find a tree, she unwrapped her hand. The laceration had swelled closed but remained puffy and red. No fresh blood escaped the wound. Instead a cloudy serum seeped from the edges. She touched it with ginger fingers and winced in pain. Amy laid flat on the ground and drank deeply from the stream, letting her injured hand rest in the coolness of the clear water. Her stomach ached from the onslaught of fresh liquid, but she drank until she could hold no more. Who knew when they would find another source? Resting on her elbows, she brushed the fingers of her good hand over the wound, massaging it and attempting to squeeze out the infection. Pain spiked into her fingertips.

Jack whistled as he approached.

She quickly slung the water drops from her hand and rewrapped it. "Ready?" A dark lock of hair had fallen from under his cap and curled over his eyebrow. Her gaze lingered on his handsome face.

He swiped a self-conscious hand over his scar. "Ready."

She hadn't meant to make him think she stared at his scar. In fact, it had become such a part of him she hardly noticed it anymore. It was his eyes that caught her. The intensity when he looked at her that stirred emotions she desperately wanted to ignore. No sense lingering on those thoughts. She spun on her heels and stomped into the forest.

With her eyes glued to the ground, she led them over the next ridge. A warm hand grabbed her shoulder and yanked her backward. Before she could realize what happened, she was in Jack's arms, and he was dragging her behind a tree. "Wh—?"

He clamped his hand over her mouth. "Shhh. Look."

Amy peered around the tree, and her eyes felt as large as tulip bulbs.

In the next dip between mountains, Red paced next to Vasper's prone form. The horse had collapsed. Though she couldn't hear the words, Red's mouth moved in a string of profanities. Where was Mattie? Her gaze darted left to right, from Vasper to Red to the empty forest beyond.

There. Mattie sat tucked behind a log. Amy's heart leapt into her throat. Mattie, in the flesh, alive and breathing. There she was! Amy's feet shuffled. She needed to get to her little girl.

Jack's grip stopped her. "We need a plan. If we burst in there now, we are at a serious disadvantage. There's no cover."

She fought a brief war within. Jack's words made sense, but her instinct pulled her to Mattie. Annoying, painful sensibility won out. She nodded. Leaned into Jack's chest and his arms encircled her. "What do we do?"

"Even if Red keeps moving, he'll be so slow trying to either carry or drag Mattie, we can follow. Let's be patient and wait until dark. Maybe we can sneak in and get Mattie without risking injury. I'm sure Red has a weapon."

His plan was logical, perfectly reasonable, but nightfall was a million seconds and minutes and hours away. How could she possibly wait any longer? She stood with her face buried in Jack's chest, urging herself to accept his plan. His arms held her up, kept her strong, held her back, and comforted her all at the same time. Her walls were melting like blocks of ice in the sun. Her fears and doubts, her shame, all dripped away drop by drop. She raised her face. He closed the gap. Inched toward her lips so slowly she wasn't sure if it were real. She closed her eyes. His warm breath swept across her brow. Her breath pooled in her chest.

What was she doing?

Jack's full lips—the ones she remembered as

being so sweet—brushed hers. Amy jerked away on unsteady feet and wiped her mouth with her fingertips.

Jack's arms fell to his sides. He bowed his head.

She stepped away from him to the next large tree and leaned against it. Her head swirled like soft serve ice cream on a cone. Delicious but mixed up. She took several deep breaths, pushing them out through her tingling lips. When she opened her eyes again and peered around the tree, Red and Mattie were gone.

Vasper struggled to sit upright. He whinnied as his head slammed against the ground.

Amy rushed down the hill to him, tossing sensibility aside. The sound of his struggling hooves hitting the ground made her stomach turn. She reached his side and placed a calming hand on his neck. "Vasper, boy. Shhh. It's me."

Tom hadn't stopped by last evening to say good-bye. Sam wasn't too shocked, but she knew he'd finish the hay no matter how upset he might have been. When the new sounds of men shouting and a diesel pickup came from the field the next morning, Sam wasn't surprised. What she didn't know was how to deal with things going forward.

She glanced out the front window. Tom, Hank, and another young gentleman were tossing bales onto a trailer behind Hank's pickup. Tom's strength hadn't faded one bit through the years. She could still see his bulging muscles move under his shirt as he easily lifted the seventy-pound bales.

She forced her gaze to the sky. *Lord, help me out here. The feelings, you know, the ones I need you to help me get rid of? This ain't helping one bit.*

How she wished she could talk to Zena. She had always known what to say to make Sam's muddied thoughts clear.

Sam's back still ached, but as long as she was careful it felt better. Not touch-your-toes better, but at least she could walk fairly normally today. She slipped out the back door and followed a narrow, overgrown path around to the cemetery. Unlatching the simple wooden gate, she entered and knelt before Zena's headstone.

"Sorry I still haven't mowed, Zena. My back gave out on me. I sure wish I could get your advice on something. You knowed how I feel about Tom. How I've always felt." Sam paused and glanced to the thunderheads forming on the horizon. A distant rumble reached her ears. "His wife left him, Zena. And I know if he comes back a second time wanting to . . . well, I ain't sure what he wants exactly, but I do know I won't be able to resist. Being near him again these last few days flared up the fire all over again. I don't know what to do."

Sam brushed the dirt off the face of the stone and sighed. "I know, I know. He's still married. It's a yellow jacket's nest of trouble."

Why couldn't the feelings just go away? She'd wished that same thing so many times through the years, she'd lost count. Prayed so hard for them to vanish. *Lord, please help me do the right thing. Help me encourage him, as a friend, to patch things up with Evangeline.*

She rose and massaged her back. The clouds drifted closer and taller. Hope the men hurry with the hay.

Were Amy and Mattie still out in the middle of nowhere, unprotected? Scared? Lost? Were they even alive?

Jack's hand gripped Amy's quivering shoulder. He would scold her later for rushing in, but he knew she couldn't help herself. Thankfully, it seemed Red had moved on, not laid a trap for them again.

The horse's nostrils flared as he tried to suck in air. His skin hung in loose folds, the ribs and backbones protruded, and his hair was dull and coarse. A deep wound on his right front cannon bled freely.

A tear slid down Amy's nose and landed on his face. "I'm so sorry, Vasper." She turned to face Jack. "We have to put him out of his misery."

Jack squeezed his eyes shut. His mouth ached with the words he needed to speak but he knew would hurt her even more. "We can't, Amy. Red will hear the shot."

"I can't let him suffer like this."

"Look, he's already calmed down. He knows you're here, and you love him. That's all you can do. I'm sorry." A screwdriver stabbing his gut wouldn't burn more.

Amy pulled her shoulder from him, but she didn't move to pull her gun. She must have realized he was right. The tears pouring freely from her eyes now made the screwdriver twist deeper. He could do nothing to comfort her or to help. What good was he, after all? He'd started to feel useful, even important, the past couple days. But now, the woman he loved—loved? He bowed his head. Yes, it was true. She was suffering, and he could do nothing to stop it. His uncle was right. Everyone was right. He wasn't a man. He was a pointless lump of clay God had mistakenly placed on this earth.

Vasper's labored breathing grew more ragged. He struggled again to right himself.

"Stay down. Just go to sleep," Amy whispered.

Her anguish tugged at his soul. He suffered with her, even though he had no emotional connection to the horse itself. "We need to go. Red's close. We can't lose him."

"I won't leave him."

And I won't leave you. He wrapped his arms around her midsection and hefted her off the ground. She didn't fight him, but he fought himself. It tore his heart in two to drag her from her dying friend, but he had to do it. Mattie was so close. Amy fell limp in his arms, but her chest vibrated with her sobs.

"I'm so sorry, Amy."

Vasper whistled and feebly dug his hooves against the ground as Jack turned his back and carried Amy away. He deposited her at a tree and raced back to the horse. It had grown still. His eyes glazed over, and his chest barely moved with his last breaths. Jack loosened the bags from the saddle and pulled them from under the horse. He patted Vasper's neck and whispered a prayer. "Lord, please help him die. Take him home."

He flung the bags over his shoulder and returned to Amy's side. He helped her to her feet. She refused to look at him but didn't pull her hand from his. He led her up the hill, chasing Red over the next stumbling block in their paths. For Amy's sake, Jack vowed not to stop until Red was in their sights again. Though the tracks were harder to follow, the emotional pain heightened his awareness. It was like Red's boot prints were stars on the ground, shining to him and urging him forward.

Chapter 21

At lunchtime, while Sam watched from her spot on the porch, the men produced a cooler and ate in the field. The rain was holding off so far, and it looked like they were over halfway finished.

She hated being idle. It didn't feel natural. Maybe by tomorrow she could manage, with the back brace, of course, to get some chores done. She needed to fill the horse trough and check the herd for injuries. They hadn't been back to the barn, but she did catch a glimpse of them this morning grazing near the fence. The stalls needed to be mucked out. The cabins straightened up. The dining hall swept and mopped. Her back spasmed just thinking about it all.

By early evening, the men had made four trips to the barn, and the field was green and empty of the lumps of hay that had been like tan ice cubes sprawled over the ground. Sam tried not to hope Tom would stop by on his way out, but she failed miserably. She wanted to see him, and she couldn't deny it to herself any more than she could deny the bulging disc that plagued her.

Hank pulled the pickup and trailer into her driveway, and he and Tom hopped out. Good. A chaperone.

"Thank you all for what you've done," she hollered from the porch as they approached.

Hank tipped his hat. "It's the least we could do, considering."

"Have you heard anything at all?"

"Not a word. As you know, Debby said Cosmo had lost the trail. We still have a search team scouring the area northwest of here, but the rain ain't helped none a'tall."

"I know you're doing your best. It's hard not to worry, is all. What about an aerial search?" She remembered what the pilot she had recruited relayed through Kat. The forest was too dense this time of year to see the ground. Unless they spotted them in a river or one of the few fields, an elephant could be hiding out there and they wouldn't see them.

"We tried. Couldn't see the ground for the summer foliage. But, I promise, Sam, I won't give up. Amy's out there somewhere and hopefully Mattie still is too."

"You believe Amy that Mattie's still alive?"

"I'm trying to." He glanced at his father's solemn face. "I'll let you two talk."

Hank stepped back into the truck and closed the

door.

"Thank you, Tom. Really."

"I couldn't leave a friend stranded." He smiled weakly. "Listen, about the other day. I'm sorry. I don't know what I was thinking."

"No need to apologize."

An awkward silence bounced between them for a good thirty seconds.

"She ain't coming back, Sam." His eyes betrayed his emotions by shining with unshed tears.

"I'm so sorry. Have you heard from her?"

"She called and said she's filing divorce papers. Her lawyer's supposed to bring 'em over to me tomorrow."

"That fast?"

"I got the feeling she already had things lined up when she left."

"That's awful." *Encourage him.* She drew a deep breath. "Isn't there anything you can do? A grand gesture, like they say in the movies?"

"I don't think so."

Sam drew a raspy breath. She longed to comfort him. To embrace him and tell him it was okay, that she loved him still. But she couldn't do that. She wouldn't. He had to fight for his marriage. "Fly to her. Wherever she is. Evangeline always was a romantic. If you made that big of an effort, surely she'd hear you out. You do still love her, don't you?"

He nodded.

"Then do it, Tom. God wants us to honor our marriage vows. It's not just a commitment to her you made, you know."

A glimmer of hope shone in his eyes. "You really think it would work?"

"I do." And sadly, for her own heart, she did. Evangeline would melt if Tom showed her how much he still cared. Her friends deserved to be happy. She had no right to voice her own desires. *Lord, give me strength.*

"You tell Hank I appreciate everything. I'm still praying for Amy's and Mattie's safe return. Tell him not to give up hope just yet."

Tom smiled. "Thanks for the advice. You have always been a good friend."

If he knew the longing in her heart, would he still feel that way?

An hour after Tom and Hank pulled away from her cabin, a sheriff's car pulled into the spot Tom's truck had occupied. Strange. Her heart dropped into her stomach. Why was Hank back? There could only be one reason. Bad news.

Sam rose from her rocker and waited on the bottom step, her knuckles turning white from her grip on the rail. But it wasn't Hank who exited the patrol car. It was Debby. Sam cocked her head sideways. "What can I do for you, ma'am?"

Debby smiled. "Hello again. I just wanted to check in on you. Have you heard from Amy?"

"Not a word in days."

She pressed her lips tightly together and nodded. "I'm sorry to hear that."

"It's awful neighborly of you to come all this

way to see how I'm doing. Can I get you some tea?"

Debby switched the radio off at her waistband before she replied. "I have some other news. You might want to sit down."

The blood drained from Sam's face and left her dizzy. She plopped onto the stairs and rubbed her hands on the smooth wood beneath her.

"The blood we found in that first glade, it came back positive as Mattie's."

"No. No, it can't be."

Debby's gaze jumped from ground to trees to sky. "I'm sorry to be the one to tell you. With that much blood loss, there's no way she could still be alive."

Sam hiccupped, barely biting back a sob.

"I wish there was a way for you to alert Amy. She's wasting her time out there." Debby gestured to the wilderness encompassing the farm.

"Will you still look for her body? We need to bring her home."

Debby bit her cheek. "I'm not sure how much would be left at this time, considering the wildlife and all."

Bile rose into Sam's throat and threatened to choke her. It couldn't be. Mattie was dead? Her body mangled beyond salvageability for a funeral?

"I'm sure Hank will tell you that we're doing everything we can to track this Jack fellow down, but if Amy has run into him first, we may have a double murder on our hands."

Would this woman's words ever stop stabbing

Sam's heart? All she could do was nod. Double murder. Amy. Jack. Debby's mouth still moved, her tone colder suddenly, but Sam couldn't make out any words. Then the car was leaving the driveway and the sun was burning the back of her neck as it peaked in the afternoon sky.

How was it that her entire world had come crashing down around her, and the sky still hovered overhead? Shouldn't it be shattering like her heart?

Hank rolled his window down and let the hot summer air dry the sweat on his brow. Maybe it would help clear his head too. Sam's plea pinged around his mind like a spiked pinball. Don't give up hope just yet. He was trying so hard not to. But where had his investigation gotten him so far? What ground had he gained? None. Debby had pulled Cosmo off the scent trail after the rainstorm, stating there wasn't anything to follow anymore. He hadn't the heart to tell Sam that part.

When he'd dropped his dad off moments before, to an empty house, the tired lines of his father's face seemed to deepen. The subjects of Mom, why she'd left, where she was, and what in the world was going on were all off limits. Hank tried. Dad didn't want to talk.

Hank saw the way Dad looked at Sam. The hint of sparkle in his dad's eyes. And he didn't like it. Not one bit. Sure, Sam and Dad had history. Ancient history. And that's where it should stay.

He chuckled. Who was he to think like that? Sam and Dad were adults. They could make their own decisions. He grabbed his phone off the dash and dialed Mary Beth. It was time to stop worrying about rejection and ask this beautiful, kind-hearted woman out.

"Hello?"

Hank pushed the end button. What if she turned him down? Truth was, as much as he liked to strut around in his uniform and pretend the women fell for it, they didn't. The next thought hit him like a horse-kick to the chest. That's why he'd pursued Amy all these years. He knew she'd never say yes. He could keep asking and know the answer was a definitive no. He'd never had to put his heart out on the end of the tree limb of love and hope he didn't fall. *Lord, what is wrong with me?*

The cell phone in his hand buzzed. His heart skipped a beat. Had Mary Beth called back? The number for the lab flashed on the caller ID, and he let out a sigh.

"Sheriff Wainwright."

"We have the results for you. The fingerprints on the lighter are consistent with Amy Dawson."

Amy was glad Jack was thinking straight. She couldn't have left Vasper of her own accord. Leaving him was awful, but Jack was right. Mattie was just over the next hill or two. She allowed herself to be pulled along by his determination, following blindly through trees and over logs. His hand kept her going and gave her the courage to dry the tears. She could mourn Vasper later.

Jack led her along, stopping rarely and muttering under his breath. She was either too tired or too thoughtful to understand his words, but she knew their meaning. Red was close, moving slow, and leaving an obvious trail. They stopped and Jack pressed a bottle of water into her hand. “Drink some.”

The tepid water helped clear her mouth of the sour taste it had acquired. She could picture her shrinking, dehydrated brain cells swelling with the new fluid, enabling coherence once more. Her thoughts began to line up with the task ahead.

The sun crawled through the sky as they hiked up and down, over logs, around curves, through low-hanging branches. The forest had lost its mysterious beauty. Now it all seemed the same. Everywhere she looked, brown with green and patches of sunlight. Unforgiving terrain that stole her energy and provided such little nourishment she felt as if her stomach had shriveled and died. It no longer growled, a fact which scared her. How she wanted to believe that Mattie was at least being fed well.

Jack bowed up and stopped in front of her, and she crashed into his back. He let out a puff of breath but held his fingers to his lips.

Amy peered through the trees ahead and caught a glimpse of blue.

Red picked his way through the brush, holding Mattie by the hand and conversing with her. His words bounced up the slope of the natural depression. "We'll be there soon." He took another drag of his cigarette and tossed it aside.

Mattie, of course, didn't respond. But she didn't look frightened either. *She's so brave!* Amy willed good thoughts their way, hoping the universe could deliver Mattie a sense of hope she didn't feel. Amy placed a trembling hand on Jack's arm, and they watched until Red was out of sight around the next bend.

"Come on," she said, tugging his elbow. "We can't lose them now."

She maintained the lead the rest of the afternoon. They caught glimpses of Red and Mattie at increments but held their position far behind. If they could stay unseen until Red made camp, maybe they could walk in and take Mattie. Thieves in the night. Red would wake in the morning without her, and Amy and Jack would be well on their way home. The police could find him later and deal with him.

No. Amy wanted to personally see the look on his face. She'd wake him at gunpoint and tell him everything on her mind. Then she'd tie him to a tree and leave him until the sheriff's department could get him. But she wouldn't tell Jack of her plan. He would object to such bravado and insist they play it safe. Red had dragged them halfway across the state, it felt, and she aimed to see his cockiness disintegrate.

A stream gurgled ahead. She stopped to make

sure Red had moved on, and then she knelt and drank.

Jack refilled the two remaining bottles, drank from the creek, and nodded.

They moved on silently. What would Amy do without him? He had been such a help, a welcome companion from the loneliness of the trip. A support system when she was ready to give up. Even though facing her emotions had been hard, she was glad he was along. The forest grew dimmer as the sun disappeared behind the tree line. She tiptoed across another four-wheeler trail and through sparse trees until Red was in view. She couldn't hear Jack's footsteps behind her, but she knew he followed.

Red placed Mattie on a log, patted her on the shoulder, and then wandered around picking up sticks for a fire.

If only Amy could rush in and grab her now!

He laid the sticks on the ground and lit them. The fire rushed upward, throwing sparks into the gray evening.

Amy was so close, she could see Mattie's little chest rise and fall with each breath. It took every ounce of reserve to hold herself behind the tree she used to hide. Jack squeezed her shoulder. The warmth from his body so close behind her flushed her cheeks.

Red dug in his backpack and produced a soft-sided cooler. He handed Mattie a yogurt and spoon and watched her as she ate it quietly. "Time for your shot, sweetie."

Though she looked for it, Amy couldn't detect a hint of malice in his words. He seemed so gentle and kind to Mattie. Not at all the monster from Amy's memory. Strange.

Mattie lifted her shirt and stared over Red's back with blank eyes.

Her gaze passed right through Amy. A shiver zinged up her spine. It was the same look Mattie brought with her when she first arrived at Camp Hope. The glazed-over eyes the child had learned to put up to protect herself. Was Mattie daydreaming or simply blocking life out? Without thinking, Amy raised her hand and waved.

Mattie blinked, and her eyes narrowed to slits. She had no doubt seen Amy's motion.

Jack's fingers tightened on Amy's shoulder. The last thing they needed was for Mattie to start acting differently and tip Red off to their presence. She shouldn't have alerted Mattie, but the poor child needed a sense of hope, a sense that rescue was on its way.

Amy's legs grew stiff as she waited in the same unmoving position for darkness to circle down around them. It floated down so slowly, she thought she might die of stress before it arrived. But finally, the fire and the stars and the nearly full moon provided the only light. A fox barked nearby. Amy and Mattie both jumped. Jack slipped his arms around her waist and held her. She longed to lean back into his arms and enjoy the moment, but she must remain vigilant. Their opportunity would be here soon.

Red made a pallet next to the fire for Mattie and covered her over. He pressed a kiss to her forehead and then paced behind her.

Her cute snores soon reached Amy's ears. Would Red never lie down to sleep?

Jack dropped his arms and tensed behind her.

Amy turned her head to look in the direction he stared. A new sound came on the wind. A truck? No, a four-wheeler. Her pulse jumped and pounded in her neck. If Red's supplier was headed to his camp, that meant certain disaster for them. They were directly between the dirt road and him. How would they not be discovered?

Jack pressed his lips to her ear. "Stay here."

Amy leaned into the tree, took a deep breath, and peered out at Red.

He stopped pacing and turned in her direction.

She froze. Would her white face reflect the firelight and give her away?

Red turned his back and knelt to check on Mattie.

Amy let the breath out slowly. The four-wheeler grew closer. Its headlights became visible through the trees, yellow flashes at first then steady beams. There was nowhere to hide, and Jack had vanished. The putt-putt hum of the four-wheeler cut off, and the forest fell silent. Every breath she took, surely someone would hear. Long minutes dragged by without sound or movement. There was a muffled groan and a thud. Then silence again.

She readjusted her feet, and the crackle of leaves drilled into her mind. She slid down the tree, its rough bark scraping her back, and hunkered into a small ball.

A figure shrouded in shadows jogged by so close Amy could have reached her hand and brushed their legs. Her heart pounded against her ribs. Was it her imagination, or did this stranger move gracefully like a woman?

Red's greeting sounded from near his fire. A feminine voice replied.

Amy peeked from her hiding place in time to witness the newcomer rise on her tiptoes and kiss Red on the lips. They embraced briefly and began a quiet conversation. From the looks of it, a serious one.

The woman's voice rose. "You what?"

"Don't worry. It burned out," Red answered.

"Someone could have seen the smoke and found you."

"I think it will work in our favor. Cosmo won't be able to track through that burned out place, will he?"

Amy raised a hand to her chest. How did Red know the search dog's name?

"Not if I don't let him. He can smell anything, but I can make it look like he can't."

The woman's petite form was outlined by the fire. Amy could not get a clear view of her face, but there was no doubt. Debby was Red's supplier. Dizziness attacked Amy's mind. All the actions of the sheriff's department swirled into muddled confusion. No wonder they couldn't get a tail on a living little girl. Their search and rescue lead was helping the kidnapper.

"Well, your stupid fire didn't work. Come here. I

gotta show you something." Debby tucked her arm into the crook of Red's elbow and led him in the direction of the four-wheeler.

Had Debby found Jack? Amy shot to her feet. Blood raced to her toes and caused them to tingle painfully. Pounded in her wounded hand. She had to do something. They'd left Mattie unattended, but Jack may be in trouble. Which direction to go?

Jack would want her to save Mattie.

Amy took a deep breath and crept to the fire. "Mattie. Mattie, wake up." She brushed a hand through Mattie's dark hair.

The little girl's eyes fluttered open.

For a moment, it seemed that Mattie didn't know how to react. But then she flew into Amy's arms and squeezed her neck so tightly Amy saw stars at the periphery of her vision. Tears pooled in Amy's eyes. She hadn't realized how empty her arms felt until Mattie was in them again. "I missed you, Mattie."

Mattie nuzzled deeper into Amy's neck.

"Let her go," Red said from behind her.

Amy clinched Mattie tighter to her chest. "I won't."

Red laughed. "I would if I were you."

She spun to face him, and her heart sank. Red held onto a woozy-looking Jack, a gun pressed to his temple. Blood seeped from a wound on Jack's forehead. It seemed as if Jack's legs wouldn't bear his weight. His pants shook, but the look in his eyes shot fire into her soul.

"Amy, don't." Jack's words slurred together.

"Drop her," Debby said.

Amy turned her head to the sound. Debby eased out of a shadow behind and to the left, with a gun aimed at Amy's back. *No. Please.* Amy squeezed Mattie tighter to her chest.

Red forced Jack to his knees. "We will kill you. Murder isn't that much more of a step than kidnapping, so why not."

Debby closed the distance and held out her free hand. "Come on, Mattie. Time to go."

"You're braver than you were as a girl, Amy. But I wouldn't push your luck. Remember what happened last time?"

Amy pressed her eyes closed. The world fell into slow motion. The sounds of Jack's raspy breaths, the crickets chirping, the fire crackling mixed together and created a dreadful symphony. She had no choice. Either give them Mattie or watch Jack die. "I'm so sorry, Mattie. I will find you," she whispered close to her ear. "I love you." Amy pried Mattie's arms from her neck and put her on the ground.

Debby snatched Mattie away. "I shouldn't have intentionally missed back there at that cliff."

Intentionally missed? Heat rushed into Amy's cheeks. The danger had certainly felt real enough. Even if the bullets hadn't been actually aimed at them, the panicked retreat they'd invoked could've killed them all. Amy's hands curled into fists.

Debby smirked.

"Move."

Amy's arms, stripped of Mattie's presence,

ached. Her hands fell limp as chill bumps shot up to her shoulders and crawled down her back. She was directed to kneel next to Jack. He took her hand in his and squeezed, then slipped his arm around her waist. Both guns were still trained on them, but Debby's and Red's gazes were for each other.

Red spat and flicked a cigarette butt to the ground. "If you follow, we will kill you." He waved his gun at Debby. "Tie them up."

Jack's fingers found the gun tucked in Amy's belt. She shot him a warning glare and shook her head. His hand dropped.

Debby passed Mattie to Red. She retrieved a bit of rough rope and bound Amy's hands behind her back.

The tiny plastic fibers dug into her skin, itchy and burning as Debby cinched them tighter. Debby moved behind Jack and grabbed his wrists. Jack spun and before Amy could shout, Debby whacked him on the head with the butt of her gun. He fell to the ground in a heavy, unmoving heap. Amy gasped and inched closer to him on her knees.

"Can't I just kill him now? The buzzards will find 'em before my dumb friends down at Sheriff's will." Debby's laugh rang out loud and nasally.

Red chuckled. "Not in front of Mattie. Come on. Let's just get out of here. They'll walk themselves to death before they catch us on that four-wheeler."

As Debby tied Jack's hands, Amy's gaze fixed morbidly on the blood elicited from his tight bonds. It was over, wasn't it? Red had won. He and Debby were going to disappear with Mattie and . . . and what? Start a family together? It all seemed so preposterous. So ridiculous. Red had kidnapped her foster child for what purpose? As far as Amy could tell, they treated Mattie like a princess. Amy looked to Mattie one last time. Tears streamed down her sweet, pale face. Her eyes dug Amy's heart from her chest. The glaze and fear were back. Amy dropped her chin and before she knew what was happening, she had a splitting pain in the back of her head, and the world went dark.

Chapter 22

Amy trudged through thick, red liquid. Burning hot, sticky stuff. The agonizing pain in her head drilled all thoughts out. It might split open like a dropped melon. Or an old pumpkin. *Open your eyes. Wake up.* The brightness of the sun stabbed pieces of glass into her eyes. Brilliant green leaves fluttered in a subtle wind framed by a cloudless blue sky. Where was she? Why couldn't she move? She raised her head and pain stabbed through her. Her vision blurred and dimmed. She couldn't succumb, though her body longed for more rest. She wriggled her numb fingers, tied behind her back. The previous night's events came into focus. Jack.

Somehow she managed to roll onto her side and came face-to-face with his bruised and bloody face. Dirt stuck in clumps to the dried streaks of magenta on his cheeks. "Jack." She maneuvered her knee around to nudge his thigh. “Jack.”

He moaned and opened his right eye to a slit.

“Can you hear me?”

His left eye was swollen shut. “You look terrible.”

Her laughter surprised her. “Oh, don’t make me laugh. It hurts.”

“I feel like my head got ran over by something very mean.”

“It did. Debby and Red. Remember?”

“I remember. We have to get moving.”

Her shoulder throbbed from lying on it. “How exactly?”

“Can you untie me if we roll over?”

“I’ll try.” Amy wriggled like a worm in a puddle trying to turn over, but she made it. She scooted closer to Jack and felt for his hands. She dug into the knots, prying and bending her fingernails backward. The rope loosened, and his hands disappeared from her reach.

“Give me a second, and I’ll get you free.” He groaned as he labored to untie his feet and a few moments later appeared in her line of sight.

Jack rubbed his wrists and flexed his fingers. “There. I can feel them again.” He knelt and untied her.

“Thanks.” She sat up and touched his cheek. “I’m so sorry.”

“You don’t have a thing to apologize for. This is not your fault.” He smiled weakly. “Let me see your head.”

With tender fingers, he parted her hair and

inspected the welt left by Debby's gun butt. "Does it hurt as bad as mine?"

"Yes."

He planted a soft kiss near the bruise at the back of her head.

Amy shivered. "Let me see your wounds. They got you good, didn't they?"

"Debby surprised me at the four-wheeler. I don't remember much after that."

She gingerly touched the pump knot on his scalp and brushed over the cut on his forehead. "Do you think you have a concussion?"

"I'd bet good money on it. You?"

"Probably." She used her shirttail to wipe the blood from his eyelids. She leaned closer.

Jack drew in a sharp, ragged breath.

She pressed her lips to his scar, savoring the feel of his skin against hers. He shuddered. Amy pulled away. She hadn't meant to do that. "They took Mattie right out of my arms." Her voice hitched. "We were so close."

"Did they leave us any supplies at all?"

Amy's gaze took in the makeshift camp. All that was left were ashes and bloody dirt. "Not a thing. What are we going to do now?"

Jack grabbed her hand and indicated that she sit next to him. "We won't give up. We are still alive, and that means there's still hope."

"Humph. Hope. That's not the word I would've used right about now."

"There's always hope. God's here with us."

Amy pulled her fingers from his grasp and tucked her knees under her chin. "God's not been with me in a long time."

"You are His child. He's never left you."

"Then why did He let my childhood happen the way it did? Isn't He supposed to protect His children? Or was I meant to be used in place of money? Sold to nasty men who held guns to my head and forced me to . . . to . . ." Amy jumped to her feet and stumbled away from Jack. She let him back into her bubble, and here he was preaching to her about a good God. What did he know? She stopped at the same tree she'd hidden behind and leaned into it. The world spun wildly, sending a wave of nausea careening over her. Her stomach heaved but there was nothing to retch.

Jack's hands swept the strands of hair from her face and held them in a ponytail.

When the episode passed, Amy hugged her stomach and allowed Jack to wrap her in his arms.

"You know that's not what I meant. There's evil in this world. Horrible evil. And you never deserved to experience it. But God is the one who can heal you, if you'll let Him. I don't know why your childhood happened, but I do know God cried with you through it all."

"How do you know?"

"When I was at my lowest, I accepted Him as my Savior. Now when I need to, I pray and I can feel him here." Jack leaned away and pointed to his heart. "I've prayed for you every day for fifteen years."

He had prayed for her? Every day? She wanted

that kind of faith. Wanted God to see her again. But how?

"I see the doubt pass in your eyes. Faith is not a doubting way. If you want God, you have to jump."

"I'm not so good at leaps of faith."

"You took one on me."

"And you left."

"I didn't want to."

She knew that, but hating him for it had been much easier. Being angry at him gave her an escape from the pain his absence caused. Amy tilted her head back and raised her hand to his cheek once more. His lips met hers, sending fireworks into her body. Electrifying sparks of green and silver danced behind her closed eyelids.

Hope.

A word she hadn't used or believed in a long time. Jack's kiss, Jack's prayers for her, his faith, gave her hope. Hope for the first time in decades. It filled her, brimmed over the sides of her heart's prison, and wrapped her in a warm embrace.

The sensation of a hot breath washed over her back. Amy's eyes snapped open. She pulled away from Jack, whose eyes remained closed. "Cobalt."

The horse whinnied in response and pressed his nose to her shoulder.

She whipped around and flung her arms around his neck. "How did you find us?" She half-expected him to actually answer. "Good boy." The reins were broken in two, but the saddle and its bags remained intact. Had the smell of the grain just out of Cobalt's reach been torture for him as he wandered through the forest? She scooped a handful out and held it before his nose. He gulped it down. Amy handed Jack a bottle of water she had stowed in the other bag and waited for her turn.

Jack handed her the bottle and smiled. “See. Hope.”

“Hope.” She tilted her head sideways. “Maybe you’re right. Keep praying for me.”

His smile broadened, wrinkling the swollen features of his face. “That hurts. Don’t make me smile.”

“We are quite a pair.”

“I don’t even want to know how bad I look. Pretty scary, huh?”

“A little.” Amy giggled.

“Well, you’re still beautiful.”

Her cheeks flushed, though she doubted he would see it under the dirt.

“Got anything to eat besides horse feed in that magical bag of yours?”

“As a matter of fact.” She handed him a granola bar. “My emergency stash.”

“They even took my mandolin.”

“We’ll get it back.”

He broke the bar in two and handed her half back. They ate quickly in the quiet morning forest. A mockingbird trilled, and a squirrel chirped.

Amy rolled the new word around in her mouth. Hope. She slipped her foot in the stirrup and swung into the saddle.

Jack took her proffered hand and mounted behind her. He circled her waist with his arms.

Amy smiled. “I know where Red is taking Mattie.” She aimed Cobalt away from the four-wheeler trail.

Chapter 23

Sam's phone rang. She didn't care. Why should she? There was nothing good left in her world. Amy and Mattie were both dead. The only call that could come now would be more bad news. She looked at the screen. Hank. Sure enough. More bad news. She clicked the green button to answer the call and placed it to her ear. Several seconds passed, but she wasn't sure if she'd already said hello or not. It didn't matter, really.

"Sam, I've got the blood results back."

"Debby already told me."

"She what? When?"

"Yesterday morning."

"That's impossible, Sam. The results came directly to me from the lab less than five minutes ago."

What? That didn't make any sense. Her heart skipped a beat.

"The blood isn't Mattie's."

Her black thoughts leapt back into the vicinity of sunlight. "Say that again?"

"The blood was animal. Not Mattie's."

"Why would Officer Debby lie to me?"

"I don't know, but I will find out."

Sam ended the call and sank into her rocker. Was Mattie alive then? If Debby lied about the blood, maybe she lied about everything. That meant she had no actual idea about Amy either. *Thank you, Lord. There's still hope.*

Hank ended the call with Sam, slamming his phone on his desk with more force than necessary. Why had Debby undermined him and spoken with Sam? Why did Debby lie? A flood of questions threatened to drown his reasoning skills. Had he been blind not to see Debby's falsehoods? Had Cosmo really lost Mattie's scent, or was Debby a part of the crime?

That didn't make sense, though. He could account for Debby's whereabouts leading up to Mattie's kidnapping. She and Cosmo were on scene at another disappearance involving a missing teen. He'd seen them himself every day for a week heading into the woods, tracking the lost hiker. Maybe Debby simply received wrong information and wanted to break the news gently to Sam?

He dialed her number. It went straight to

voicemail.

His desk phone jingled, and he lifted the receiver. "Sheriff Wainwright."

"My office now." Click.

She didn't identify herself. There was no need. He recognized Mayor Hardy's voice.

Every trotting step Cobalt took rattled Jack's head, like angry hornets digging into his brain. Having his arms around Amy's waist brought a measure of comfort and at least a distraction from his beat-up state. "Want to tell me the secret now?"

"What secret?"

"Where are we going?"

Amy pulled back on the reins. "Do you hear water?"

"No."

"Come on. Let's take a quick look. I swear I hear a trickle."

She'd changed the subject in less time than it took for him to ask the question. Apparently she was going to keep it to herself a bit longer.

They dismounted. Amy charged away from him, pulling Cobalt behind her.

He followed with his gaze to the ground. His neck ached from holding the same position for so many hours and days in a row. It would be heavenly to sleep in a real bed. With a pillow. The dried blood on his scalp, neck, and cheeks itched. His hands were no longer tan but rather black from filthiness. His clothes no longer recognizable as his own. Maybe the water would be deep enough to clean up a bit.

"Here!"

He hurried in the direction of her voice. A trickle of water cascaded over a rock ledge and dripped onto a flat stone before trailing downhill under the leaves. "It's almost dried up."

"It'll slake our thirst."

Amy drank first then cupped her hands and caught water. She brought it to Cobalt's nose and repeated the action a dozen times until Cobalt turned his attention to the scant vegetation.

Jack leaned his head under the small stream flowing off the rock. Its coolness calmed the throbbing. He gently scrubbed his hands, hair, and face. Every touch to his wounds brought new pains, but it was worth it to remove the blood. He opened his mouth and let the sweet water fill it and dribble down his cheeks. He felt Amy's eyes on him. "What?"

She averted her eyes.

Was he dreaming, or did those eyes possess deep feelings for him? She had returned his kiss, but how did she really feel? Hard to tell when he could only open one eye and had a concussion jumbling his thoughts. He turned his attention back to the water and drank until he could hold no more. He felt a bit refreshed at least.

Amy mounted Cobalt. "Okay, let's go. Help me stay on a northwest bearing."

"I will. You won't tell me where we are going?"

"Elgin."

She helped pull him onto Cobalt's back, and he slipped his arms around her. "I won't ask why."

"Thank you. Are you familiar with Elgin's location at all?"

"Never heard of it."

"I have no idea why I remember this, but I know Elgin is directly northwest of Briceville. I think we must be fairly close."

Curiosity begged him to question more, but he tamped it down. He trusted Amy, and he needed to prove she could trust him. He had no doubt when she was ready, Amy would tell him the story of how she knew where to go.

Sam felt ridiculous driving her truck to the barn. It was such a short walk, but she didn't want to take a chance of stepping in a mole hole or rain rut and torqueing her back. Fingers crossed, it actually felt pretty good this morning. Her toes were still out of reach, but she sat up with minimal pain this morning. Good thing boots were easy to slip on.

Emotional pain plagued her more than physical today. The constant whirlwind, back and forth, rollercoaster of thoughts and hopes, fears and despairs, made her mind and heart ache. Was Hank right? Were Amy and Mattie really going to be okay? Why had Debby lied? The answers to those questions seemed to be held by a greedy phantom just out of her reach.

Lord, I'm sorry for my doubt. Help me go on. Give me some sort of sign that everything will be okay.

She stepped out of the truck into the thick summer morning and cinched the back brace in a bit tighter. *Thank you, Lord, for the healing you've given. That at least, I know.* She knew she wasn't out of the woods. A bulging disc didn't just unbulge, especially one as bad as hers, but she'd at least bought a little more time.

She carefully climbed the ladder to the loft and grinned. The sight of a full supply of hay was a good thing to see. Thank goodness for good friends.

Friends. And nothing more.

Tom should be on a plane headed for Montana about now. Headed to patch things up with Evangeline. Like it should be.

She picked her way back down the ladder and grabbed the manure fork and wheelbarrow. As long as she didn't bend at the waist and remembered to use her legs, she should be able to clean the stalls. As soon as Amy returned, Sam would like to bring the horses back in and prepare for things to get back to normal. If she returned. And if they could ever discover normal again.

Sam didn't have to work long to bring out a sweat. The temperature in the barn rose steadily all morning until the heat and lack of breeze became unbearable. She flipped on the overhead fans and flung open the doors.

That's when she smelled it. Smoke. Just a faint tinge of it in the air. Her first thoughts flew to Amy.

What if a new forest fire had broken out? It was a few short years ago that the entire mountain chain along Briceville and Royal Blue had burned.

The hill between the main house and the barn provided a good view of the horizon. She scanned it for signs of smoke, but no gray plumes seemed to be present. Her gaze returned to the barn. No! Her heart dropped to her toes. A thin tendril of smoke rose from the peak of the roof.

The hay.

She never got it fluffed properly and dried out after the last rainstorm. She should've warned Tom. In everyone's haste to get it in before the next rain, and with the distraction of the kidnapping occupying everyone's minds, no one must've checked to be sure it was completely dry.

She whipped her cell phone out and dialed 911. The operator said she'd dispatch the Briceville Volunteer Fire Department, but Sam knew even coming from the closest town it would be too long.

She ignored the stab in her back when she broke into a run. It didn't matter. If she could save the barn, it would be worth her pain. She grabbed the fire extinguisher in the tack room and climbed the ladder again. She stepped onto the loft floor and froze. The air, filled with thick white smoke, instantly made her cough. Flames devoured the bales all around and leaped up to lick the rafters. She pulled the pin and discharged the fire retardant onto the nearest flames, but it didn't make a dent.

It was too late. And she'd provided the air

circulation that fed the flames by turning on the fans and opening the doors.

The intense heat and smoke threatened to overtake her. She dropped the empty extinguisher and turned to climb down.

From the tack room, she rescued as many saddles as she could carry and drag at one time. There was nothing left to do but back up and watch as the flames began shooting out of the roof. *Thank you, God, that the horses aren't in there.* That, at least, was a blessing.

She heard the tanker approaching, its engine groaning with the steep ascent up the mountain, long before she saw it. Every moment it drew closer, the flames grew higher and encompassed another part of the barn.

Suddenly, she was surrounded by vehicles and men shouting. Most of them slipped into their fire gear only on the lower half of their bodies. Their actions slowed once they realized the barn was too far gone to save.

A gentleman around her age with salt-and-pepper hair approached and removed his hat. "Ma'am, I'm sorry but there's nothing we can do but contain the fire. It's too late to salvage it."

"I know. Thank you. If we can keep the fire from burning the whole farm, I'd appreciate it."

He tipped his chin and spun to give orders. The volunteer firefighters grabbed shovels, pickaxes, and rakes and started working to form a perimeter line around the barn. They chopped the dry weeds and dug out a berth several feet wide. A moat of dirt.

She was so helpless. It was all too surreal. The barn, engulfed in white hot flames against a backdrop of blue, sank inch by inch as boards crumbled. A perfectly normal summer day. Other than the major disaster in front of her. All the hay gone. The beautiful, expensive barn gone. Supplies gone. How would she break it to Amy once she returned?

She spun at a tap on her shoulder. "Hank."

"I'm so sorry, Sam."

"It's no one's fault. Hay fires happen. That's why it's called spontaneous combustion. I just don't know what we'll do." She clasped her hands together and wrung her fingers until the knuckles ached.

He looped his arm around her shoulder. "We'll figure something out."

She swiped at a tear rolling down her cheek and sniffled. "Your dad make his flight okay?"

He hugged her closer. "Yes. And thank you. I know you talked some sense into him."

If he only knew.

An hour and a half into the fight, a group of women arrived with waters and Gatorades. Sam recognized many of them as wives and girlfriends of the volunteers. In such a small community, and one she'd lived in since she was a teenager, it was hard not to know almost everyone.

Ms. Simmons approached and handed Sam a blue Gatorade. "Figured you might need a drink too."

"Thanks." She hadn't moved from the spot since the ordeal began. The ache in her back grew to a throb.

She needed to sit. She plopped onto a saddle and motioned for Ms. Simmons to join her.

"Any word about Mattie?"

Sam shook her head. "We have no idea where they are."

The two women stared at the barn, which teetered on the verge of full collapse, in silence.

Ms. Simmons sighed. "I was hoping to return as a volunteer when Amy came back. I thought maybe you all would pick up where you left off with that first group."

"I was hoping too." She gestured to the fire. "I'm not so sure now."

Ms. Simmons placed a reassuring hand on Sam's knee. "I haven't given up hope for Mattie and Amy to return safely. And I just know we can figure something out about the barn."

Sam's eyes filled with tears again. She was trying hard to hold onto her hope too. But she was losing her grip. It would careen off a cliff out of her reach any moment now.

"Can I pray with you?"

Sam took Ms. Simmons's hand and squeezed. If anything could help, it would be prayer.

"Lord, we know that sometimes trials happen. We also know that you are always with us, through all of them. Thank you for staying near and giving us strength. Please bring Amy and Mattie safely home. Please provide a way to rebuild so that this beautiful camp can continue to serve the children of our community. Help Sam to cling to hope in You and never give up. Amen."

A sense of peace washed over Sam with Ms. Simmons's beautiful prayer. She was right. God was with her and with Amy and Mattie. If Sam gave up hope, she'd be giving up on God. And she would never want to do that. Why Debby lied to her, Sam couldn't understand. But she would cling to hope in Him.

People paraded on and off the farm throughout the remainder of the day. Somehow pizza appeared, and she managed to eat a slice. Ms. Simmons never left her side.

With early evening came the hoarse calls to retreat from the creaking, groaning remnants of the barn. The firefighters scattered in different directions.

It came to Sam in slow motion. The men running away like beetles from a turned-over board. The slow toppling of the red-hot pile. The thunderous rumble of wood cracking and crashing into a pile of rubble. She squeezed Ms. Simmons's hand as the once beautiful barn collapsed to the ground. Sparks rocketed heavenward, lighting up the navy blue sky like cruel fireworks. Pieces of embers exploded on impact and shot out onto the dirt moat. They sizzled and faded to smoldering charcoal. Flames flared up to consume what was left of the tinder.

Sam expelled a massive sigh. That was it. The barn no longer resembled the integral piece of their farm. It was gone. What would they do?

By nightfall, a pile of smoldering red embers was all that remained.

The salt-and-pepper-haired chief approached,

looking haggard and covered in black ash. "Ma'am, we will stay until we are sure the fire won't spark up into flames again. But you should get some rest. May I walk you up to the house?"

"Su-re," she stuttered. "But I actually live in the cabin over there."

"Then let me help you to your cabin. You look plumb wore out."

She looked worn out? He was the one who looked as if he might collapse. Ms. Simmons squeezed her shoulder and sent her a look that said, "Go on home."

"Yes, um, thank you."

"My name's Monty."

Sam took the hand he offered to help her stand. "Sam."

"It's nice to meet you. Not great circumstances, but still nice." A tinge of pink colored his cheeks under the streaks of black.

What was this tingly feeling that streaked up her arm?

She allowed him to support her elbow as they made the short trek to her cabin. When he helped her sit in the rocker, she realized how truly exhausted she was. Her legs felt weak and her arms heavy. The pain in her back had escalated again sometime, and she couldn't even pinpoint when.

"Oh, the saddles." She started to rise again. "I can't leave them."

Monty held up his hand. "Let me. I'll bring them up and leave 'em on your porch."

"That would be very helpful. Thank you."

He tipped his chin and walked into the night toward the barn.

Sam hoped she'd see him again. Her eyebrows rose. Interesting. She really did hope to see him again. No more fires, though. What other excuse could she come up with?

Chapter 24

By the time night arrived, Amy's pounding head begged her to stop and rest. The full moon rose, a silver orb in the navy-blue sky, and provided enough light to keep traveling. Jack's grip on her waist grew weaker and weaker, and yet she continued.

Red's words—the ones that spawned her memory—replayed in her mind. *The last time.*

He had to be referring to the summer when Jack stopped Red in the barn. But what Jack didn't know was Red made another attempt and almost succeeded in attaining what he sought. The longing to get that memory out of her mind overtook her. She jerked Cobalt to a stop, ignoring the sliver of pain in her hand as she tugged the reins tight. Jack nearly tumbled to the ground. She grabbed his arm and corrected his teetering.

"What is it?"

"I need to share another story with you. One I

haven't told you before."

She took his silence to mean he was listening.

"Remember when you stopped Red in the barn?"

"Yes."

"The next day he cornered me again. He pinned me to the hay and kissed me. He told me he would 'make an honest woman out of me' if I'd let him. Take me to his family's hunting cabin and keep me safe. But that was the last thing I felt with him. Safe. More like terrified. The look in his eye was the same as all those men in my childhood. Hungry, possessed almost. Like they were starving for me and would go crazy if they didn't get what they wanted."

Jack's fingers dug into her sides, but it elicited no pain. Instead, it encouraged her to keep talking.

"When I refused his offer, he said he would drag me there. That the cabin was a short ride to the south of Elgin off an old TVA road. And he'd keep me prisoner, then, since I wouldn't go willingly. That I'd learn to love him. He leaned in for another kiss and I bit his lip so hard my teeth clanked together through his flesh. He pulled back and put a shaking hand to his mouth. It was like the blood I brought forth only added to the look in his eye. He smacked me. Hard." Amy hiccupped. Jack's arms encircled her and squeezed gently.

"In that brief moment when he was paying more attention to the pain in his lip than me, I slipped away. When I made it to the house, Aunt Zena saw my eye and asked what happened. I lied. Told her the horse had hit me with his head on accident. The next day

Red was gone, and I hadn't seen him again until now. I was never more thankful to Aunt Zena or more relieved to see a man disappear."

"That's how you know where to go."

"Once we get to the town, I won't know how to find the cabin, but maybe some of your prayers will help."

"What about yours?"

Her prayers? Maybe she should give that a try. "Can you ride a little longer? We have to beat them there or my plan won't work."

"Keep going. I'll manage."

Amy squeezed Cobalt's sides, and he stepped into a walk. She made no move to pull free from Jack's embrace. The warmth that spread up her back and into her neck brought her comfort. A sense of safety she'd never found before, and she wasn't ready to let that go just yet.

She let Cobalt have his head. He picked his way carefully through the bright, haunting forest. Mattie was out there. Somewhere close, and Amy didn't intend to lose her again.

At last, they stopped on a mountaintop and looked down on a city sprawl, like a luminescent caterpillar crawling its way through the black mountains. The sounds of vehicles on the roads echoed to their perch.

Amy sighed. "This has to be it."

"What are we waiting for?"

"I don't know which way to go."

"You said Red told you the cabin was south of

the town. If we circle around, maybe we'll get lucky."

"The power lines."

"What?"

"He said the cabin was off an old TVA road. That means power lines. The only reason they cut roads way out in the middle of nowhere is to maintain towers. Right?"

"If we find a set of large lines heading up the mountain and follow it, we should find the cabin. Right?"

"Exactly. Thank goodness for the full moon."

Jack chuckled. "Not goodness. God. He provided what you needed."

Jack's right. Thank you, God. Amy spurred Cobalt along the mountain ridge, skirting the limits of the town below. Soon the forest opened ahead and power lines rose a hundred feet above their heads. The grassy clearing shimmered in the moonlight. She halted Cobalt and surveyed the long, narrow cut between lines of dark trees. Though the moon was bright, figuring out where the old road cut away would be challenging.

Jack leaned close and peered over her shoulder. "Which way?"

"I'm not sure." She squeezed her eyes shut. Where would someone build a hunting cabin out here? They'd need privacy. And game. Deer would spend their time eating the easy grass rather than foraging through the trees for scraps. It would provide the perfect hunting ground. The lines to the right would intersect with the town. "Left." She touched Cobalt's sides.

He reacted slowly, his front hooves scraping the ground as he moved them forward.

Amy leaned over his neck and patted his mane. "I'm sorry, boy. You must be exhausted. We're almost there. I hope. And, I promise, when we get home you can have more grain and hay than you ever dreamed of." She leaned back.

Jack's arms circled her waist.

"Keep an eye out for any sign of a road. I have a feeling the hunting cabin will be near this right of way. Red seems too lazy to walk far to hunt." What if she was wrong? What if they didn't beat Red back? What if they couldn't find the cabin? *Praying is awfully new to me, Lord. If you're there, please help us. I have to save Mattie.*

A faint stirring in her heart made her smile. She hadn't felt that touch since she was a small girl, before the abuse started. If only she had clung to Him instead of pushing Him away and blaming Him for her situation. She could've had so many more years enjoying His comfort.

What would happen to Jack after this was all over? Would he still feel that wanderlust and insist on leaving? Did she have the courage to ask him to stay?

"There."

Jack's excited voice made her jump. Her gaze followed his finger to the edge of the dimly lit trees. Sure enough, there was a break. A red dirt road half-covered in leaves. "How did you see that?" She felt his shoulders rise and fall in a shrug. "Let's pray we are lucky."

They ducked under the low hanging branches, like arms guarding the entrance to a rustic castle. Not two hundred yards down the road, a pink ribbon tied around a sapling indicated the presence of a side road cutting perpendicular off the TVA trail.

Amy flicked the reins on her knee. "It could take us until dawn to explore all the side channels. Red and Debby know exactly which way to go."

"Yeah, but I bet they thought they'd lost us for good and stopped for the night. Strange as it may seem, they treated Mattie well and probably wouldn't push her too hard."

"I hope you're right."

"We'll find it. Just don't give up."

Jack's reassurances buoyed her spirits. Hope felt good. Something to cling to in times like these. Prayers felt good too. *Please show us the way.* A strong breeze rose and ruffled the ribbon on the tree. Amy smiled. *Thanks, Lord.*

She directed Cobalt onto the narrower road. It wasn't nearly as well maintained, but it was manageable, even with a tired horse. They wove between the trees and around hills until ahead the moonlight reflected on a tin roof above a dark cabin. Parked out front was a truck with a light bar on its roof. "That's a pretty clear sign, eh?"

Jack chuckled. "Again, God provided." He slid from behind her. His feet thumped the ground hard, and his knees buckled.

"Are you okay?"

"Plumb wore out. And stiff. I'll be all right. Just gonna walk the rest of the way to the cabin."

Amy dismounted and took the reins in her right hand. With her left, she scooped Jack's stiff fingers into her own and squeezed. This was it. Their last chance. When Red and Debby arrived with Mattie, they would be ready.

Chapter 25

Amy turned the knob and pushed. The door of the cabin swung open to reveal darkness so thick she couldn't see a foot past the threshold. "Hey, can you hide Cobalt for me?"

"Sure." Jack walked off the porch, unlooped the reins from the banister, and disappeared into the forest.

She stepped into the room and paused to let her eyes adapt. It didn't do much good. With her right hand, she palmed the wall and flipped on a light switch. A lone fluorescent bulb hung from a string over a scratch-topped kitchen table. Papers cluttered one end. Two rooms, nearly bare, from what Amy could see. No decorations on the log walls. A fireplace in the corner that looked like it hadn't been used in years and a sagging mattress on a frame made up the contents of the living room. One doorway led off the wall by the fireplace. Amy padded to it and listened.

There were no sounds on the other side. She turned the handle and peeked through the crack.

The door jerked out of her hand. Out of the darkness of the next room, a low growl raised the hairs on her arms. She backed slowly to the table as Cosmo stalked from the bedroom with his teeth bared.

"Easy, Cosmo. It's me, Amy. Remember?"

The dog dropped his head lower and pinned his ears back.

What commands had Debby used to make Cosmo obey? Were they English? German maybe? "Sit, Cosmo." No. Think, Amy. Think. She pressed her hands to her temples.

Cosmo stepped closer.

"Seek sitzen!" It didn't sound exactly like Debby's command of the words, but Cosmo stopped and his behind hit the raggedy brown carpet. Amy heaved a sigh. "Good boy." Without turning her back on the dog, she opened the refrigerator. Surely there would be something to entice Cosmo back into the bedroom. On the top shelf sat an opened can of dog food with plastic wrap rubber-banded around the neck. She removed it and ripped it open. "Come on, Cosmo. Let's go back to the bedroom."

Cosmo wagged his tail and followed her into the room. Best friends now that she was feeding him.

Another frame with an old mattress and mismatching sheets was the only furniture in the small room. A bathroom led off of it, and on the floor were Cosmo's bed and bowls.

Amy dumped the can in his empty bowl and shut

the bathroom and bedroom doors behind her.

"You turned on a light?" Jack spoke from the open front doorway.

"I couldn't see."

"They will notice when they come back."

"Sorry. I wasn't thinking. I'm so tired, my brain is shutting off."

Jack closed the gap between them and wrapped his arms around her. "Me too. I bet I'll sleep for a week after this is over."

She snuggled into his chest. "Agreed. Cosmo's here."

"What? Where?"

"Bathroom. He nearly ate me when I opened the bedroom door."

"What's the plan?"

"Do you still have your gun?"

"No. Debby took it at the four-wheeler."

"I've got mine. I don't know how they missed it. It'll have to do." Amy explained her idea and then turned off the light. She went to the bed and hid on the opposite side.

Jack slipped out the front door, closing it behind him. He would stand guard until Red and Debby arrived and wait for Amy's signal.

Cobalt was safely tucked away several hundred yards from the cabin, secured to a tree and happily resting. Amy was hiding in the cabin and waiting for the impending confrontation. Her plan was sound. As sound as it could be in the situation, anyway. Jack was perched on a knoll near the cabin that guaranteed he'd be the first to notice when Red and Debby arrived. They had taken every precaution afforded them to make sure things went their way given the circumstances. So why did he have this agonizing knot in his chest? Too bad the cabin didn't have a phone. They could have the cavalry waiting when Red returned.

He settled his back against a broad tree and forced his eyes to stay open. The moon raced across the sky and melted into the horizon. Still, there was no movement, no sign of life anywhere in the dusk. His heavy eyelids drifted down and snapped open so many times he lost count. The sky lightened behind thick, gray clouds, and a soft rain plinked through the trees.

Jack rose to his feet. Maybe Amy's hunch was wrong. He stretched his contracted and sore muscles and took a few steps toward the house. A faint drone reached his ears. He dove behind his lookout tree and waited. The sound grew closer and closer. A four-wheeler popped into view down the lane. Red and Debby. The knot in his chest tightened.

Lord, please keep Amy safe.

Red and Debby stopped beside the truck and climbed off the four-wheeler. Red carried Mattie's limp body.

Jack's blood leapt in his chest. What had they done to her? He balled his fists and leaned into the tree. It would have to hold him back because he longed to dash in and grab the poor little girl.

Red paused at the door and spoke to Debby, the words inaudible from where Jack waited. Debby glanced around and put her hand on her gun.

Jack's breath caught in his throat. Cobalt's prints. How had he forgotten about them? They littered the area around the porch steps. If Debby or Red spotted them, Amy's sound plan would take a terrible turn.

Long seconds ticked by while Debby's gaze took in every detail of the forest's edge. Jack held perfectly still behind the undergrowth, fearful of breathing. If he could pause his heartbeat, he would have. If only Debby didn't look down at the ground beneath her feet.

Debby's hand dropped to her side. She and Red disappeared into the cabin.

It's up to you now, Amy.

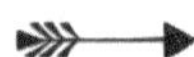

Amy's heart thumped a wild beat in her breast as the four-wheeler drew closer. Then there were muffled voices and footsteps at the door. The front door flung open and the dullness of the room brightened with the gray reflection of the clouds.

"Everything's like we left it, Deb. Why do I have this feeling we ain't alone?"

"I'll get Cosmo. If someone's here, he can find them."

Now was the only opportunity to act. Amy bit

her lip and leapt from her position behind the bed. She aimed the gun at Debby's head. "Don't move."

Red and Debby jumped and spun to face her.

Mattie's unresponsive, little body in Red's arms made Amy's insides turn. What had they done to her? "Hands up."

"She's bluffing." Debby's hand moved slowly for her hip.

"I wouldn't if I were you." Amy fired a shot at a cup on the counter. Splinters of porcelain flew around the room with the echo of the gunshot. Luck must be on her side to hit the target she aimed for first shot. Her ears rang with the intensity, but Mattie still did not move.

Debby's hands shot up.

"Put Mattie on the floor and step back."

Red did as he was instructed, raising his now empty hands.

"What did you do to her?"

"We ran out of insulin. She needs a doctor." Red's voice quivered.

Amy's heart skipped a beat. Not this. They'd survived all this. Mattie couldn't die now. "Haven't you got a phone?"

Debby nodded but didn't make a move to produce it.

Red's chin dropped to his chest after a slight nod. "Give it to her, Deb. Mattie needs help. The jig is up."

"You're just going to give up? After all this? I've ruined my career and risked everything to help you and you're going to just let them win?" The shrillness in her voice added to the ringing in Amy's ears.

A tear slid down Red's nose. "Help my little girl, Amy."

What was he talking about? "Your little girl?"

"She's my daughter. DCS took her from me. I didn't know what else to do."

Seriously? He'd thought this was going to work? "Why not just do their plan and get her back the honest way?"

"I ain't capable of all that stuff. They woulda had her adopted to you before I could ever finish."

Amy rolled her eyes. She tightened her grip on the gun. They were wasting too much time. Her arms ached to scoop Mattie off the floor.

Debby edged backward and suddenly sprinted for the bedroom door.

"Stop!" Amy's shot hit the wall near the door. Not her intended target, but Debby's hand paused.

Out of the corner of Amy's eye, Red shuffled toward the door.

The dull, gray light creeping in the open doorway darkened. Jack stepped into view. "I wouldn't do that if I were you."

Red startled and froze, defeated.

Amy gritted her teeth and forced her finger to release the trigger. "Give Jack your phone, Debby, and your gun or I'll take your hand off."

Finally, Debby did as she was instructed, placing both items on the floor and sliding them toward Jack.

Jack grabbed them, punched 911 and held the

phone to his ear. "We need an ambulance and the police." He described their location, the situation, and gave descriptions of himself and Amy and hung up.

Hank's stomach growled again as he looked over the laminated menu. He hadn't ever eaten at this little diner on the outskirts of Elgin, but the salty scent of potato wedges frying in oil mixed with the heady, deep aroma of a pot of coffee brewing somewhere behind the counter made his mouth water. He flagged the thin waitress down.

She greeted him with a smile and pulled a pencil from behind her ear.

Hank handed her the menu. "Bacon cheeseburger with chili cheese fries and a coffee, please."

She winked at him and patted his shoulder. "Sure thing, hon."

Was she flirting like this with all the customers? He wasn't even wearing the uniform that usually attracted attention from ladies. She was beautiful, but something about her mannerism caused him to shy away. He really needed to call Mary Beth. And, maybe, not hang up when she answered.

The bell over the door jingled behind him. June's Diner buzzed with the lunch crowd. Hopefully, that meant the food was good.

A strong hand clasped his shoulder.

Hank jumped and spun in his booth.

"Sheriff Wainwright, old buddy. Ain't seen you

in ages." The officer's rounded cheeks split into a broad smile.

"Wyatt Bowman." Hank rose from his booth and clasped the chubby hand. "How ya been?"

"Same ol', same ol'."

He hadn't seen Wyatt in more than ten years, probably. He was wider than the last time, and balder. But his infectious smile hadn't changed. "It's good to see you. Join me for lunch?"

Wyatt glanced at his watch then at the counter and back to Hank. "Sure. Ain't much goin' on in the town today. Thank goodness."

Hank slid into the bench and watched Wyatt approach the counter, chat with the cashier, and place his order. He carried two trays back to the table and laid one in front of Hank with the smile on his face never flagging.

"You ain't working today?" Wyatt popped a fry in his mouth.

That was a story for another day. Hank frowned. "Nope. Well, not in an official capacity. Up here following some leads on my own. Been over at Norma this morning, then Robbins. But the strong smell of French fries lured me right on over here."

Wyatt chuckled. "They are pretty good." The radio on his shoulder crackled to life.

"Requesting all available officers to TVA Service Road number twelve. Possible hostage situation. Search and rescue and fire have been contacted. EMS en route."

Hank's stomach clenched. Hostage situation?

Could it be Amy?

Wyatt wrapped his burger in a napkin and depressed the button on his radio. “Officer Bowman responding at 11:52.” He paused. “Sorry, old friend. I’ve gotta run.”

Though his tongue felt plastered to the roof of his mouth, Hank managed to squeak out his request. “Need some more backup?”

“Could always use your expertise. Come on.”

Hank left his plate untouched and raced out the door behind Wyatt, with his thoughts in overdrive. Hostage situation? Amy? Mattie? *Lord, please.*

With the gun trained on Debby’s prone form, Amy’s eyes met Jack’s. “How long?”

“At least half an hour.”

Amy chewed on her lip. “That’s too long. Tie them up, Jack, please.”

Jack disappeared and returned with a piece of rope. He made quick work of lacing their hands behind their backs and fixing them to the sturdiest post on the porch.

“Here. Take my gun. I’ll take Mattie and meet them at the road.” Amy handed her weapon to Jack. How had she not noticed the quivering of her hands before now?

He stepped back and held Red and Debby in his sights. “Go.”

Amy scooped Mattie in her arms and jumped

onto the four-wheeler. She cradled Mattie's head in the crook of her right arm and sped down the bumpy road. At the pink flag she turned toward town and kicked up leaves on the TVA road. The sound of a siren squealed above the hum of the four-wheeler. A white four-wheel drive truck with a red light bar on its roof appeared, crawling up the mountain with its knobby tires. She pulled the ATV to a stop and waved at the men in the search and rescue truck.

The passenger door swung open, and a young man in a paramedic uniform jumped out.

"Please help her. She needs insulin. Type I diabetic, four years old. Please." *Lord, please.* Amy handed Mattie to the man.

He took her light form easily in his arms and climbed into the back of the covered bed as the driver came around to meet him. "We don't have a fully stocked ambulance supply back here. We'll have to get her into town."

The driver nodded and motioned for Amy to join him at the front of the truck. "The police cars can't make it up here. We were supposed to post nearby and wait for sheriff department reinforcements. We can't help you with the kidnapper situation."

"It doesn't matter. Just help Mattie."

"Yes, ma'am. We'll be back as soon as possible."

"Thank you." Amy squeezed his forearm and retreated to the four-wheeler. The thought of leaving Mattie's side again stabbed into her, but what could she do? Mattie would be in good hands. Jack was facing down two criminals alone. He needed her more than Mattie. “You’ll come back, right?”

The driver stepped up onto the runner board and smiled at her over the open door. “I promise. And we’ll have the cavalry with us.”

Amy started the four-wheeler and turned in the direction of the cabin. The drive back seemed to take an agonizingly long time with her heart torn in two different directions. When she pulled into the yard, Jack held the same rigid position as when she’d left him. Arms stretched out with a gun in each hand. Debby and Red appeared to be arguing. She shut off the four-wheeler and strode to Jack’s side.

“I thought you’d go with Mattie.”

“She’s in good hands. I wanted to make sure you’re okay.”

Jack smiled. “Never better.”

He handed the gun back to her. She took it and turned her attention to the argument between the two kidnappers.

“I can’t believe this.” Debby shook her head.

“You knew the risks.”

“My plan would’ve worked if you weren’t so incompetent.”

“Me?” Red struggled against his restraints. His face turned blood red.

Amy chuckled. “You two really should stop talking. You’re making yourselves look even worse.”

A siren wailed in the distance, grabbing every ounce of her attention as it grew closer.

Red and Debby stiffened and dropped their

heads.

The same pickup Amy met on the trail pulled into the front yard. The driver stepped out and smiled at Amy. From the passenger seat, Wainwright, in plain clothes, exited and gave her a quick nod.

"Wainwright! Thank goodness. Is Mattie at the hospital?"

"She's on her way, Amy." He stopped at her side and crossed his arms over his chest. "Guess you were right all along."

"I'm just glad we caught up to them."

"Me too." He reached for her weapon. "I can take it from here."

She released the gun to his grasp and flexed her fingers. It was good to be free from the awful weapon.

He tucked it in his belt and produced two pairs of handcuffs.

Amy sighed. It was over. Finally.

Jack remained motionless, Debby's gun in hand, like a mountain. Unmovable. Unchangeable.

But he had changed. Amy took stock of his features. Dirty and haggard looking, but confident. A look she hadn't seen shining from him before. She never would've succeeded without his companionship, encouragement, and prayers. She'd have to remember to tell him that later.

His gaze darted her way. It seemed he was trying to send a message, but what? He tipped his head ever-so-slightly in Wainwright's direction and widened his eyes.

How had Wainwright gotten here so quickly?

Dread the size of a giant's fist filled her. "Wainwright?"

The sheriff glanced at her.

"How did you get here so fast?"

He cringed. "Now, don't look at me so, Amy. I can't stand those thoughts that are bouncing around your head."

"Tell me."

"It's not what you think."

"Out with it."

"I went to the mayor. She wanted a report. And she fired me for letting you go."

Amy brought her hand to her chest. "No. You love your job."

"I believed in you. And I was right."

"Thank you. It still doesn't explain how you are here now."

"I just told you. I believed you. I studied the maps, the direction you headed, and made a guess. I've been checking all these little local towns, asking questions, hoping to get lucky. And I just did."

"Did you know about her?" Amy nodded in Debby's direction.

"That's a whole different story. Sam will tell you all about it. I cannot believe I was that blind. A crooked cop right under my nose and me without a clue." He shook his head.

Sam? How was Sam involved? She touched his arm. "Thank you, Wainwright. Truly. You're a good friend."

"I'll take it." He stooped to untie Red and

Debby, switching them to handcuffs instead. He escorted them to the truck and opened the rear doors.

Red turned back. “Take care of my little girl, Amy. My little girl. Your sister.” With that monumental statement, he disappeared into the cab.

Amy’s mind whirled. Sister? How could that be? Her legs quivered and she sensed the earth rising up to meet her. Then she was in Jack’s strong arms and the world righted.

Chapter 26

"Amy, wake up."

Jack's voice splashed into her subconscious and gently urged her awake.

"We're here."

The hospital. Already? The long ride on a cushy seat in the cool air conditioning had lulled her to sleep. She lifted her head from his shoulder and smiled. "You make a good pillow. Thanks."

He tipped the bill of his cap with two fingers and opened the door.

Her legs still felt like pudding under her, but they pulled her into the hospital, into the elevator, and into Mattie's room. Her little . . . sister . . . looked tiny in the massive bed. The staff had clearly cleaned her up a bit, and Mattie's cheeks shone like red ornaments against a white tree. Amy placed her hand on Mattie's forehead. The girl's eyes fluttered open.

"Amy?"

How amazing that voice was! Tears sprang to Amy's eyes.

Jack's hand tightened on her shoulder.

"I'm here, and I'm never letting you out of my sight again," Amy choked.

Mattie's arms flew around her neck and squeezed.

She had spoken her name. And it had never sounded so sweet. Amy enveloped Mattie in a long embrace. Her arms knew the slight frame, the feel of the little ribs underneath, the sensation of her long hair brushing over them, and they rejoiced.

Who knew what the future held? Was DCS still angry with her? How was Mattie her sister? None of it really mattered. Because Amy would fight to keep Mattie in her life, to be her guardian, and to raise her with hope.

A nurse entered the room with a laptop. "Are you the guardian?"

"I'm her foster parent." Amy hated to release her hold on Mattie but satisfied herself by holding onto Mattie's little hand while the nurse checked vitals.

"She's doing great. Such a trooper after all she's been through. Her blood glucose is stable. She's eating well. The doctor is discharging her now."

Amy squeezed Mattie's hand. "Good. We are ready to go home."

Sam stepped out onto her porch. As promised, the saddles were stacked neatly against the front wall. The air still stank of smoke this morning, and a haze hung over the field. An ugly reminder of yesterday's events.

Sam picked her way carefully to the barn and found herself alone, staring at the remnants of a once beautiful structure. Sometime during the night the crowd must've slipped away. If it weren't for the giant pile of smoldering ashes and water-soaked mud, she'd have never known they were there.

The entire herd of horses stood at the gate nearby. They each watched Sam's movements quietly. It was as if they knew their home was gone. Sam strolled over and petted them. "Sorry, guys. You'll get to stay out a while longer, though."

R.C. stamped his front hoof and nuzzled her hand.

"I know, bud. It looks bad, doesn't it?" She chuckled mirthlessly. "What am I saying? It is bad."

She hung her head. The barn burned on her watch.

A truck rumbled up the driveway.

Sam moved to the knoll where she'd watched the barn burn down and waited. She didn't recognize the vehicle, but it pulled up right next to her.

Monty exited with a smile. "Morning, Sam."

Sam's heart fluttered. "I didn't expect you this morning."

"Just thought I'd come make sure everything was still just smoldering. A fire that hot, it's hard to get all the embers out."

"Seems to be. Thanks for checking."

Monty looked down at his boots. "I know this is terrible timing, but I was wondering if you'd like to go to dinner with me sometime."

Sam tugged at the braid dangling over her shoulder. "I'd like that."

"Friday?"

How could she explain how much she wanted to go, but that she needed to wait until she knew Amy and Mattie were safe? "I can't."

His smile fell.

"I would really like to. It's not that. It's just complicated right now. But as soon as it's not complicated, I'd love it if you'd call me."

He slapped his hat back on and smiled. "I'll get out of your hair. But not for too long, I hope." He winked.

Sam giggled. Giggled? Really? Like a school girl. But she couldn't help the excitement blooming in her heart. It might take time to let all her feelings for Tom go, but this could be exactly the start she needed.

Monty drove away, but her smile lingered. Had she really been asked on a date?

Sam patted Moonpie one last time and sighed. She needed to clean the main house a bit, so she started the short walk uphill. Her cell phone jangled in her pocket. She didn't recognize the number on caller ID.

"Hello?"

"Sam, it's Amy."

Her pulse bounded. "Amy, thank the good Lord.

Are you okay? What about Mattie? I've been worried to death."

Amy laughed. "We're fine, Sam. We're coming home. Both of us. And Jack."

Thank you, Lord! Spontaneous tears erupted and poured down Sam's face. Her throat constricted with emotion. "That's . . . wonderful. I can hardly believe it. I'm so relieved."

"Believe it. I know your prayers helped. I'll tell you all about it soon. See you in a bit."

Sam pressed end and put the phone back in her pocket. Her entire body shook. "I can't believe it." She wanted to jump and scream and dance, but instead she collapsed to her knees and prayed. "Lord, you are the most amazing, gracious, perfect Father. Thank you for bringing my family home to me."

Lighter steps than she'd had in days brought Sam to the house. She flung open the doors and windows to let fresh air in. Mattie was coming home. Amy was safe. And Jack. She had doubted him, but he was coming home too. The runaway teen she remembered as being a good soul was a good man. Another thing to be thankful for.

She made Mattie's and Amy's beds, cleaned up the kitchen, and swept the foyer. She knew they wouldn't care how clean the house was, but her excited energy had to be expended somewhere.

"Oh, I bet they're starving." She raced back to the kitchen and opened the pantry and every cupboard. She'd fix a meal they wouldn't soon forget.

Before long the kitchen smelled of fragrant

spices, baking bread, and sweet tea brewing in a pot on the stove. If only they'd hurry up! Her arms longed to embrace them. Her eyes begged to behold them.

Did she hear a vehicle? Sam's stirring spoon paused midair. Definitely the sound of crunching gravel. The spoon clattered to the counter, and Sam sprinted out the front door. The sight of Amy and Mattie exiting the truck in the driveway froze Sam's feet to the porch steps. It was really them. She brought her hand to her mouth as more tears streamed down her face. Dirty and disheveled, but in one piece. *Thank you, thank you, Lord.*

The search and rescue driver offered to deliver them safely home. She and Jack held hands over Mattie's lap in the backseat and fought to stay awake. Mattie leaned into Amy's side and soon her soft snores and Jack's louder ones filled the cab. Amy smiled at the driver in the rear-view mirror, but her eyes too drifted closed once again.

When the truck stopped and cut off, Amy peeled her eyes open. They were home. Sam appeared on the front porch, wringing her hands and swiping at tears. Amy scooped Mattie into her arms and stepped out of the truck into the sweet summer air.

The driver fidgeted with the truck keys. "Wainwright is bringing your horse home in the morning, ma'am."

"Thank you. And thank you for all you've done."

Amy hugged him with her free arm and pecked him on the cheek.

His chest swelled as his face burned crimson.

“It was nothing a’tall, Miss Amy. We were proud to help. This will make the front page of the Elgin News.”

Amy chuckled. “You’ll be regular old celebrities.”

He left her with a beaming smile.

Sam bounded down the stairs. “You’re killing me, here.” She wrapped Amy and Mattie in a firm hug. “I was so worried about y’all.”

The lines in Sam’s face looked as if they’d borne a year’s worth of fear rather than a week’s. “We’re okay.” Amy cast a glance at Jack and touched the bandage on her hand. The nurses had insisted on letting a doctor look at it. Probably a good thing too. They’d given her antibiotic and tetanus shots and prescribed a round of medicine.

Sam raised an eyebrow. “I want every detail.”

“Can we eat first? I can’t remember the last morsel of food in my mouth.”

Sam’s throaty laugh filled the front yard. “Chicken and dumplings sound okay?”

Jack moaned.

“I think that’s a yes.”

With Mattie tucked into a chair between them, Amy and Jack took turns regaling Sam with their adventure, of how they’d come to meet up and overtake Red. Sam whistled low at the announcement of Amy’s near drowning and snakebite. Her eyebrows shot up so far Amy thought they might escape her forehead at the news of Debby's involvement.

"That explains an awful lot about Debby."

"Wainwright said you had a story of your own to tell."

"Debby about had me convinced all of you were dead."

Sam filled in details of Debby's visit and lie that made Amy's blood boil all over again. "That skunk." She paused and drew a cleansing breath. "You know what, she doesn't matter anymore. Wainwright took a chance letting me go, and I'll always be thankful for that. He even searched the towns up that direction after he lost his job."

Sam took a bite of dumpling and shook her head. "That mayor didn't know what a good man he was. Shame he lost his job over all this."

"He'll get it back, if I have anything to say about it."

"Well, Amy, what's got into you?" Sam giggled. "I dare say I like the change. It's 'bout time you let that spunk out free."

Amy felt heat rise into her cheeks under the scrutiny of Jack's smile. She was glad too. It felt as if she was herself for the first time. Free to embrace life, and hope, and God.

Seated around the table with their bellies full, Sam could hardly believe her ears. The tale they elaborated was beyond words. It was like a story in a book. All they'd faced this past week and the heroic showdown and rescue. It had really happened, yet she couldn't wrap her mind around it. Her gaze returned to Mattie over and over again. As if she couldn't believe the beautiful child had truly been returned and needed proof every five seconds.

Amy glowed each time she glanced at Jack. The love they'd begun long ago seemed to have blossomed. *Good for you, Amy.*

"Well, that's the whole shebang, Sam. Can you believe it?" Amy beamed.

Sam shook her head. "I really can't." She took Amy's hand across the table and squeezed. "I'm so thankful you're home. And everyone's okay."

"One of the best parts is I found God again out there. He is so good. I never would've survived without Him and Jack." Amy blushed at the mention of Jack's name.

"That's wonderful."

"Tell us what you've been doing. Besides worrying."

Sam dreaded this part. The barn wasn't visible from the main house. Amy had no clue it was gone. She drew a deep breath and fiddled with her glass. Best way to get it out was to just get it out, she supposed. "Well, I kind of burned the barn down."

Amy started to laugh, but when she realized Sam was serious, her smile disappeared.

"The horses are fine. I had let them out to pasture after you left. It was the hay we put up. At least some of it must've been too wet. I'm so sorry, Amy."

Amy's response was slow in coming, but when she did answer, it was exactly what Sam needed to hear.

"It's just a barn. We," she gestured to the four of them, showering an extra wide smile on Mattie, "are all okay, and that's all I care about. The barn can be rebuilt."

"I managed to save some saddles too."

"Thank you. This place has been too much for me to expect you to care for alone all these years. I'm sorry too. You are a strong, amazing woman, but you need some help. I've been afraid to hire a man—or anyone, really—in here too long. That's going to change." She winked at Jack, who raised his eyebrow.

Amy had a plan, Sam could tell.

"That's good news. Because the other thing is, I hurt my back a few months back. I didn't tell you because I didn't want to let you down. But the doc says I need surgery."

Amy stretched her arm across the table and grasped Sam's hand. "You should have told me. I'm sorry if you felt you couldn't. I've been pretty hard to live with my whole life."

"You have not," Sam chided.

"I have. I've put my fears and needs above everyone else's. You schedule that surgery, and I will be your personal nursemaid. Deal?"

Sam chuckled. "Deal."

"Now, we need showers in a bad way. I can no longer smell my own stink, and that is a bad sign."

"Y'all are pretty ripe."

Laughter filled the kitchen.

Sam pulled Mattie from her chair and squeezed her until she squirmed. "I'm so happy you're home, little one."

"Me too," her tiny voice replied.

Sam felt her eyes widen. "You talked."

Amy smiled. "She's going to be just fine. We all are."

With everyone safely home and Red and Debby behind bars, Sam could focus on the future again. She wasn't looking forward to surgery, but the relief it would provide would be worth it. And she could say yes when Monty called. That part, she was looking forward to. With all her heart.

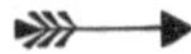

Amy had to wash her hair five times to get the dirt and knots out. It fell over her shoulders, slowly dampening her clean t-shirt. The smell of laundry detergent and soap was the most refreshing thing she'd ever known. With a mug of steaming coffee in her hand, she watched the stars appear in the clear sky from her perch in the rocking chair. Her body ached for the comfort of her bed, but her mind wouldn't shut off to allow sleep. It seemed she must rehash each detail of the past days in order to make her brain calm. To make sense of everything that had happened and properly catalog it before she could sleep. At least Mattie, after a long soak in a warm bath, was safely tucked into her bed under Sam's watchful, loving eye.

"May I join you?"

The quiet tenor of Jack's question brought goose bumps. "Of course."

He took the seat next to her and rocked slowly.

Each breath that passed, she longed to reach for his hand. Things were different now, though, weren't they? Life had to go on. They weren't alone in the woods with one goal in mind. What would happen tomorrow? Surely Jack would leave. She couldn't ask him to stay when all she could offer was a tiny room above a garage. She felt like a new person, but it wasn't enough to make him stay. "I have some cookie jar money. I'd like you to have it."

His chair stopped moving.

"I couldn't have succeeded without you. I will forever be grateful for your help and friendship." She refused to turn her head. He wouldn't see the tears pooling in her eyes at the thought of his departure.

"I don't expect payment."

"But you have nothing left. They even took your mandolin. I want you to have a new one. Please, let me help you." Her great uncle James's clothes hung loose over his stout frame, but she could still tell his muscles tensed.

"You want me to leave?"

No. Why would her tongue not cooperate with her heart? "I want you to be happy."

"I'm happy here."

"I can't offer you anything."

"I'm not asking for anything."

His warm, sturdy fingers enveloped hers, sending a shiver up her arm. Her voice, barely a whisper, shook as she spoke. “Stay.”

Epilogue

July 16, 2016

I like to think I am like the green spring grass. Short, yes. But also never cut. Never cropped. Full of goodness and nutrients. Growing. Changing.

I am not.

I'm much more akin to the tall oak tree. Lush green leaves in the middle of summer. Roots deep, long, touching the well far underground. Arms stretching for the vast expanse of clear blue sky.

Sturdy. Strong.

Hopeful.

Amy closed the pencil in her notebook and scooped Mattie into her arms. "Good morning, sweetie."

"Hi."

Still only a word or two at a time, but that was progress. The veil of uncertainty had left Mattie's eyes. Replaced with a soft light Amy intended to do everything in her power to foster.

Sam stepped around the corner. "Some campers want to see you." She motioned behind her, out of sight.

Two bowed heads with short ponytails peeked around the house.

Amy rose to greet them and planted Mattie on her feet beside her. "Elise, Gretta. It's good to see you again. I'm so glad you could come back."

Elise spoke first. "We're sorry, Miss Amy. For the way we treated you."

Amy took each of their hands in her own. "Girls, there's nothing to apologize for. You were absolutely right. Things are changing around here." Amy winked at Jack as he appeared in the yard. "What do you say we go for a swim?"

"Yeah!"

"Sam, cancel crafts and tell all the campers to suit up. We are breaking tradition today and starting off with a bang. It's hot, and the pond is cool. Time to throw that schedule out the window."

Gravel crunched as a vehicle pulled into the driveway.

"I'll catch up."

Sam took Elise, Gretta, and Mattie to change.

Wainwright met her at the top step. "I don't know how to thank you, Amy."

"Please, you've said that ten times already. The

mayor was happy to reinstate you once she learned the whole story."

"I have something for you." He reached into his back pocket and pulled out a stack of folded papers. "Here."

Jack clomped onto the porch behind her and slipped his arm around her waist.

She took the papers and read them slowly. "You didn't. How?"

"You talked to the mayor for me. I talked to DCS for you."

"It's really true, then? Mattie is my sister?"

"Half-sister. I've seen your mother. Apparently, Jewel and Red had a brief fling that resulted in the blessing of little Mattie arriving."

"Unbelievable."

"They've both named you as appropriate guardian and, given your relationship to Mattie, DCS has agreed. In a few weeks, the lawyer will file the papers to name you adoptive parent."

Amy's breath flew from her lungs. "I can't believe it. Thank you."

Jack's strong arm squeezed her hip, sending chills and happiness dancing along her bloodstream.

Wainwright's phone rang in his belt holder. "Excuse me, Amy."

She nodded as he turned his back and headed for his patrol car.

His voice floated on the summer breeze. "Mary Beth, hi. I'm glad you called."

Amy smiled and gazed out over the lush farm.

The new barn's bright red tin roof peeped out from behind the hemlocks' tops. How amazing her little community was, offering manpower and funds to raise a new barn for them. And she was a part of it. After all these years, the walls around her heart were down, and she melded with a group of friends she barely knew. Yet it felt comfortable. Natural. Fulfilling. *Thank you, Lord.*

Laughter from the campers drifted in on the next breeze. She looped her fingers through Jack's and breathed a contented sighed. Life was certainly becoming something she had never dared wish for. More than she ever hoped for.

Until now.

And not only *so*, but we glory in tribulations also: knowing that tribulation worketh patience; And patience experience; and experience, hope: And hope maketh not ashamed; because the love of God is shed abroad in our hearts by the Holy Ghost which is given unto us.

Romans 5:3-5 (KJV)

A Special Note from the Author

Dear Reader,

I am thankful for your support! Thank you for reading, *Camp Hope*. I've been so blessed to see the first two books in the Love, Hope, and Faith Series released within a year of each other. What an amazing start to what I hope is a long and fruitful career. I love writing for the Lord, and I love hearing from readers. If you would like to connect with me, please feel free to visit my website, www.saralfoust.com, and send me a quick hello or a prayer request. If you haven't read book number one, *Callum's Compass*, it's not too late. Though these books share a series, they work well as standalone reads too.

I would be honored if you took the time to leave a review for me on Amazon and Goodreads. It makes my day reading your feedback and truly helps an author's budding career. I also send out a newsletter with giveaways and news, and I'd love to have you.

Finally, look for the third and final installment in the Love, Hope, and Faith Series, *Rarity Mountain*, available now! Keep scrolling or turning the pages for a special sneak peek at *Rarity Mountain*. Thanks for sharing this journey with me.

Acknowledgments

I couldn't do anything without the prayers and support of my friends and family. I am blessed beyond measure to have a wonderful web of support surrounding me. Thank you to each person who has encouraged me along the way. I wish I could name each of you, but it would take pages and pages. Just know, I am thinking of you all as I type this thank-you note. A special thanks to my two Beckys. Your feedback has been amazing, and you've both helped shaped *Camp Hope* into its current form.

Thank you to my original publisher, Kathy Crestinger, who has answered at least five-thousand-fifty-six questions from me over the years and for being patient with my impatience. You are a blessing to me! Good luck in retirement!

About the Author

Sara is a multi-published, award-winning author, freelance editor, owner of Silver Lining Literary Services, LLC, and mother of five who writes surrounded by the beauty of East Tennessee. She earned her bachelor's degree in Animal Science from the University of Tennessee and is a member of American Christian Fiction Writers, The Christian PEN, and Sigma Tau Delta English Honor Society. Sara finds inspiration in her faith, her family, and the beauty of nature. When she isn't writing, you can find her reading, camping, and spending time outdoors. To learn more about her and her work or to become a part of her email friend's group, please visit www.saralfoust.com.

Find Sara at:
www.saralfoust.com

Also by Sara L. Foust

Kat Williams's brother died in a gruesome accident in the mountains of East Tennessee. She blames herself.

Ryan Jenkins's fiancée was murdered. He couldn't protect her.

With the death of her brother, Kat believes she is unworthy of love from anyone—even God. When a good friend elicits a promise that she will stop living in the past, then leaves her clues to a real-life treasure hunt, Kat embarks on an adventure chock-full of danger. To find the treasure, Kat will have to survive wild animals—and even wilder men. Can she rely on Ryan, the handsome wildlife officer assigned to protect her…without falling in love?

Ryan swore off love when his fiancée was murdered, but feelings long buried rise to the surface around Kat. He volunteers to help with her treasure hunt, vowing to keep her safe. Together they venture deep into caves and tunnels…and even deeper into the depths of their unplumbed hearts.

Available on Amazon and wherever books are sold now.

Sneak Peek of Book 3

In the

Faith, Hope, and Love series

Rarity Mountain

Chapter 1

Dr. Fern Strongbow settled into a folding chair across the desk from Dr. Sylvia Greenlee. Fern popped a flower into her mouth and smiled as her friend and mentor grimaced. “Dandelion?”

Sylvia shook her head. “You eat some strange things, Fern.”

“They’re delicious.” Fern ate another yellow top and smiled. “What’s on the agenda for our weekly session?”

A dog whined in the next room, drawing Fern’s gaze to the office door. No doubt Max was having trouble awakening from his dental surgery. Pentothal did some strange things to their patients in recovery.

"I'm sure Kaylee can handle that."

She was probably right. But what if Kaylee was otherwise occupied? Fern leaned back into the cold metal and sighed. "I miss the old chairs."

"Well, they were worth $50 at the farmer's market. Paid the water bill last month."

Max whined again.

Fern's gaze once again darted to the closed door. "You sure Kaylee isn't busy with something else?"

"Max will be fine. We need to talk."

Sylvia's gaze landed on the wall behind Fern's head instead of greeting her head-on in that penetrating, straightforward way Fern had come to appreciate long ago. Strange. Did she have more news about the clinic? Fern's pulse skipped.

"As you know, things have been tight around here. But I haven't been completely honest with you about how bad things are."

Fern's stomach flip-flopped. Her chewing mouth stopped. "Oh?"

"I know I promised you partnership in another nineteen months, but we aren't going to make it that long."

Wait. What? Her pulse swished in her ears, thumping like the poor dog's tail against his crate-prison in the next room. "What are you saying?"

"As of today, I'm seeking a buyer for the clinic. I'm sorry."

Words ping-ponged around in Fern's mind, but none of them found her mouth. She swallowed the bitter flower.

"You'll be fine, Fern. You're a survivor."

Her neck stiffened. "Survivalist. There's a difference. We've discussed it a million times."

"I mean it. You are a survivalist, but you're also a survivor."

No, she wasn't. She was a mess inside. Barely keeping it together so no one noticed. Where would she go now, with her dreams of part ownership in Knox Highway Veterinary Clinic dashed? Her safety net yanked away, feet dangling over open space, a chasm of uncertainty yawning below. How could she remain in control when everything was being turned upside down?

Simon Fincuff returned his attention to the strips of flooring. Not a hard floor to lay, but one that required his best work, considering the customer. Arnie reminded him of that every morning when they arrived.

Mrs. Golden's nasal squeak sounded from the other room. Growing louder with each word.

Upset again. Why didn't that surprise him? Was it his imagination or did he hear her spit out his name?

Arnie's muffled argument ended with the slam of a door.

Simon glanced up as Arnie entered the room, reading the words on his boss's face before they formed on his lips.

Arnie shook his head. "I'm sorry, man."

"Not your fault."

"It's different this time."

Simon's motions froze. The next words coming, the sentence forming in Arnie's mind would change everything, wouldn't they? Again.

"I've got to let you go, Simon. She insisted. I'm sorry."

Heat burned Simon's cheeks. "Not your fault."

"She did a background check of her own, you know. I didn't tell her."

"I know."

"If I have another job, I'll call you."

Yeah, that's what they all said. Once he'd been let go, he never got that follow-up call.

Simon gathered his tools and tucked them into his canvas bag. He didn't say goodbye to Arnie or the job site. No one would miss him after a few days passed. Why couldn't people see past his past? Yes, it was dark, but there was light underneath. One he wanted to shine brighter than the penned ink of failure.

Another job lost. Another uncertainty looming. What was he supposed to do now?

"Come in, Betty." Gregory Vanderbilt, III, laid down his pen and took the chewed lid from his mouth. "Don't hover."

"Sorry, sir. I didn't want to interrupt."

"We do this every day. What exactly did you think you were interrupting?"

"I don't know, sir. Sorry."

Gregory held out his hand. "List."

Betty's hands shook as she gave him the clipboard.

She wouldn't last another week. He'd bet money on it. "This is all of them?"

"Yes, sir."

"Buy. Pass. Buy. Buy. Pass."

"Sorry, which ones?"

"Good gravy." He picked up the pen and scribbled in the margins. Buy veterinary clinic. Pass putt-putt course. Buy television station. A good buy, that one. Buy the gas station. With an overhaul of its front appearance, it should be profitable. Pass on the bank. He owned enough banks already. Well, his dad did anyway.

Gregory thrust the clipboard into Betty's hands and waved her out.

The Knoxville Sunsphere's copper sides glittered under the gaze of a late summer's sunset. Would Pops be satisfied with his purchases today? How would he react if he wasn't?

Fern slipped her key in the lock, jiggled it, and swung open the front door. Hard to believe she would be leaving this place soon. A cacophony of barks, whines, and thumps greeted her.

"Good morning, furry babies."

Max yelped his reply. She would miss him the

most. Most clinics had resident cats. Max loved the attention of being the sole resident dog. But he would go with Sylvia. Fern sighed and knelt in front of his cage. "Hey, bud, want to get out of there?"

His tail wagged in a blur of motion.

Fern massaged the soft spot behind his ears. Tears pooled in the corners of her eyes. No. She wouldn't let them come. Kaylee would arrive any moment. Fern couldn't let her see weakness. She'd lose the young girl's respect. Lose control. Max would be fine with Sylvia. And Fern had her own pets to console her. What she needed to focus on was finding a new place to work with a mentor as kind as Sylvia.

As Fern exited the rear door with Max, Kaylee stepped from her car and flashed a smile. "Good morning."

"Morning. I need you to get started in the kennel right away. Some of the animals are out of water."

Kaylee's smile fell. "Yes, ma'am."

Kaylee didn't need Fern's prompting, but Fern couldn't help herself. Issuing directives was an easy way to avoid small talk. Avoid intimacy with subordinates. With everyone. Kaylee may not like her much, but Fern preferred dislike to disrespect any day.

Sylvia pulled into the parking lot and waved. "I've got news."

Already? Fern's stomach turned cold.

"We've found a buyer."

How could Sylvia's tone be so upbeat while Fern's chest ached so?

"Deal closes Friday. We have to get on the phone

with clients now and refer them elsewhere. Find new doctors to transfer care for the inpatient ones."

Fern narrowed her eyebrows to a painful crease. She wanted to argue. To say no. Would it do any good?

"I know this is hard, Fern. But I could use your help. I know you want to make sure these guys are cared for."

"I do." There were those dumb tears creeping in again. Why? Why did they have to show up today when they hadn't been a part of her eyes in so many years?

Gregory leaned against the hood of his dark gray Mercedes, crossed his arms over his chest and his legs at the ankles, and waited. Always waiting, wasn't he? Waiting for Pops to arrive. Waiting for Pops to leave.

Waiting for Pops to approve.

He shook the last thought from his mind with the flick of his hand and the recrossing of his feet. The television station proved to be an interesting acquisition. Whether Pops liked the idea or not. Jenny would've understood his desire for this project. Too bad he hadn't seen her in ten long years. Wonder what she was up to? She was married, Gregory knew from a weak moment of Facebook stalking a few years ago. To a man whose smile seemed genuine and tattoos proclaimed a touch of hippy in his blonde-haired, free spirit. Good for her.

He could see his cheesy movie now. He would be wearing the typical director's hat, the silly-looking thing with a bulge above the forehead and the bill at the back. Holding a megaphone and yelling orders from the linen-backed chair loudly pronouncing DIRECTOR in bold script. A smile curved the corners of his lips. Could he really make it happen? Finally use his psychology minor to put into play the dream he'd held since he was a boy?

Except it wouldn't be a cheesy movie. Maybe a game show. No, a wilderness survival challenge. Ooh, that was good. Setting player against player in the most extreme situation he could muster, and watching them struggle to survive, striving for the grand cash prize.

It would need to be somewhere remote. Somewhere challenging, yet full of natural resources—

"Son."

Gregory's daydreaming snapped out of view, replaced by his father's scowl.

"I've spoken once already. I shouldn't have to speak twice."

"Yes, sir." Gregory took his father's carry-on bag from his outstretched hand. "How was the trip?"

"Good. Bought that warehouse dirt cheap. It was on its last leg, so they didn't have any room to negotiate."

As usual. His father swooped in, snatched up the struggling, and dug in his talons.

"What have you accomplished while I was away?"

Ah. There it was. Time for the inspection. And it

had only taken four point five seconds for him to ask. A new record. “Acquired several businesses.” Gregory opened the door for his father.

“I assumed that.” He sat in the passenger seat and aimed his gaze out the front window. “Details, son.”

Gregory shut the door a bit harder than he should’ve and made his way to the driver’s seat. “I bought the veterinary clinic and the gas station.”

“Good, good.”

“And a television network.”

His father’s silence yelled at him. Was he ever going to respond?

“Sell it.”

Chapter 2

Fern crossed her legs and uncrossed them. Crossed them again. Folded her hands in her lap and took a deep breath. Could it really have been a week already? They'd rescheduled all the appointments and transferred care to a veterinary clinic in Fountain City. All the animals were taken care of. Max with Sylvia. Kaylee at another clinic. Sylvia on an extended vacation. Fern alone.

The door opened behind her. She forced a smile and turned to greet the office manager.

"Sorry about that." He returned her smile and sat at the desk. Straightened his tie and slid papers from a file.

"I understand. It's a busy day."

"Yes, well, let's get right to it. I've looked over your file. You graduated in 2013 Summa Cum Laude. Very impressive."

Fern shifted in her seat.

"But you only have four years' experience, in one vet hospital. I'm afraid what we're looking for right now is . . . Someone with more varied experience." He rose from his chair and extended his hand.

She flinched. Robotically rose to meet his grasp.

"Thank you for coming in."

All that preparation fixing her hair and changing outfits five times. Calming her nerves and driving with shaking hands. For less than five minutes of face time. And a rejection. Couldn't they have called her to tell her no thank you?

Fern forced herself to nod. "Thank you for your time."

She let herself out of the office into the plain lobby. The receptionists ignored her as Fern stooped at the water fountain. She raised her head and swiped the back of her hand across the drops at the corners of her mouth. Her fingers froze. A blush crept onto her cheeks. So close she almost bumped into him, a man with a thick brown beard and piercing eyes waited for a turn at the fountain. "Excuse me."

"Take your time."

Straight, white teeth cut through the brown, and his face was transformed. Handsome. Striking. Her pulse skittered away from her normal self-reserve. She slipped past him and almost ran for the door. When had she last noticed a man in this way? Not since that night had she looked upon the male sex with anything but scorn. They were all deceivers. Selfish manipulators. She needed to force these current emotions into submission, but her heartbeat didn't seem to agree with her.

Simon chuckled as the beautiful woman skirted for the door. He hadn't meant to frighten her. In fact, he was dressed nicely for a change. Trimmed his beard and everything. Showered. Brushed his hair, though it did need a trim. Surely he wasn't such a scary sight?

"Mr. Fincuff?"

"That's me."

"I'm ready for you now. Right this way."

Simon followed a shorter man in slacks, dress shirt, tie, and loafers to a small rear office with no windows. Not a very practical outfit for a man working with animals all day.

"Have a seat."

"Thanks." He settled into the armed chair.

"You are applying for a kennel position, I see."

"That's correct."

"Do you have any experience in this field of work?"

There it was. The question. The question everyone asked and seemed to put so much importance on. "No, sir. I am a skilled floorer but have never worked at a veterinary hospital."

"Why the sudden interest?"

Desperation made men do all sorts of unexpected things. He cleared his throat. "It's time for a change, sir. I may not have experience, but I am a quick learner and good at taking directions."

"Well, while the kennel position doesn't require specific degrees and such, we do prefer candidates with at least some experience. Have you ever owned a pet?"

"I grew up with dogs and cats, sir."

"Yes, well, thank you for your time. I will keep your file and let you know once I finish interviewing all the candidates."

Simon rose first and extended his hand. "Thank you. I'll look forward to your call."

He escaped the stuffy room before the office manager could reply. Simon wouldn't hold his breath.

Back outside where he could breathe, Simon unbuttoned his tight collar. The image of the woman at the fountain played in his mind. Her long, black hair had been pulled straight back so tight he wondered if she got headaches. But there was something about her. About the way her almond-shaped, Jacobean eyes reminded him of the color of his favorite flooring. He would most likely never see her again. But he wouldn't soon forget her.

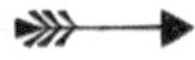

Behind Gregory, the heavy door swung shut with a loud click. His footsteps echoed down the empty hall. Where were the light switches? He felt his way along the wall until his hand struck an eight-switch panel. With an upward sweep, he turned them all on at once.

Fluorescent bulbs fluttered to life, casting a bright yellowish glow over the entire building. The television station awoke in a quiet jumble of dusty desks, piles of equipment, and cameras on tall stands looking forlorn and forgotten with their faces pointed toward the floor.

Gregory's chest swelled at the thought of the possibilities.

Sell it. Humph. This one time, just this once, he was going to have to disobey his father. He had tucked the information about this acquisition into a corner of Z Enterprises he hoped his father would never check. Maneuvered some unpurposed money around. Covered his tracks fairly well, he might say. It wasn't like Pops did any of the accounting himself anymore anyway.

He would need to buy more equipment. Some smaller, motion-activated cameras with live-feed ability. And outdoor protective stuff for the gear. Whatever it was called. He'd learn about that as he went. Maybe he should hire someone who knew these things. That way he would free up his mind for the creative angle. His college roommate, Turner, would be perfect. Last Gregory had heard, Turner was free for hire, working freelance and not getting many gigs. He'd probably be happy to have some work and lend his skills.

So much to do. Thankfully, Pops was leaving again in the morning. This time for two weeks. That should give him plenty of time to interview players and get the filming started. Gregory rubbed his hands together and then whipped out his phone. "Betty?"

"Yes, sir?"

"Copies ready?"

"Yes, sir."

"Great. Meet me at the curb in twenty minutes." He would post the flyers himself. It had been a long time since he'd done something as menial. He flipped off the lights. A lilting whistle escaped his lips.

When was the last time he'd felt such enthusiasm spark?

She might as well have one more cup of the good coffee while she still had some money in her savings. Right? Fern slid into a patio chair at Old City Cafe and sipped her white mocha. A man in a light suit stepped in front of a car on the small side street. The car honked, but the man smiled and waved. He continued to bounce toward the cafe with a handful of flyers. She stifled a giggle. What in the world was he so happy about? He must not be worried about job hunting or paying bills.

He stopped at the cork board and pinned up a colorful paper, whistling as he pushed the thumbtack in.

There was something about him that held her attention. Though he was handsome, it was the grin that fascinated her. He returned to his dark Mercedes and sped away.

Fern grabbed her coffee. She had to see what he posted.

Calling all Survivalists! A great opportunity to

audition for a new television series. Survival Tennessee. Show up at 202 Market Street Friday, July 7th, 2017, ready to exhibit your skills. Prize money? $500,000 each.

Her eyes widened. Half a million dollars? Was she meant to see this flyer today? Had some fate of the universe placed her here at exactly the right time, with exactly the right skills, with exactly no career? She pulled the bright purple flyer from its pinned home, folded it, and stuck it in her pocket. Two days from now a different sort of interview awaited her.

Simon scanned the board filled with flyers of all different sizes and colors. Old staples held tiny strips of torn paper like announcement confetti. Concerts on University of Tennessee campus. Special deals on textbooks and CDs at McKay's. Roommates wanted. Pet sitters available. No job postings. It had been a long shot, he knew, but he was getting more desperate. Two more "no thank-you" interviews this week. No returned calls. No leads.

A bright green flyer in the corner caught his eye. A survival challenge? With a huge prize? Now that could prove promising. What did he have to lose at this point? He was a talented hunter and camper. At least he had been before . . . He shrugged. Skills like that were like riding a bike, right? Surely old experiences would count for something. And if he spent the next two days watching YouTube videos on survival skills, maybe he could bluff his way through the interview process. It was worth a shot.

He jotted the address down on the back of a business card from his wallet.

With $500,000 he wouldn't have to worry about any more interviews. About the call backs that never came. Wouldn't have to worry about his past that never left him. He could start fresh. Maybe move far away, like Alaska. Somewhere no one knew him.

But what about Lance? His younger brother was sinking into their pasts. Burying himself in guilt. How could Simon leave when he was the only one who knew the real truth? The only one who could protect Lance.

Gregory chewed on the blue pen lid as he read over the questions his new team had compiled from his dictations over the past twenty-four hours. He had woken at least a dozen times during the short night to record slurred but exciting ideas into his phone. Not to mention the morning hours spent letting his imagination run wild.

Five young interns squirmed in their seats around the marble-topped conference table.

"All right. Let's get started. We don't have much time. Intern number one," Gregory pointed at the woman directly to his left, "you will be sitting on the panel with me. I want detailed notes of each person that comes to try out for the show. But I don't need your input, so silence will be expected." Was it callous he hadn't bothered to learn the interns' names? Maybe, but it didn't seem necessary. They'd only be here until auditions were complete. And he was paying them handsomely. He moved around the table clockwise. "Number two, you will be at the door as participants come in. You will hand them a copy of these rules." Gregory held up a thick stack of papers. He'd stayed up late into the night typing them. Not his secretary. Him. He raised his chin a bit higher. "You will also need to ensure we have enough copies made ahead of time."

"Yes, sir," number two answered.

Ah, one of them did have the courage to speak to him. Surprising. "Number three, you will be charged with making sure auditioners are separated and kept that way as long as they are in the building. I don't want them talking to the ones still waiting." He didn't need the other two. "Four and five, you can go home."

The five interns exchanged wide-eyed glances. Four and five raced out of the room.

"I will need you each to sign this nondisclosure agreement. It absolutely forbids you to speak of the interview process, the questions, the television rules, et cetera. Under no circumstances will it be tolerated should I hear that you have leaked information to anyone, family included. You will face criminal charges." He took a moment to lock gazes with each one of them. Hopefully, it would be enough to keep everyone involved quiet. And keep word from ever reaching his father. "You three will be here at seven o'clock tomorrow morning. Understood?"

They nodded.

"Copy room is down the hall to the right."

When none of them moved, Gregory resumed munching on the lid and turned his chair around to gaze out the window. The interns shuffled papers and feet behind him as they left the room. But he was already miles away. He needed the perfect pair of contestants. Ones who had skeletons in their closets they were terrified would come to light. Ones who would be skilled survivalists but also push each other's buttons. The only way a TV show of this type, this tired, overdone type, could stand out from the rest was if it was different. And different meant conflict. Lots of it.

Gregory dialed Turner. Their conversation had gone well the day prior. "You ready?"

"All set. I looked at your video equipment. I need money to purchase more, man."

"Done. Come by today and pick up my Visa."

"See you in an hour."

Everything was falling into place. Turner in charge of filming and hiring the few members of a crew. Interns helping with auditions. And he was scouting locations this weekend. As long as he could keep Pops in the dark, his plan was coming together. A couple more days and Gregory would take his show far away from the offices of Z Enterprises. And, if all went according to plan, the first time Pops would hear of it would be when the debut episode aired. Piece of cake.

Chapter 3

Fern swung open the tall glass door, sending a shaft of ice-cold air past her shoulders into the sweltering morning. Waves of heat radiated from the pavement over downtown Knoxville. The lobby of Z Enterprises, covered in glass and cool metal sculptures, wasn't necessarily inviting. The deep red color of the reception desk added little to its hospitality. Fern's resolve wavered but for a moment before she bolstered her confidence. She was the most competent candidate, no doubt. Her childhood primed her for such an adventure as she faced now. How many backwoods East Tennesseans could say that?

The receptionist greeted her with a smile that didn't reach her eyes.

"I'm here to audition. For the survival show."

"Nineteenth floor. Take the hall to the right."

Fern nodded. This was it. A half-million would

buy her very own veterinary practice. She pushed the silver button and waited while the elevator hummed and slid open. Red carpet and pale lights overhead made the small space feel claustrophobic. Soft music played, doing little to temper her nerves. Just stay in control of the conversation. Stay in control of yourself. She took a deep breath and let it out slowly. The doors slid open silently, ushering her into a wide hallway.

A woman with a clipboard stopped her outside a set of large, wooden double doors. "Name?"

"Dr. Fern Strongbow."

"Take this packet and read over it. You can wait over there."

The short brunette directed her to a waiting area filled with plush chairs and magazines. The walls were covered with massive photos of a silver-haired gentleman shaking hands with all sorts of professional-looking people. She didn't recognize any of them. But she got the impression she was supposed to.

Was she early? She double checked her watch. Nope. Why was no one else waiting for an audition?

Maybe it was all a hoax? And she was a fool.

But if it was a joke, the receptionist would've laughed. And Fern wouldn't be holding a mini-novel on her lap wondering what she'd gotten into. She flipped open page one and began reading.

Rules of Survival Tennessee. Please read thoroughly. If you are chosen and accept a position as contestant, you agree to abide by the following rules:

1. Both contestants must complete the challenge together in order for the prize money to be awarded,

$500,000 each upon completion.

Both contestants. She'd have a partner? Why hadn't that occurred to her before? She could control her own actions but not those of another person. And that person would have the chance to make or break her odds of winning. This was a bad idea. She couldn't survive with someone else. Too much outside the bounds of her control.

Fern jumped from her seat. If she could make it to the elevator, she could sneak away, and no one would know what a clown she almost made of herself.

"Dr. Strongbow?"

The deep voice behind her made her wince.

"We are ready for you now."

Smile. Act like somebody. You can always decline later when they offer you the gig. Fern took a deep breath and turned. "Thank you."

A young man with glasses led her through the doors into a spacious conference room. The table stretched long between her and what she assumed was an interview panel. Like a barrier of judgment. And stern frowns. And loads and loads of serious glares.

A gentleman in a dark suit and colorless tie spoke first. "Thank you for coming. I am Gregory Vanderbilt, creator and financier of the show. This is Turner. He's in charge of the filming crew. We'll get right down to brass tacks, as they say."

Fern sat in the lone chair on her end and took in the attire across the table. Gregory's outfit spoke of wealth, seriousness, power. Turner, though, in his t-shirt and slouching shoulders told her he was a bit more laid back. She'd bet he wore shorts and flip-flops under the dark table. Who was the quaking wisp of a woman to the left? Probably unimportant. She needed to direct her smiles to Turner, her business tone to Gregory. She may no longer want the position, but she wouldn't appear the fool she felt she was.

Gregory stuck a pen lid in the corner of his mouth. "Tell us why you are qualified to appear on the show. I assume you read the instructions."

She had barely had time, but she couldn't show weakness. "I am a veterinarian. I was raised on an off-the-grid homestead. No indoor plumbing. No electricity. I spent the first seventeen years of my life hunting, butchering, and preparing meat. Building shelters, starting fires with bow drills and flint. Tracking. Sleeping under the stars. My mother was an expert at edible wild herbs and plants, and she passed that information down to me. I doubt you'll find a more suitable candidate."

"We will judge that, Dr. Strongbow. Though I am impressed with your background. What skills can you demonstrate for us today?"

What? She'd not planned to improvise outdoor skills in a tall, stiff building nineteen stories above ground. She glanced around and cleared her throat. "Anyone have a pocket knife?"

Turner produced a yellow-boned folding blade from his pocket and slid it across the table.

"See that box?" Fern pointed with the opened blade to a blue plastic tote marked recycling.

The gentlemen nodded.

With a flick of her wrist, the knife flew across the posh space and sunk deep into the box's side. "I can procure food in the wild. Easily."

"Impressive. We have several other candidates. We need you to fill out an extensive questionnaire, medical release, medical history, and permission to request prior medical records. Once you finish those, we have more questions. We will give you twenty minutes to read over the materials and fill out forms."

Medical history? How far back would they check? Surely they couldn't get those records. They were sealed because she'd been a minor.

"You can be excused."

"Thank you." With legs that quaked a bit, she returned to the still-empty lobby and began leafing through the papers. She hadn't expected this. Why had she dreamed she would march in, talk a bit, and walk out with a role? Of course they had to protect themselves in case something happened. And she didn't even know what to expect on the show. Wait. Was she considering saying yes now? Would she get a chance to ask questions?

Maybe she should go home. Mr. Vanderbilt's actions belied his words. He hadn't been impressed with her. Rude. Belittling. Not wowed.

And did she want him digging around in her past? Exposing the details she fought to hide from everyone? She began to read the instruction packet.

Are you in a relationship?

Why would they need to know that? No.

Can you leave for thirty days or more?

She guffawed. Yep. Nothing to hold her anymore.

Do you have any debilitating fears that would prevent you from finishing the challenge?

Debilitating? No, nothing she couldn't handle.

Do you consider yourself a loner or a team player?

A loner, but could she put that and still have a shot at being chosen?

She read the reminder at the top of the sheet again. "Honest answers are required. We will pull details of your past."

Loner.

The questions went on for the length of the page, followed by a medical disclaimer, which she signed, excluding Z Enterprises, Gregory Vanderbilt, III, and the television show from indemnity should she sustain injury or die.

Die? Her heart skipped a beat. She should leave. Get up and walk out. Why was she still sitting in this comfy chair, answering these crazy questions?

The dream she'd had the night prior came back to her again. Cycling around and around, the image of her own practice. Run her way. No chance of being "let go." No boss. She could be in control of every aspect.

The next page included the medical history release form. She tapped her pen on the clipboard. If she gave her current primary care doctor's name, that's all from whom they would request records. Right? She scribbled her signature.

She filled in the questions about her major medical histories and issues. None. As far as she knew, she was in perfect health.

Now, to read the show details in more depth.

Participants will be challenged by a series of questions, tasks, and puzzles in order to earn survival supplies and find the prize, which will be hidden somewhere nearby. Cameras will record every minute of the challenge and be watched live by a team of behind-the-scenes crew members. If participants are suspected of lying or cheating in any manner, supplies will be removed. On top of the challenges imposed by the show's producer, participants must also fend for themselves in the wild and survive for as long as it takes to solve the riddles and find the prize money. Don't think this will be a short stint, an easy task. It won't be. Prepare yourselves for a month's stay at minimum.

A month?

Survivalist participants will be given the opportunity to bring two items with them to begin and have the chance to earn a number more.

There will be wild and dangerous animals. Bears, bobcats, elk, and venomous snakes. There will be someone watching you at all times, but you will be alone with your partner most of the time.

Alone with her partner. What if it was a man? What if she couldn't stay in the alpha role?

Half a million dollars to each participant is waiting somewhere. Tucked away. Hidden. You won't find it without the clues. Don't even try.

The money. So tempting. So life-changing. She could handle anything this Gregory guy chose to throw at them, as long as her partner could.

She signed the bottom of the page without reading the rest of the booklet. It didn't matter what it said. Her mind was made up. She was going to win that money. And prove to the world she was capable of this challenge. Or drive her partner crazy trying.

He held the door for a slim blonde with disappointment streaking her mascara. Simon smiled politely, but inside he hoped that it meant less competition for a spot.

Once he exited the stairwell into a plush lobby on the second to highest floor, he was directed to a small room with a coffee pot and a few chairs around an octagonal table. No other contestants?

Good. He'd brushed up on his skills as best he could yesterday, but if the audition required him to demonstrate fire making or shelter building, he'd be sorely under-prepared.

He leafed through the thick document presented to him by the clipboard woman. Nothing too surprising. They'd delve into his past. Like everyone. Would his record knock him out of the running here too? No matter what that cruel file said, he wasn't a bad guy. He'd prove it today. Turn on all his charm. Fire up the big words dictionary in his mind. Impress the loafers off those TV gurus.

He read through the rules and signed the proper places.

"Simon, we are ready for you, sir."

"Wonderful." He added a smile to the bubble he hoped shone through in his voice.

In the conference room, he slid into the chair, folded his hands on the table, and aimed his attention on the gentleman opposite making introductions.

"We have an extensive list of questions for you. Are you ready to begin?"

"Fire away." Pun intended.

"What do you feel is the most important quality in a partner?"

"Dependability."

"What are your unique talents as they pertain to this type of show?"

Simon renewed his smile. "I grew up hunting and fishing with my dad. We camped a lot. I learned primitive skills from him early on. It's been a little while since I've had the opportunity to use them, but I look forward to breaking them out once more." He probably shouldn't have said that last part.

"Do you feel two people in a relationship should be honest about their pasts?"

A relationship? Like a partnership, they meant. Surely. "Yes."

"Good, good. Are there any secrets you would never share?"

Yes. One. "No, sir." They could never know that truth. No one could. But it wouldn't affect some television show or Simon's ability to survive in the wild, so it was a nonissue. No reason to even begin to dive into it.

"Good to hear. If cast on the show, you will be put to the ultimate test. Physically and mentally. How would you rate your ability at solving riddles and puzzles? On a scale from one to ten."

"That's a hard question to answer. If it involves a math problem or logical thinking, I'm very good. I've spent the last several years laying flooring. It requires precise measurements and an eye for patterns, like fitting together puzzle pieces."

"Any objections to working closely with a woman, alone, for an extended time period?"

"No, sir. I'd look forward to it." Simon winked, which earned him a smile from Mr. Vanderbilt and Turner. He figured it would.

The questions continued for another half an hour, ranging from skills and abilities to preferences in partnerships.

"One last question, Mr. Fincuff. Are you single?"

"Why does that matter?"

"We want to be sure your family ties would not prevent you from completing a long stay in the wilderness. Homesick. Missing family and all."

"I'm single, sir. I may miss my parents and brothers, but not enough to leave the challenge prematurely."

Mr. Vanderbilt and Turner exchanged Post-It notes.

"Very well. We will take your completed forms and let you know if you make the final cut."

"Thank you. How soon should I expect to hear something?"

"Tomorrow."

"Wow."

Mr. Vanderbilt raised his eyebrow. "We need to move quickly on this project. Will that be a problem for you?"

"Not a problem at all." Maybe this one time, he'd hold his breath. Just a little.

The sun's evening rays bounced off the Sunsphere and lit up the conference room. Gregory's favorite time of day. Beautiful. And he had the quiet office to himself and his own pursuits. "Well, Turner, what do you think?"

"I think you've had a lot of eager people in here today. Hard to tell which ones are being honest about their abilities without testing them."

"Oh, I can tell." One of his specialties, reading people.

"All right, so which ones weren't feeding us a bunch of bologna?"

"Simon, Timothy, Anders, Jolene, Katelyn, and Fern."

"Six out of twenty-five?"

"Yep."

"My favorite of the men was Anders. Women was Fern. That knife flinging of hers could really help her out there. Both with the critters and her partner, if you know what I mean." Turner's coarse laughter filled the room.

"I liked Fern too. Something about her. Let's put her on the final list for the women."

"Agreed."

Gregory munched on a lid. "Not sure Anders would make a good partner for her, though."

"I thought you wanted drama?"

"I do. But not the sort that would make. He'd antagonize her all right with his macho attitude. But I don't think they'd get past that to mesh well enough to complete the show."

"You don't want them to fail? I thought the point of this was to create good television."

"Failure doesn't equal good television. Just shorter filming and a disappointing ending for an audience. Trust me. I know what I'm talking about."

"That whole psychology degree mumbo jumbo stuff again?"

"Precisely."

Turner crossed his leg over the opposite knee and leaned back. "Did your dad ever find out about that psychology degree of yours?"

"He doesn't need to know. How about Timothy?"

Turner chuckled and held up his hands. "Fine. We won't talk about your dad now. Or ever. Like usual. I liked Timothy. Talented with outdoor abilities, it seemed. If you're right, and he wasn't bluffing."

"He wasn't."

"You make the calls first thing in the morning.

I'll pack the gear and we'll get up there to scout the location Saturday."

"Excellent."

Turner padded from the room humming a Jimmy Buffett song.

Things were coming together well. Pops would be home in a few days and by then, he'd be "on vacation," filming on location from his director's chair. Would the candidates survive the way he hoped? Would they be a good match? He grinned. What a surprise they were in for once the challenges started. They'd think he was trying to kill them. Perfect.

Rarity Mountain is available on Amazon and wherever books are sold now!